DARK SIDE of the Sol

MIRANDA SPAVENTA

This is a work of fiction. Names, characters, businesses, places, events, and incidents are either the products of the author's imagination or used in a fictitious manner. Any resemblance to actual persons, living or dead, or actual events is purely coincidental.

Printed in the United States of America
First Printed October, 2023

Published by:
Between Friends Publishing,
1080 GA Hwy 96, Suite #100,
Warner Robins, Georgia 31088

ISBN: 978-1-956544-59-6

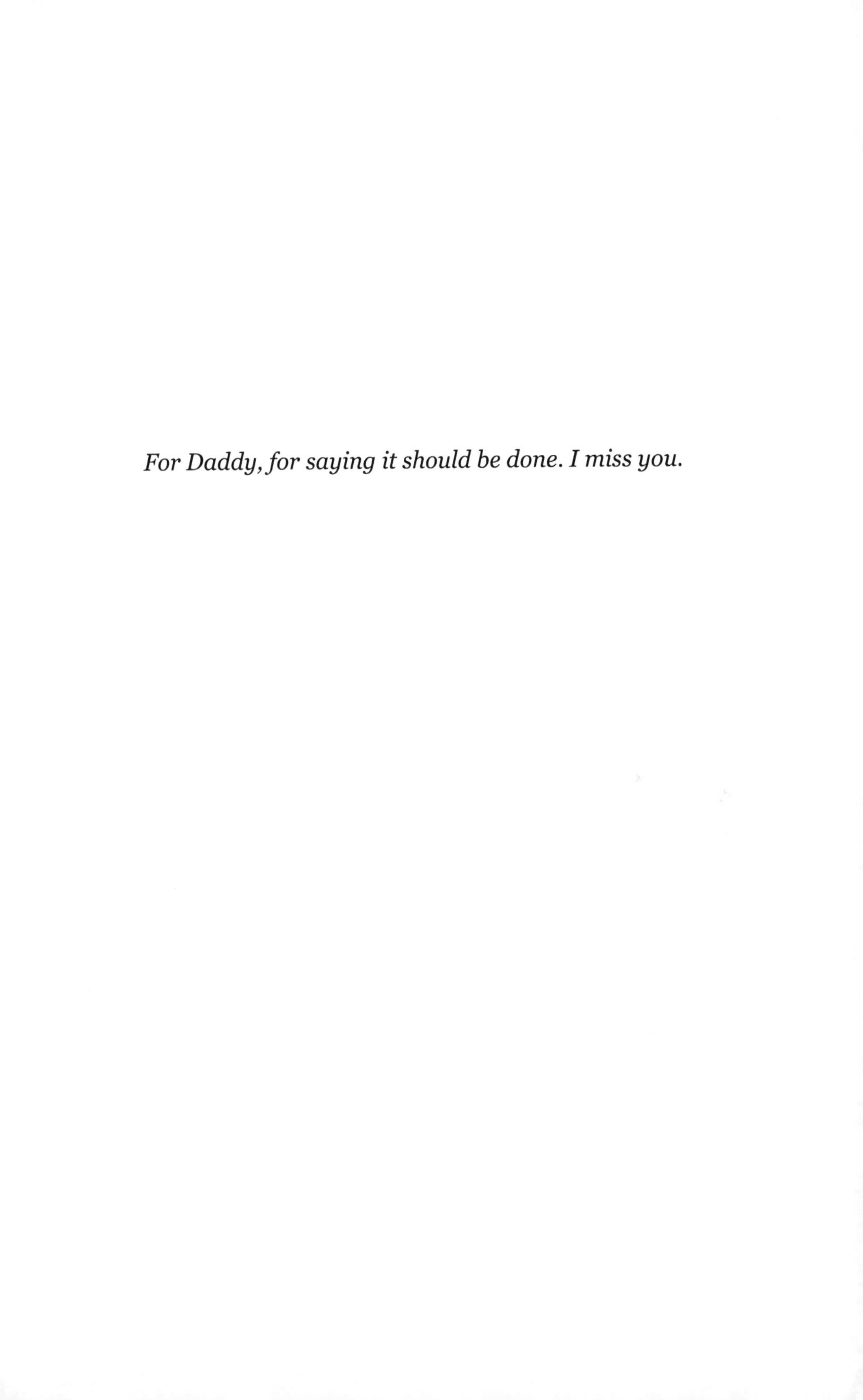

For Daddy, for saying it should be done. I miss you.

PROLOGUE

"Come on," someone whispered. A large hand landed on my shoulder. "We have to get out of here. If it's her, then we will know in the morning."

I looked out over Abruzi, a city of beauty built among a landscape of dreams and cleared my throat. "Yeah," I muttered, as a dark figure passed in front of the door that I stood watching. My chosen brother waited for me with understanding marking his features.

"Yeah, let's go." I turned from the building as another, larger, darker shape appeared, filling the doorway and blocking my smaller female frame entering the building before him. "It's just, are you sure? You know the target is Syndicate without question?"

When he didn't answer, I turned to stare into the dark where my second stood. He was already beginning to fade into the highlands where we were to meet with the others. "If it's her, it changes everything," I began.

The shaman stopped, barely turning his head to me, and mumbled that there was no other way. "The double crescent moons will not be out again for several weeks, and the world doesn't have the luxury of time on its side," he explained. He refused to look back, but I heard all the unsaid things in his disappearing footsteps.

"Then I hope it is all worth it in the end," I sighed out loud to the pitch-black sky as I walked toward the tree line of the highlands, toward whatever tomorrow would hold.

I

The tongue on this Veiliri scum was the only thing keeping it alive; warm and soft as it hit the nerve on the bottom of my nipple. The pointed teeth clasped on and dug in. "Fuck that feels good," I whispered.

When they went for the nipple first, it made them harder to kill. But the morning always came and the morning ushered in death at my command. The tug of rough tongue caught on my breast again, harder this time, and tested how far I would go. I leaned into it, pushing his face in with silent demand. I dropped my head back and arched in further, closing my eyes, lingering on the first bursts of heat flushing throughout my body. The male latched onto the rawness there and brought me back to the reality of my moment: my assignment. I took in the dark room again, noting the tall ceilings and single door. They always thought they were so safe in the penthouses, soaring into the skies along the mountains weaving above the city and the sparkling sapphire of its night.

Clothes ripped to shreds left us naked, a cool breeze drafting by was the only light caress of tonight. Luminescent glow of the lanterns that marked the sides of the buildings barely slithered through the floor to ceiling windows covered in satin lined curtains. Shrouded in shades of black and wrapped in shadows, of course, to match the obsidian theme throughout all the other living spaces. Another poor attempt at recreating the luxurious beauty of the empires recently murdered and exiled from their reign over Tannira. The unctuous feel here was nothing like the warmth of that sapphire and sable crest of the Azullon families that had built these lands into a wealthy nation over millennia of fairness and true undiluted love for their people.

Another tug, a bit harder this time, nearly drew blood and got my full attention. My slickness dripped down my sex and trickled; the muscle of my thighs shimmered in it now. One finger drew enough back to easily soak me from behind. "Bite it," I demanded, my voice heavy with power.

His black eyes lifted from his place as he knelt on the bed, briefly questioning my command before clamping down. Soon he was sucking like he would give up breathing just to get my entire tit in his mouth with his tongue hitting the nerves bundled under the peaked nipple. His hand found the other, preparing it for a soft massage before the main course.

That is what made the good lovers harder to kill. I would let this bastard suck me raw waiting on the sun to rise, cumming from just that, many times. A kiss of cold lingered on the budded nipple briefly. His attention was moving to the peak now hardened between long, thick fingers still rolling and pinching there. I suddenly tensed, tingling and anticipating the warmth and the pain that made me throb. His black eyes flickered again, but with intention this time, not asking to hurt me first as tanned hands shot up from beside him catching both breasts, thumbs to middle and hands cradling the overflow. His head dropped, his inky hair blocking me from viewing myself when he made the first lick. A long dark tongue, nearly black in this lighting, shot out and hit the wettest part of me. He was fucking me, literally. "Fuck me, all of me," I encouraged him.

His tongue is why I remained here. The creature with his mouth on my apex and dark tongue deep inside of me beckoned me onward. Black silky movements curved around my center, taking turns between lapping me up and hitting my peaks in a rhythm only this type of assignment was good for.

I have always had a love-hate relationship with the little bastards on tonight's docket. I loved the insatiable appetites and sex drenched tight bodies, but the fact that they were vicious fodder in a war that was taking too long to finish infuriated me. Their drive to feed and take the energy from their prey until nothing remained was maddening. They fed at every double crescent moon, then fucked, and then killed. Each time the crescent moons met casting the lands in complete dark, I hunted on behalf of the Order of the Old Gentry using skills that I shouldn't have. I got my release to calm the constant heat of recently inherited powers and then I got to take another monster off the streets.

The long, dark tongue had gotten rougher, scratchier, taking its time circling me from the front to back. I leaned onto my stomach, arms stretched across the bed. Satin linens rubbed against my aching breasts. I almost missed the inhale through his teeth; it was so slight as I arched my back up to open all of me to the Veiliri monster. The forsaken-tongued mouth hovered above me. With one long wicked lick before pushing itself in from the back, his face was slick with the drip from his work inside of me.

Most Assasjines, what the Gentry call people in my distinct line of business, don't want to enjoy this part of the job. This was the part I lived for, though. It's the ultimate high before the kill. I reached behind running one hand inside myself where his tongue had just been, inviting him in, bringing him closer. Just a little more, filling me up and dancing with a touch of pulsing, pleasing pain.

After the job was done, I took my time looking around the room. It was at the top of a long spiraling staircase with elevating steps the draw you straight up to the top floor. The landing of the stairs was open to an unlit fireplace and filled with dark orchids and night blooming roses that mirrored the ones growing against the stone bordered courtyard in front of the buildings dense front doors. Out of the windows lining the southern wall was the city of Abruzi, with Blue Mountain standing tall as the backdrop for the buildings built to hug the landscape and withstand the test of the magic of the communities within its varied walls. The longest arms of the mountain tumble for miles out from its base to mark the natural passes into the city. Large lines of rock end abruptly in piles of leaning spires that mark the valley's center, the outskirts of Abruzi.

There was food and a few clothing items, but the quarters were otherwise empty of any intelligence. I searched for a few moments longer than I normally would, noting the swirling tattoos on the body before tossing a sheet over it, then marked it for cleanup. I'd notify Vance and he could have his grunts search the rest of the room and report back with what they found so that Arike, our renowned leader, could find some way to make me feel bad about doing a good job. It was never enough with him, but he had been a steady presence since I came to the Gentry and for that I was thankful. I would have stayed to harass the team or cover every inch myself if it weren't for an urgent need to receive a message someone had been trying to get to me.

I doubted that the informant would still be out this late on a night of hunting, but when the sex was good, you lose track of time. I checked the clock in the tower of the building across the street, all but the clock face was shrouded in the darkness and the fog cascading from the mountain tops behind it, to see that its still early enough that he could still be near the market.

I reach into the pocket of my customary black jacket and feel for the communicator I left there. Its cold flat surface palmed easily into my hand for me to check for messages of trouble from my partner, not that I needed a partner, mind you. The Veiliri in Abruzi were all the same, and directing their attention across a bar or from a dark alley was the easiest part of this job. It's like they want to be run through by the tip of my blade. The fact that we both take to the streets to hunt one another every few weeks like contestants in some ancient public game is really all you need to know about the current state of Abruzi.

Men and women who once ran establishments of grandeur or directed commerce into the markets now serve their penance for being successful by scrubbing the blood out of the streets in the early hours following hunt nights, I should feel bad about that but it's hard to focus on pity when rage was always threatening to find its way forward.

Ordinarily I would use my magic to trixxt - or jump through space - to get myself back to my ship, but tonight the reward outweighed the risk of going by foot and this loft was perched upon a building at an intersection of footpaths just around the corner from where I need to be. I grabbed a cloth from the small shelf beside the plain, sunken tub and wipe my blades clean before sheathing them back into their holsters. I cross back across the cold room and head toward the quiet staircase, opening just an exit door to take them down two by two rather than waiting on the magic of the lift to carry me to the floor.

The front doors were open to the silence of the night, the only sounds coming from the ticking of the bell tower clock and the scurrying of rats across the cold stone streets. I stepped from the warmth of the pale light beyond the front doors and into streets cast in darkness. I could use my light to shine a way through the streets, but the dark was my playground, and I always looked for a chance to pull my daggers when Veilri scum littered the avenues. There were few streets between here and the edges of the darkened corner market and from there it wouldn't be a long walk to where the Gentry were parked below the Gardens, so I may not even have the chance.

Tucking the faux black locks behind my ears, I put my head down and tried to listen past the wind picking up as it rushed the alley I turned into. Only a few buildings separated the loft's building and the eastern market, but the paths were built to minimize large caravans and protect the stillness there. The resulting alleys fight for space between the buildings and exist in a black darker than their surrounding paths. A few feet in and the sounds of bodies sliding in the night find me. Rough sounds that were a bit too barbaric to be humanara slipped down the slick walls toward where I stood.

I loved being wrong when it meant I got to slice up another Veilri, this one with giant leathered wings. You could see their edges drawn against the dark, silver tips gathering any stray light to them above his shoulders.

I dropped my tingling fingers toward the hilt of my blades, more like the Gentry's blades since mine were lost years ago, and grasped the hilts tightly. I began to move toward their writhing mass when a whimper reached my ears and stopped me. The girl he was feeding from was still alive, and if I did this in the dark I could kill her, too.

Deciding to risk drawing others to me if it meant saving a life, I eased the blades back down and took a small breath, clicking the fingers of my left hand and illuminating the alley with its light. I thrust my casting hand up to blast the demon with a small stun to stop his attack, but I shouldn't have bothered. The beastly winged soldier continued his feast. The glow only served to highlight the terror on the young Abruzi girl's face.

I took a few steps and slid my blade into his neck without him lifting his head. I jumped back to avoid the venom from his talons and let his body drop to the dark ground away from the crumpled form of his lover. I gave him a quick kick out of the way after making sure he would never get up and turned to the girl. She was brunette and small and wore a chain about her naked hips with tiny brass balls that clanged loudly when she shook the correct way. Or so say the disgusting people that wear them to attract the attention of the Veil, hoping for one to slip up and let slip the secret of how Telseneir found their way to bring down the entire continent of Tanirra through a slip in the gates years ago. Some started out as spies, and some were delusional with hopes of leaving for a better land for a life that didn't exist anymore. I wasn't sure which kind of fanatic this girl was, but she didn't belong in the streets tonight with her lifeblood draining from her in places that made contact with the Veiliri. It was disgusting and I leaned to the side before bending and placing my jacket around her shoulders.

"Get out of here," I offered her my hand but she pushed it away with a look of shame.

"He said he would fly me out of these streets and to the gates and through the portal to Telseneir. Straight to its city of gold," she whimpered and tried to straighten, her legs taking several moments for the feeling to return. I held her with my dagger hand while she reached for her garments and slid a light shift over arms that were ghostly pale in the dim light I held close to us in the other hand.

"There is no city of gold and no Veiliri here willing to take you past the dumping yards where the bodies will be pulled at first light and sent back to their own people to tally the cost of tonight's hunt. You'll be faded to nothing more than a number," I whispered. I tried to say gently, my eyes taking in her bare feet and loose summer gown now pooling just along their tops.

"But there is. I've seen the gold, the jewels of Telseneir, delicately forged unlike anything we can find here, even before Tanirra fell," she said. Before I could reach to help her across the winged body, she dropped unevenly to his side and pushed, grunting with the effort to move his body to its side. I didn't offer to help, but I didn't leave either. I stood watching the exits for threats while she dug around in the pants and cloak hidden under his fallen body.

I was almost ready to give up and leave her there when a quiet sound of triumph sounded into the night. I crouched to bring the light closer to the item she held in her closed hand. For a moment I forgot the alley, the bodies around me, the danger in the streets and focused on the small golden compass opened in her palm. Its face lit with the customary N at the top. Moving the light closer to the piece I could see that the design was flawless. Etched into golden pieces stacked around the center were runes, old spells, and any number of personal enchantments set into it's glimmering base. It had to be an amulet of a mage who liked to travel well prepared.

There were a thousand reasons why the Veiliri would be using it to entice pretty young girls into alleys, but the simplest was also the most logical. They were monsters. I offered to walk the girl to a safer location and paid her for the compass, tucking it deep into my empty jacket pocket. From the other I pulled the slim square communicator and sent another location for the crew to handle.

II

I walked the girl away from the offending body and dropped her off at a door at the end of the alley that I hadn't seen hidden against the building walls from where we stood. We stopped in front of it, a small light from inside trying to escape the door frame when it swung quietly open. The sound of weapons being slid from and back into holsters eked out from just inside a moment before the door slammed shut in my face.

Just as well, had she been less rude I may have wasted time talking to her about her insane mission to befriend the Veiliri. I stopped trying to haul in recruits from these groups to our rebel outfit because they were desperate to be saved. Unfortunately, I've learned that no one was coming to save us.

I stomped off through the street and check that it was clear before extinguishing my light, cutting across to the small globe of flickers swinging on signs that marked the bazaar's entrance. I dropped my chin and hop across a small pile of rubble dropped on the path and jog alongside the sign to the circular doorway into the tents and stalls.

I couldn't see any of the details as I walked straight toward the center of the covered tents but I didn't have to see the blue and purple and green colors of their silken roofs to know exactly what they looked like. I thought of seeing them from the path we would follow into town when I would visit as a child, their colors like skirts waving in a dance among the low, misty clouds of the mountains. I walked for several moments before reaching the end of the smooth wooden walkway winding from the entry through the first round of vendors. I paused to listen then lit the room up with a snap, my other hand gripping my blade again.

I hoped I didn't have to pull my blade; its shine was still dulled with the life I'd taken moments ago. I pulled up short under a tent with five tall points and smooth cloths draped over piles of goods and veered right toward a wall with an armoire that rose above my head and spread across a dozen feet in width. I walked up to it and rapped on the door twice, then twice again.

I stepped back to let the door open and was rewarded with a small creak before light began to spill out, mixing with my dimming globe. Through the slice of light, I could see a curtain separating stairs that must lead to a lower sitting room. A spell to make their space bigger. Clever. A small face peered up at me through low dancing lights and waved for me to enter. I put my light out and bent to follow the tiny horned female through the doorway.

We came to the stairs beyond the curtain, and I waited at the top while she moved elegantly through the furniture to a stack of envelopes on top of a low table. Shuffling through them she pulled one out and frowned then held it out to me slowly.

"Are you sure this is mine?" I looked at the stack on the desk and back to her soured expression.

"Yes, but there should have been another update tonight. I expected my partner back by now and he has not returned. If you will still be on the ground tomorrow, maybe you should check back," she offered.

"Ah. How long has he been out," I asked.

"Just a few weeks, headed up to the border with some of those Gentry flunkies and a small group of the LD's boys. Said they had a lead on someone who could provide images and critical intelligence to the effort, but they had to track him down."

"How do you know he will be back tomorrow. Do you keep comm crystals?" I asked because most homes don't have them if they aren't military. They make the Veiliri nervous and bring unwanted attention to their doors.

I looked around the open room while she settled herself into a swinging cocoon of cushions and turned slowly in the low flicker of the candles back to face me after settling in.

"No. We spotted their group setting up to enter the cover of the mountainside this afternoon. From the top of the clock tower my neighbor spotted them, with her raven perched on her shoulder and eyes rolled back into her sallow face, she announced down to the crowd that they would make it into the doors of the cliff well before the night took over."

"Fine," I sighed and turned to her crackling fire pit in the center of the room to read and burn the message. Maybe the contents will be enough of an answer.

I read through the message a few times and tossed the parchment into the blaze. Handing the envelope back to my informant I promised to try and visit tomorrow to see what I could get from her partner before I stepped lightly back out of the armoire and onto the shortest path to the exit opposite the open-air square.

I let my gaze drift through the tents to where the Gentry is anchored on the other side, outside of the market and across a field of waving grass dotted with little tables and benches nestled against towering trees and angled to give its guest a wide-open view of the glowing peaks of the surrounding Blue Mountain.

The sun would be up soon enough, so I walked quickly toward the edges of the bazaar and kept my eyes moving between the left and right displays making up the lines of the aisle out. Once I thought I spotted movement and a flash of gold slits glowing like eyes between the flowing ribbons, but in a blink, it faded into the inky dark. I shined my light in its direction and moved so close to the side that I lightly brushed against the white tents of the apothecarists on my way out.

Once I cleared the market, I aimed for the carrier and just cleared the doors to the receiving bay before the mages began to stand and walk toward their seats to take us home.

III

On the way in I stopped for cheesy toasted sandwich with sliced tomato and buttered herbs. The Gentry believed a well fed member was a healthy member and I couldn't ever remember disagreeing with them about that. The smell of the butter still stained my fingers as I tossed a hair piece onto the vanity. Black curls toppled off the edge where I throw the whole hair piece as soon as my inner suite doors opened leading to my bedrooms. My extension from last night was heavy and the first thing to do was to free my long white locks immediately upon getting home. I hate the hair pieces the most. Actually, they were really the only part of this job that I hated. The glamours were far more comfortable and took almost none of my magic, but if I let my magic slip when I climaxed, then I could lose my full grip on a glamour. I don't want to hide who I am as I make my kill, but "life over vanity" and all these other bullshit mantras the Order of the Old Gentry uses to control us mandate it. I give them certain illusions of control, and they mostly leave me unbothered. Unbothered is how I will survive to end the war indefinitely.

The small hazel-colored gems come off easily and I immediately wash them down the rough marble and geode sink, changing my eye color back to its natural blue. I face myself in the mirror hung above the soaking tub.

I turned away from the mirrors and back into my rooms, across rugs of white and faded yellow, past squat, overstuffed chairs in front of a smoky hearth, and into a small area set up for tea and preparing small meals. I snapped my fingers and set a small fire under the domed top of the heating element. I let the candle burn for a moment before setting a small cup of water on its roof. The candle grew in strength, and I left it to boil while I finished undressing.

I remove my filthy leathers and set them aside before settling back against the small settee at the end of my bed. I let the breeze dance on my bare skin before a shiver drove me to wrap in the heavy cream blanket from the foot of my bed.

I sat watching the flicker of the flame under my tea and thought back to the surprisingly cool summer breeze that tousled the dark lengths I wore tonight on my brisk return walk to the doors of the ship, and I realized how desperately I missed the luxury of being able to dream about before. I drifted on the memory of the wind, its currents carrying me gently home and allowed my heart a moment to freely ache.

I only allowed it a moment though. Tonight, I learned something that will require my focus. Not from my target – he was an idiot – but my informant's partner. I was surprised to arrive before him after I received a message from the owner of a pub that sits in a quiet corner of The Gardens. Now he was late to show, delaying some answers from coming to me. Despite that I had received confirmation that another group of rebels had yet to show at their rendezvous, bringing the total to seven. Which is six too many.

Yes six, one of the groups was made up entirely of cave spiders and one handler to travel with them and I was glad to see those bastards go.

The difference is that this time we know where they went missing from, the report coming to me with a tiny, dotted map and urgent note that put them miles off target and much closer to the Northern borders than they should be.

I needed to get this to someone who could do something with it in time to help them. Someone who wasn't blocked from using their power to sneak on and off this ship. Someone willing to risk it all despite his home doubling as his own prison, complete with Veill security to keep an eye on him... when they weren't masquerading about his property as proper members of Abruzi, of course.

The Gentry had a ban against me trixxting myself directly off the ship and I try to abide by that. They also have bans against my interrogating people alone, eating directly from the cook's tables in the little kitchen, hiding pets (this one is dumb) and flying, among others that I'm sure I've forgotten about.

You wreck one tiny flyer, and they get all hot about it, apparently. It's not that I don't have the skill to fly, it's that I'm just not supposed to be doing it alone after I left a flight mage on the ground and used his pod as battering ram to run through a group of winged Veiliri descending on a small fishing village. I rolled my eyes and sighed again at all the silly rules, but I know, despite my reckless behaviors in the streets below, that I need to stop pushing Arike to be annoyed with me about Gentry business. Signing a flyer out against his instructions would annoy him greatly.

I grumbled and realized that I needed help. I have to keep my head down and keep myself from becoming a problem for the organization.

I stood from the settee and wondered briefly if any of the group hiding in the mountains tonight with my informant were there when the seventh group were lost. Maybe they crossed paths and maybe they saw something that I could use so I decided to drop in on him the next day. I also gave my word that I would, which I suppose counts for something still.

I carried the tea back into the bathroom and set the cup down on the edge of the tub while it filled itself with heated water. I gaze again into the mirrors and light the candles, watching as light now bounced lightly around the ice-opal frame. Mine is the only full length one on this part of the ship. The ship is my home. Home. Still a strange thing to admit, but this is my home now.

The original peace deals meant battleships were turned into luxury homes in floating suburbs above the clouds, a separation from the debauchery and sinister rule of the cities below. Long before the bases of the Gentry became a mixed society of trained members living alongside Tanirra's refugees in this opulent, floating home, I was a priestess. I lived free among the winding rivers of the valleys and practiced my magic in small doses under the instruction of others like me. Since the night that life was ripped from me, I'd been here weaving an image, another illusion stained with influence of the Gentry all around me. I give a lot to my people, some nights I take just for me, but my jobs are always perfectly executed.

The slight bruising of teeth marks from last night were already faded. Indigo shimmer and candlelight gently mist the midnight black walls behind me in time with the tilt of the ship as it takes off to dock in The Gardens. My reflection is caught in the dancing of lights for a moment, giving the illusion of a halo glowing briefly atop the silken strands of the hair of my mother's people. I look angelic. True, in some ways I am. I stare at the body in the mirror, perfect now, free of scars, bruising, blemish, and blood.

The blood from last night's job had run down my back after I finished him. To be fair, I let him finish me first, then the small dagger found its mark. The memory of that heat covering me thrummed through, peaking more needs.

I put aside thoughts of duty and plans and focus on working my body into a pleasant exhaustion, enjoying the memory of the night.

No, I decided the halo would remain hidden along with all my other truths for now. I dropped my hand to test the water and another to test a different wetness to take my mind off the job. The kill is the thrill? I throbbed at the thought. No, pretty sure the Gentry said it was that you find happiness in honor. That's also true, but honor doesn't turn me on the same way.

The small circles I make around my apex turn into slightly larger ones, steady, pushing in gently. I use one hand to steady myself on the steps down into the sunken quartz and amethyst tub lined on one side with hewn seating with gold flecks fully reflecting the layer of candles now. The other hand is already moving to push inside.

One finger, now two. When the water hits and the warmth laps around my waist, I push in three. Flicking those fingers once makes me groan and sends a shock of magic into the bath, scenting it with night jasmine. Glowing aqua eyes stare back at me from the mirror. My back is flush with the tub now and taking in my own beauty. Heat, night jasmine, and churning water washes all the other sins away, but my hand touches against the slickness again building between my thighs. This one I like. Wash the sins away per Gentry doctrine, but this one, this sin I keep. It is the sin that I need to stay sane.

IV

After tossing and turning under the pile of white linens on my bed for a few hours, I decided to get dressed and try to grab breakfast from a shop in the commons that made excellent wrapped eggs and sausage. I left my room and made it to the Garden commons in time to see the sun rise above a small group of elemental mages training for mobility on the grassy areas between the storefronts. I dropped a coin to pay the breakfast items I picked up for myself and Vance and headed back into the ships to pay my partner a visit, though I could have watched the graceful movements of the mage for several more moments.

Once inside the halls again I ducked inside of a small alcove to magic myself a fresh look. I doubted that seducing Vance to fly to me to Abruzi would work, but I'd used all of my other tricks on him and I was getting antsy. I shook out my hair and flowing skirts before knocking on his door.

I'm not surprised to find Vance dressed in loose linens and lounging in his rooms when I arrive. He couldn't have been back for long though, having needed to clear two of my kills and catalog them, along with whatever else the Gentry sent him out for the night prior.

"Thank you, Skarlet. It's not often you come looking for me. What can I do for you," he asked.

"Take me down."

I stared at the blue eyes of Vance as I walked toward the foot of his bed and leaned against the smooth chaise lounge of deep ivory threaded with pure white positioned there. Making a show of taking a seat and stretching my long legs, my feet languidly wound against the bottom post of the enormous bed in his suite. I curl my toes into the cream-colored cashmere blankets piled high across his bed. Split skirts of dusky red spill open with the movement, one panel of gossamer slips, showing the creamy skin of my thigh where panties should be.

"No," he bit into his breakfast and shook his head for emphasis.

"I'll owe you a favor. We can make this a real fun game, you and I," I teased.

"No. I am ignoring you and your scent. Your incredible deliciously shaped lips. All of it. You know the rules," Vance hissed. He flushed with the restraint he maintained, not falling at all for my advances.

He finished his meal and offered me tea, which I declined.

I needed to get out of the ship. Vance could operate fliers with unrestricted access, which was something I wasn't allowed to do by Gentry doctrine. It probably helped that he was already a winged master of the skies, flying aircraft for missions rather than need. The red pout of my lips was natural, but I licked them to add an extra incentive before purring at him. "I didn't say go down on me. I asked you to take me down. You galaxy males really should get laid more. It would help with your hearing issues," I grinned.

The dimples he tried to hide lit his face even with his head down. His eyes were anywhere but on me.

It's just a tiny request," I continued. The slit on my other thigh slid open so that both hips were now on display.

Vance was a gorgeous male. He was a galaxy fighter, once Commander of the Sky Knights, and a natural born hero with rugged good looks. The dark blonde of his hair was always clipped close which set off his stunning eyes that were the color of a clear sky. Maybe someday I really would take him to my bed. He was much more to me than that though. He was a friend if it could be said that I even had any of those.

I knew he was a good male from the moment we met. He rescued me. I was there, free falling through a sky full of war and blood with nothing left to cover my exposed body in the gore that surrounded us, but then there was Vance. The Knight Skies of the First, his own god, must have sent him soaring on the wings of steel that swept around me. He moved like lightning and commanded a war-pod around us with no more than a flap of those storm-stained wings, flying it to land us here where we have since lived and trained with so many others with similar tales. It was an unspoken rule that the Gentry's chosen had secrets they would kill to protect, so we never discuss those stories.

Since that night, Vance had left lingering looks on my skin when he thought I didn't know, but he's never once advanced. My first true memory here was of myself standing nude, terrified, and completely at his mercy after our first landing so long ago. A savage battle of will and want burned in those blue eyes, and the energy of battle still vibrated from his massive body. Still, there was never a physical inclination from him.

Back in the moment, he curiously lifted those eyes of shocking blue to me, skipping over the body on display to peer into my face, and I feel utterly exposed from the inside out, in the only kind of intense nakedness that I shy from now. I often wonder how much he knows of the girl he saved from the skies that night.

"My unit is out with all stealth fliers and their mage units on patrol or in drill, Skarlet, all I have are my wings. Where do you want to go?" he asked. The corner of his lips lifted slightly.

"I know, I saw them gearing up when we came in this morning." I respond, avoiding his question. "I didn't see you, though."

"I wanted to stretch my wings after cleaning up the Gentry's messes all night. I've been back long enough to wash the night off of me and get things straightened up."

I looked around his room and gave a little scoff. Books like uneven bricks leaned in stacks across most of the surfaces and maps hung like pictures across an entire wall. Swords, daggers, and scimitars lean against a weapons rack placed against the other wall. Smaller weapons clung to the wooden surface of a desk between bunches of parchments tied with ribbon.

I turned my head back to his to find him watching me. I leveled him with a direct gaze and tried to reason with him. "I can't tell you because you would draw much attention trying to help me your way."

He knew I would not freely give my destination, not when it meant an escort and public appearance of me with a Galaxy Flier that would draw way too much attention. Even in the blinding dark of the nights we hunt together, I don't acknowledge him outside of our comm crystal. He knows me well; knows I avoid being seen in common areas of the cities of Abruzi below us during the daylight. Outside of this ship and outside of jobs, I never go out without precautions, glamours, disguises, and a damn good reason.

"Skarlet, I'm on your side, in whatever it is that you're up to." He offered. "But you have to let me in."

"You're a beautiful sort of bastard. A mean, cold, ass, but so beautiful. If you won't offer your help unconditionally then don't bother." I leveled him with a cruel smile as I lifted to make my exit. "Do be sure to check that you lock your door tonight, Sir. I have a few ways of changing your mind if I find myself stuck on this ship because of you," I reply.

The male knew. He had always known at least one of my secrets and probably guessed more. I tossed a feline grin his way and bit playfully at

Vance on the way out of his door. Vance had proven loyal, and I trusted him. I think he might be the only fool to try to get close enough to be a friend, and without ever touching me.

There are many allies on this ship, but none I have allied myself with. Vance had been it from day one. If someday that changed and he became a liability, then I promised myself he would die happy. I could give him a good ride before I slit his throat. I chuckled to myself at the thought. The grin stuck with me amongst a wash of annoyance and the soft snap of white light from one palm had the red gown replaced with blood red flying leathers. A glamour would have to work when I got to the city.

"I have to find another way to get to Abruzi," I sighed and ducked out of the halls of the ship's living quarters. At least I can say I tried to find another way when Arike summoned me for my thrashing about this.

The halls that led to the docking bays were as ornate and ostentatious as the rest of the ship. I guess it took a lot to cover up all that grey and bloodshed. Passing panels of embossed metals etched to depict stories of great battles fought and of heroes claiming their titles, I kept my eyes straight but visions of shallow graves beneath a towering mountain push their way in. Visions not represented in any way on the newly placed murals on the hallway walls.

Thoughts of that night assault me and I pick up the pace. I glance to the left and take in a tale about the building of the gates, laborers and mages and the Gentry all represented there, but no moonlight touched priestess could be seen standing beside them. All of the temples and their priestesses fell the night Tanirra was overrun and there were none left to tell their story to the artists.

Well... there weren't supposed to be any left but here I was, trekking past the washing of my people's history from print to steal a flyer from my guild so that I could sneak into a city that doesn't want me there to save people who aren't looking for me to come for them.

"I need a fucking day off." A sliver of annoyance glows across my face. "And it probably won't be today."

One more bend to the bay to see what the crews have ready for me. The brightness is almost blinding coming from the open drop pads where Vance's squads were entering and exiting in perfect formation. The sun throws a sparkling glint from a beautiful speeder. The wicked flyer proudly displaying its deceitfully delicate blades, and recently restocked, is a Golden Beezer. It is tiny; it blends into the day itself and is not visible by discovery shields since it's powered by solar energy alone.

The Gentry owns one of only two left intact after the battle. The other is kept by Prince Dekren Charsee of the Golden Aisles. Rumor is he uses this Beezer's twin to shuttle his mistresses in from other lands or within Veill itself, though that last part was thought impossible before the gates blazed to life that night. Regardless, all of Dek's women are of extraordinary beauty and all are to be treated as royalty during their stay with the prince. Truly, Dekren would be a great catch for some young Lady, despite there being rumors of his occasionally callous response to refugees entering his lands, and with the ongoing fight against the Veill to keep his lands beneath from being overrun. He is good for an occasional tryst as well and not hard on the eyes. The tall, tanned prince was due a replacement princess soon if our last brunch was any indicator of his timing.

"Hello beautiful, Mama is here to take us for a little ride," I grinned and jogged to the corner where the flyer waited.

It may not be a day off, but stealing a chariot made for a sky queen will make things far more like a vacation. I winked at the knight walking toward me with his hand outstretched for my fly orders. I flash a hand and trixxt myself into the seat, not bothering to open the locked door to get in before slam a hand against the solar powered panels to bring myself and the tiny Beezer to just outside the ship. The knight stood looking out from the bay now barely more than a speck across the galaxy from this distance. The Gardens stretched below me across all of the landing docks for non-battle ships. They call it "Bay of the Gods." They'll say anything to comfort their countenance, their tolerance, and even their loyalty; Whatever is needed to help them forget everything that we all had lost.

Community areas and towering buildings melt into a fairy tale shaped blur as I let the Beezer take flight. Since the ships of the fallen aristocratic have been converted, so have lavish amenities been added to the skies. Because of the peace deals, it's all docked her now, outside the flying reach of the Veiliri who now control most of the continent of Tanirra.

V

A vista of rainbow piercing through high altitude chelcei and golden rutilated quartz rise up before me. Peaks gilded like the eyes of gods topped ranges for miles and the shimmer of color almost hid the silver lining my eyes. A home that boasts of this kind of beauty would be found nowhere outside of these lands. Even the city of Abruzi, the largest on the continent, built itself up around the Mother's natural works.

The chelcei gem clusters form the tips of the mountain ranges, making them difficult to mine and worth at least a dozen times more than the diamonds that they look so much like. Often the size of a dragon's egg, the chelcei, once removed from under the sun, will shine forever with that same warm essence despite the many pieces it is broken into. The glowing gems are often set as jewels for rings and elaborate hilts.

The ruling family of Azullon, while they were still the power of the Mountain and all the lands past the valleys, had shamans and smithies that were able to form them into knives that remained eternally sharp. One alone would set a family of the valley above his station for his life and the lives of his legacies. Once a year, before the fall of that sapphire valley and the last ruling Azulli into the demonic hands of the Veill, a week was spent by every able body surrounding the Mountain in attempts to obtain a chelcei stone. The treks were dangerous, and precious few made it up far enough to mine a jeweled peak.

Other allies were made though, friends of the folly-of-the-mountain and entire families were bonded over frozen lakes and soaring vistas. Any who could reach one would be entitled to the fortunes of its sell. A great feast would be hosted in the valley for the conqueror and his or her family. Days of revelry that would stretch on and on and carried on still for the years to come in new tunes sang by traveling troubadours.

My heart ached to look upon it now, to know what was lost and what there still was to lose. A familiar anger rumbled up my body before I could push it away again. The air I drew stuck in my lungs as if I were physically trapped in a nightmare. Swimming under the currents of anger and anxiety, I loosened my grip on the Beezer to circle me back towards the location of today's meeting.

Thinking on the last time I'd been inside the mountain, I'd like to say that I immediately joined the fight against my home but at first, I ran, straight to the Azullon Keep, under Blue Mountain. I was too late and the scenes I stumbled into are the ones that chase nightmares into my nights now. Bodies lie strewn across the courtyard, dead or dying. Fires blazed, destroying curtains and furniture and nipping at the skirts of still bodies. Screams tore the evening air and echoed through the pillars and out of the large temple mezzanine, its theater sunk down carved steps and into the mountain so deep that the pool in the center of the altar was fed by an underground mountain stream. One voice cut through all the others, urging me to come to her, accompany her body while her spirit left for Asti's kingdom. I turned my back on the burning temple and ran to the grassy bowl at the base of a small knoll where the last of my family lay dying. I leaned down to gently kiss her farewell and was knocked unconscious by the gift she siphoned into me. Her magic, left to me like an overwhelming gift that I am never quite sure what to do with. The memory of her death chills me to the core and I shook my head to bring myself back to the present.

"I have not given enough. I have not been enough," I said hastily. I pushed the stale air out of me finally as the mountain ranges zipped past. The blue valleys shifted, and I banked into the countryside of Abruzi. There was no time, no place even, to have any doubts of what needed to be done. Before coming into sight of the landing field, I pulled up above the mists of low hanging clouds, aiming for a little more cover.

Another flash of light and the sound of hands rubbing together were the only things that broke up the solemnity in the Beezer's beautiful cabin. Thinking of the landing just moments away threatened to push the thought of Blue Mountain back up. I straightened again and tossed up a glamour to mask my natural creamy tan skin and white hair. Blocking out the intruding past, I reminded myself that grief was a weakness nearly as strong as pride. I would not fall to any weakness again. I needed to focus only on the itinerary of the day; the right now.

"It's time to have ourselves a little chat, honey," I insisted. I calmed the boiling feeling inside me and reminded myself that emotions had no place in duty.

Merlot-stained lips pulled back to reveal a dimple in the face that now looked a little softer, ears rounded, and button nosed like the girls from humanara lands. Skin was more tanned to reflect the glittering gold bangles and cuffs up my wrists and arms; a glamour to look like a sky princess, to match the chariot landing in the sun-drenched fields of the glittering countryside of Abruzi.

"An escort of Veill plus regionals, how classy of him," I thought. I denied the urge to roll my eyes. Golden blonde curls nearly the same shade of dandelions and sunflowers in the fields surrounding me shifted as I peeked into the reflection of myself in the polished instrument panel. Well, don't I look just delicious. Like a bowl of peaches and cream. I am nothing if not a little narcissistic. With a shrug of admission, I push the doors of the Beezer up, opening myself to view of the oncoming envoy.

When the landing field was first built, the Lord of the estate used a combination of elements to keep the sun from warming the stones so that any kind of flyer could land here, whether on bare foot and winged or under the arms of a great ship.

The breeze from the mage mingled with the coolness coming from under her feet. The only heat saturating the bronze slippers and tight bodice of a coral gown came from the sun above. The eyes of the commander walking towards Skarlet didn't lift from her breasts until he was nearly toe-to toe with her. They lingered past the plunge of delicate coral lace that reached her navel, not bothering to hide his appraisal. Hazel eyes finally drifted up to her glamoured baby blues as he came within five feet of her.

"This is private landing only and I don't have any registered flyers coming in. Nor do I have a record of anyone declaring emergency protocols. What is your name?" Said the man I recognized as Veil Commander, Siel,. "What do you want?"

I closed the distance between us, not missing the looks of curiosity and anger briefly crossing his face. Pushing my breasts firmly against his own chest made my stomach roil a bit, but my nipples peaked against the light fabric covering them at the touch. Forcing my face into a small smile, I caught his gaze before it dropped to where our bodies met. "Commander, I had nearly forgotten how beautiful the Veill gentlemen are." Leaning into his body a little more, I whispered, "And such a good fuck, too?"

Commander Siel was definitely not a regional, not with the stature of a chiseled piece of art and pierced pointed ears. He stared down at my chest even as his erection pushed against me. My smile brightened as I said, "Please tell your host that he has a visitor with a message from the Gardens."

The Commander growled before pushing his massive body away from me. He shot me a look of raw, seething heat: desire or hate or maybe a mix of both. As he turned to go, he seemed to have a change of heart and leaned back into my body and whispered, “Ya best watch that bouncing ass, little tease. I will bury myself into it for hours the first chance I get. I can’t promise I will be gentle at all, Gentry, and I am no man.”

Dropping my smile just enough to widen my mouth, I brought my finger to my teeth and winked at him. He would be first on my list next hunting day.

The mage that brought me down from the little golden flyer stepped smugly in front of me. Wrapping me in that gentle wind, not bothering with the Commander’s introduction or even a hint at a goodbye, he whisked me straight to the opulent estate offices of Lord Drake.

VI

My visit hadn't taken long and wasn't worth the large assembly that greeted me on the rustic tarmac to begin with. Lord Drake had long been held under Veiliri rule but continued to command a strong rebel team of non-Gentry allies. As a widely public figure in the philanthropic corners of Abruzi, his life was spared in return for keeping all his financial gains. Well, they thought it was all of it. Lord Drake had supporting forces working against our oppressors from the beginning and despite the very real danger to his life, he continued to do so by slipping bits of information back to me.

Normally he sent an associate, but this meeting was the exception. I had information to deliver to him that couldn't wait. Lord Drake's associates operated outside of the control of the Gentry before the Gentry were removed as the top military operation in Tanirra and continued to do so. No one really trusted the Gentry's ways then, and now that some of its leaders have been exposed as traitors who aided the Veiliri, it's been difficult to recruit under their new direction. Lord Drake had not had the same problems with that, so most new people went through his guys. It's these reasons that dragged me here today; he had the resources to send in a few associates to extract our missing teammates once he got my information into the right hands. Hence the visit, and the reason for not telling Vance. His appearance at my side would have been impossible to hide and I'd never had made it in to see LD.

The Golden Beezer soared above the clouds of late afternoon as I left his estate. I didn't bother changing into my red leathers, opting to stay with this smokescreen for my market visit, and instead slouched back against the smooth, curved seat, pulled a cloak around my bare shoulders, and shoved my chilled hands into the lined coat pockets. Intense energy suddenly assaulted my senses, heating up my insides with unspent magic. Focusing on the luxury of the flyer and a breathing technique used in the high altitudes of the Blue Mountains helped to reign it in.

It had been days since a good training. Worthy opponents have been getting harder to find as more Assasjines are being sent out on hunts during single moon phases. The activities of the Veiliri have spiked in the last few weeks with more of them entering remote cities and claiming those territories for additional territory of the Veill. There shouldn't have been many left with the rate we destroy each other on hunts but it seemed that two took the place of every one that I took down. With no Azullons in power and dangerously few other powerful families willing to strategize against these actions, they were meeting little resistance from the locals.

The meeting with Lord Drake was fast but all I needed was enough time to pass my message along. He would share what he knew when he could and I'd take whatever he passed along. With still no sign of the Veiliri Prince that led the ambush on Tanirra from the shadows, intelligence had begun to thin, even coming across as negligently false at times. He was target number one and I'd been trying to find out who he was. Everyone in the Gentry was trying to identify him so that we could take him down first, followed by his people.

The last known image of the ruler of Telseneir, capital city of Veill, was of his father, Tristan, Leader of House Kai. Tristan was a male who ruled up until a short time prior to the insurgence. None of the Veiliri would give up the new heir's identity. All records of him had been sealed in Veill and just outside of our reach. Being unable to speak openly with the Lord set my blood singing before I even left him to circle back down to the fields outside of the market from last night.

I came in near the white apothecary tents. The lines they stood in reached far past the edges of the stalls and left no room for them beside the shoppers that squeezed between the waiters. Their hands were full of goods that often dinged the garments of the others as they try to slide through the gaps.

The Veiliri must have taken much from the people last night for them to being running terrified into the markets in droves on a day where most should be headed into one of the Abruzi's many beautiful buildings to do whatever they do for income.

Despite the breakfast I'd downed earlier, the smell of the food coming from the square made my stomach rumble in anticipation. I denied myself the luxury and managed to avoid looking at what was on offer as I cut through the center and angled for the tent and armoire.

I spotted the tent's odd stillness from across the center and began to push the crowd aside so that I could make the last few steps to the inside of the canopy. The cloths from last night lay covering the goods in the same way they had when I left. I pushed up to the armoire door and put an ear against it before knocking twice. Then twice again.

After a few moments, no answer had come. I didn't want to barge into someone's home, but technically they live in a closet so the rules here are vague. If something were wrong I didn't try the locks, I know it would always haunt me that I could have done something.

I reached for the smudged handles and settled my fingers into their cubbies before yanking mightily. I nearly busted my ass. The doors flew open with ease and staring back at me was an empty closet. Nothing more, not even a sign that they had been here.

What an absolute waste of time. Now I'm annoyed and hungry and still have to push my way through this crowd. The smashing of the tables I now had to straighten had drawn attention to the space and I couldn't afford to magic my way back to the little beezer from here with everyone watching.

I straightened the table just under my legs and made a dash into the square, hoping to lose the stares before getting to the exit. I'd almost made it when an idea came to me. I stopped in front of the apothecarist in the white tent and asked the attendant what he could tell me about the vendor with the armoire.

I thought this idea was going to get this terrible day back on track, but when the gangly man turned leering yellow eyes and a matching snarl on me and uttered a vial, deprecating retort, I knew my day was about to get much, much better. Only I could not kill him with all the eyes that were on me, so I sent the buttons of his tunic and pants flying and leaned over a table to push him back. He stumbled and his pants dropped to pool around his feet. Mothers covered the eyes of their children and ladies turned from the sight, and everyone gave me a wide berth while he scrambled to redress. Grabbing a small vial of poppima and a few lovely tonics from his shelf, I ran to the doors of the little flyer and aimed for the sky.

VII

Landing the Beezer back in the bay was not as hard as I had imagined. There was only one knight on duty, and one that I knew favored my blonde look the best. A simple smile and a few sweet lies combined with swift touches across his horns had him melting. I walked away boiling with indignation upon realizing the only reason I got away with this little stunt was Vance. Knowing that he chose this guard means he followed me to Abruzi despite denying my plea for assistance.

Frustration continued to fill me as I stalked toward the Cohenesh hoping to find a Cohein, a priest or priestess, to train with. The Cohenesh temples were sacred themselves, but the Cohein that practiced within them were not of a prude nature. Like any other Gentry official or member, they believed in self-expression, and some even performed and taught a practice called Dojari with stretches and meditation that often ended in euphoric climaxes, which they considered the only acceptable emotion.

Reaching the stairs that led down into gardens, reflection pools, and close body combat training of the Cohenesh levels, I drew short. I couldn't help but think of the trip to Abruzi, the battles of the skies, my Blue Mountains, and my people; all of the things I couldn't control.

I turned in a tight circle and made short work of the distance toward the upper-level staircases and decided on a different kind of release. Swaying through the crowd already gathered at the dance floor of a three-tiered lounge area, I tried to keep my steps light and straight while sways of curved hips matched the sultry beat drawing tension from my body in waves. Walking through the people of the Gentry, from Assasjine to determined refugees, that crowded the dance floor was an exhilarating experience. I allowed the pure energy to take over and take me away. Music always had that effect on my magic when I needed a release. What is music if not magic that answers the questions you couldn't ask?

The mezzanine that served as the second floor overlooked the dark, cavernous room lit by lamps with intricate carving and gold or jeweled overlays. Pillows were scattered about lounge areas surround the whole of the dance floor. Refreshments of all kinds littered serving areas throughout the seated spectators with some trays floating amongst the dancers on phantom hands. At the back of the tavern, the walls opened to a massive staircase that wound itself up the rest of the rooms. The release I needed was heavier than what dancing could offer. I made my way towards the stairs. The top floor terrace entrances and the dance floor walkways were the only two acceptable passages to the fighting nooks and arenas on the second floor

"One who could not love or dance freely will never fight for true freedom. You cannot desire only to serve yourself in your home or your community, nor can you be selfish on the battlefield." The Gentry were a paradox of rules, regulations, and secrets, but they believed that one who cannot give freely to their instincts will never fight with the same love of victory as those who do.

I reached the stairs at the far end and as the beats faded, I regretted that I couldn't stay longer. Tomorrow I would dance until my body hummed a song all its own. Tomorrow.

Hitting the second-floor landing and taking in the tapestries had my body heating again. More carvings of myth, lore, and half-accurate legends illuminated by cruder versions of the first floor's lamps were visible in the light from the bobbing orbs. The halls branched off and darkened again. Slipping into a small divot in the wall where training weapons normally hung, I reached into the pocket of the loose linen pants I now wore and pulled out a tiny ribbon of shimmering red and white circles.

I silently thanked the apothecarist who so indelicately extended his offer of free product if I would only offer him my product for free and thought of his face as his trousers hit the ground. Yes, its childish, but I could have killed him..

Placing the ribbon onto my tongue, I lay my head against the smooth cool stone of the wall. Before I could think of why I even bothered with the drugs, an intense feeling came over me. I could still think, but not about things that mattered. I pushed forward from the wall and sprinted towards the lit stairs again to take me up into the floor darker than the two previous. Stepping away from the small lamps that served as the only light on this landing, I turned down the dark as midnight in the Veill hallway, which caused a chill to course down my spine.

I could feel my body loosen as my eyes adjusted to seeing the heat of other bodies in the room. A breeze caught my nipples under the flowing silken top that fluttered just above my navel. The poppima intensified my craving for release. I wanted to feel that light touch of chill everywhere. A light thud sounded as my clothes hit the ground, leaving me bare.

The winds from the terraces blew clove and vanilla scents in through jeweled curtains covering the dozens of private alcoves. Some large enough for more than two, but all soundproof and luxuriously accommodating. A low growl rumbled at my side and I knew right away who I wanted to control me tonight. He sniffed, scenting my need as a different kind of heat lit me up.

I needed a male who would sink into my center and take control. Tonight, in the arms and tethering magic of this rogue, I would not have any responsibilities. I would not be the one making the decisions. The poppima's rapture intensified and all emotion melted away. There was nothing but primal need tonight as he pushed himself into me wherever he desired. I would just be a girl getting her body and her magic drained, and not a girl who let so many people down.

VIII

Standing in my door, Vance dodges the knife to his left just as I launched another to his right, which he caught without moving his blue eyes away from my face. A small smirk tried to break free of the rigid, disappointed look he stared me down with. "I told you no," he stated.

Dropping the sheet from around my body, my skin still salty and gleaming from the work of the rogue hours before, I stalked toward him. His eyes bore into the aquamarine and silver of my own. "I heard you, boss, I chose to ignore you and you followed me anyway," I replied. I raised my voice despite our closeness. "So, you bust into my quarters at sunrise to what? Lecture me? Are you going to master me now, Vance? Really try to control me?" Annoyance flashed across his features. "Finally come for that taste you lie and say you don't want?" I teased.

Vance's height grew and the solid pillars of his legs vibrated with his restraint. He gripped my wrists as I reached for his blond hair and we tumbled into the room. I was intent on antagonizing him. My wrists were caught in one of his hands and he used the other to brace against the wall. A knee shot up between me, drawing me legs further apart. Stretching my arms out to the sides caused my back to arch, pushing my bare breasts further into his view. I laughed and leaned into his form. Vance released his hand from the wall, muscles growing taught through the training shirt he still wore, working to keep his balance. He reached for a discarded blanket and threw it around me before pushing me into the bedroom and taking a few steps back to the door.

"Skarlet, don't fuck with me. You stole an aircraft, an incredibly expensive one, went dark for most of the day and came back with drugs. Which part of that should I include in my report this morning? I am summoned before the Gentry Assembled in less than thirty minutes. You're trashed from last night. I can still smell him on you. Still smell it on you. I will do my best to mitigate this, but you're to be in attendance as well.

Wash the stink of stupid off of you and cover your tits. I will see you there," he stated coldly. The double doors slammed with the power of the gods as Vance made his exit.

"Sky Knight scum!" I screamed at the door as his footsteps faded. The blanket went flying across the bed right before I fell backwards on top of it. Vance was right to be furious with me. His concern for my safety is what annoyed me most. I would accuse him of stalking me if he had ever actually made any sexual advances toward me. I accepted him as a friend, but it seemed Vance had committed himself to be my constant companion even when I didn't want him to be. Someday, when my whole world exploded, he would regret the day he decided to play hero. The flames would take him down with me.

The bath wasn't long enough or the night was too long. I could never tell after a few rounds of poppima and orgasms. The Gentry Assembled were usually whatever few ranking members happen to be in attendance when someone had done something that requires discipline or direction outside of common orders. Meetings of regular business were held by crystal projection to include those who were away. Each member either were Magi or had a magic wielder with them on travel.

The senses still fogging my brain were clearing slowly, only to be replaced by a banging pain each time a boot echoed off the long stretch of common halls. It was too early for most members to be awake except for those who managed breakfast halls and little cafes on the guest landing bay of the ship. Those few I crossed paths with on the way toward the middle of the ship were likely just coming off assignment. They all aimed toward to the same halls where I worked so hard for this headache. Considering where I am headed, I am certain I would make the same mistake again given the chance, if it meant getting me out of this meeting.

The smell of a blazing fire mingling with glasses of neat bubbly wine cut with juice and leather chairs meet me as I make my approach to the mahogany door. It was so loud. The murmuring of voices and languages on the other side of the carvings of flags of all nations that covered the door handles in the shape of embracing hands was overwhelming. That poppima had to have been poorly farmed. It sounded like the whole Gentry was babbling just ten feet away from me.

Vance stalked around a corner and tightened his mouth as his gaze found me rubbing my fingers into my temple and out to the still wet white hair I left hanging freely. The roll of my eyes added urgency, or was that real anger, to his steps. He reached me before I could get out a good huff and pout combo.

Noises erupted abruptly, drawing his attention from me to the mahogany door and the sound of a large party beyond it. Honestly, I thought I had imagined it.

I slid my eyes left and up Vance's giant form. He kept his wings hidden when on the ship, as though it would make him any less terrifying when he already ducked into doorways and looked down upon everyone. "You're cranky. Maybe you should visit the markets in Abruzi, too. I'd never judge."

Turning my body to throw a wink his way, I stopped before the full rotation. He stood utterly still. Storms rolled across his eyes boring holes into the door as though he could see the universe through them. I didn't see him move before he leaned in to whisper, "Skarlet, hear me and obey me. You stay out of this. Whatever it is, you keep that pretty pout shut and hide behind me, literally, if that will keep attention away from you." Vance had absolute authority in this moment. A hand fell upon my lower back and suddenly the poppima fog was gone. Feeling his breath leave my neck as he straightened left me standing like a Knight beside him, strong and completely devoid of fear.

The door swung open on my command and every color and shape of eye turned our way. It was not quite the whole Gentry, just all its ruling members. I had never been in the room with them all at once. Hell, I'm not even sure they had all been in the same room at once since the fall of Tanirra.

As my eyes adjusted and Vance's hand dropped from my back, the smells hit me. All at once I imagined beaches of cobalt sea lapping against them with islands of exotic fruits that ripened upon touch. The smell of Abruzi mixed in with a heavy scent of perfume and pine from the Northern Prince's forests. Spell casting materials left a myriad of floral notes on the robes of the Magi in the room to mingle with the headier scent of the steel carried by the Melee Rangers and Knights. The fires burnt logs gifted from the Thula to the West where forests sing to their people and the branches smelled of happy memories when burned.

Every sound stopped right along with my heart as all eyes turn our way. So much for being a fearless Knight. Vance dug his fingers into my back as if to say "I have you. I am right here."

Every bit of acidic anxiety and burning magic came rushing back, lighting me on fire. It took a mere second to remember to drop a glamour over eyes that would glow with the buildup. Every single Gentry ruler and his region were represented here.

Oh Mother, did they come for me? If so then I have failed. The thoughts pushed up from the place I keep my terror hidden and right into my broken soul. My hands shook with the possibility for only a few seconds before Arike appeared.

Auburn hair and blazing golden eyes move forward first: Arike Arliga, first line of The Order of the Old Gentry, and technically mine and Vance's true Commander, stalked toward me. His dark skin was lit by the lamps floating about, which made him seem to glow as he approached. Looking down his nose with a tilt of the head, he smiled.

"Skarlet Lior, always such a treat to gaze upon those divine features. Such a violent creature, with the look of an angel." The room behind Arike lifted their voices in a loud cheer.

Something was definitely not right.

Vance pulled me closer, and panic tried to rise with the heat of the room. Ignoring it I stepped an inch closer to him. If Arike knew what I was really doing under the banner of the Gentry then this group wouldn't be cheering.

I really needed to release my magic on a larger scale and if they knew, truly knew that secret, if that was why we're here then I would take this whole group down with me as I let it out. I always knew this would end in martyrdom; I just didn't think it would be so early in the day.

Our Commander allowed the cheer its moment before raising a delicate hand.

The entire room was so silent suddenly that it was impossible that anyone even breathed. Arike's smile grew to show perfectly white teeth gleaming under a long nose. Pointed ears peek out from behind the sheet of Auburn as he turned his back to me.

"All of your excellencies, please take a seat and let us break our fast while we speak of real business." Arike's grab of my hand startled Vance just long enough for our First Commander to shoot Vance a scathing look before pulling me forward and out of the Knight's reach.

My hand was lifted, after we have cleared Vance by a few feet, and placed upon the nook of Arike's elbow. He meant to escort me. From the way the room cleared, I was the only one there surprised by that. As soon as I settled to Arike's left, chairs were pulled out at once for every other member.

The scents of each region seemed to settle and were taken over by plates placed upon the table. Stacks of sticky cakes, smoked meats, poached eggs, and every fruit and bread desired by the wealthy was made. In this case, it felt like almost all of them. I picked up the orange bubbling wine and shot a curious glance toward Vance's spot halfway down the table on the opposite side of me. His shrug of confusion was barely even a movement.

Arike's second, a commander of the melee team, stood and slid a sticky maple sauced tart onto my plate himself, though there were no shortages of servers bustling through. "No peaches and cream today, Khiry?" the second tart dangled in his still hand. Arike grinned at the flush creeping up his second commander's cheeks.

"You know I just love all the juice of a good, firm, peach." The lick of my tart off my spoon sent him back to his seat as more than a few tried to stifle a grin. I began to relax, just enough that I could sit back without trembling.

What was I here for if not for reprimand? These thoughts kept blocking out all other rational ones.

Vance spoke up on my behalf. He was ever the galaxy hero trying to cement himself in my corner. "For the Gentry and for order," he brought a fist to his chest. Other leaders returned the salute, giving him audience while they ate. "This feast is amazing, and will cost me extra time in training, no doubt." A salute of forks went up in agreement. Vance continued, "When I was summoned along with Lady Lior, I could never have imagined such an honor to dine with all my brethren." A low nod in my direction and a few more faces lit up along with a "Here! Here!" chant from around the room. "In the name of good graces, might we know of what we all gather here for so jubilantly, and at such a very early hour?" Vance lowered back to his seat at the last words left his lips.

Arike nodded toward Vance before standing with his own salute. "We are gathered so very early to celebrate an excellent kill of Lady Lior's."

"All of my kills are excellent, Commander," I breathed. I didn't miss the warning look Vance shot my way.

Arike's pointed ears shifted again with his smile. "True. This kill has just been reported as a Court kill, and an unexpected wealth of information comes with that."

Was I so distracted by my own mission that I missed all the details at the scene? How did a new court member make its way into the Abruzi city for me to kill when we'd had no activity reported from any gates.

I thought back to our last hunt and the gorgeous Veiliri with the excellent tongue. The rooms seemed a little more luxurious than others I have killed in, but nothing stood out as being absurdly different. No hidden vaults or portals. I had checked, hadn't I? Had there been a portal I certainly would have saved the energy of walking to my next location and used it instead.

Arike caught the look of deep thought tightening my mouth before I could replace it with a sultry grin. He cast a knowing stare upon me, searching me from my unbound hair down the red sweater and black fleece-lined bottoms I had thrown on this morning. I realized I was tragically inappropriately attired. It was too late for a glamour, everyone had seen me at this point and to change it would draw too much attention, giving them the impression that there was something about a female's body that we should be ashamed of. The glowing gaze lingered long enough to cause a soft push against my sweater that reminded me I had also forgone any binding on my breasts, not thinking to be in here long enough for it to matter.

Our Commander averted his smoldering gaze to raise a glass. "To a kill well executed." Another cheer. "Lady Lior, you have brought us a great gift." Arike paused for the air to still entirely. "The Gentry has the body of a ranking member of the Court of Veill, with Veiliri tattoos marking him as a Syndicate member to study. We also have a lead on finding the identity of its Prince. He is not in Veill as we have long believed. Since the kill is yours, the first chance of victory is yours by right. You will leave tonight, along with Vance and Marli of the North, to hunt."

"Why do we need another partner," I tried to interrupt Arike's toast but he just quieted me with an aggressive whisper. "To guide you," he hissed.

This time, as Arike drank from his goblet, there was no quieting the roar of cheering coming from our table. I stood, all my curves on show as goosebumps took over my pale skin. A slight bow was all that I could manage under the torrent of thoughts coursing through my mental shields.

"Who is Marli," I tried to ask but Arike gave me a warning look that again kept me quiet.

Vance came to his feet to rescue me again. "Commander, it is the highest honor which we humbly accept. As it pleases the Gentry, so it pleases me." Everyone repeated and cups were refilled. My friend shot me a look that said we would discuss this later.

I took my seat and was bombarded with questions about how it felt to bring the Veiliri down.

I don't remember my cup being empty at all for the remainder of the meal and it was well after noon when we left the room. Revelry and alliances abounded all of the morning, reminding me of a poor man's version of the chelcei celebrations. My head fogged with the need for a nap right before Vance caught me slipping into my suite. His eyes were lit with determination. "Skarlet, be in training this evening. Then you and I will speak alone."

With a final squeeze of my arm, he was off toward the bays. Stumbling into bed, the last thought I had was of Vance, but definitely not as my Commander. I hated leaving an ache unattended, but sleep was the ultimate victor this afternoon.

IX

Jasmine scented fog from the bath rose in a steady torrent of steam up and surrounded the room as water mixed with my magic. I needed one last long soak before heading out for a long flight. Arike informed us that our covert team would go in first and communicate any new information in real time.

The need for stealth wouldn't allow us to send an entire squad in, but that meant we were up against a ticking clock. The death of the usurper would far outweigh any of our lives if we took too long and the Gentry were forced to bring in a larger force. Knowing this annoyed me.

Honoring the Gentry code by giving me this assignment was a mix of stubborn principle and a quick way to start another war with such a large target as the Prince of Veill. We could allow no errors. We would be completely alone until the Gentry decided to intervene.

My nap earlier was not nearly long enough, with one of Vance's little grunts banging on my door and demanding I join them in the Cohenesh. "Now," he had muttered with an edge of apology.

I managed to slip into training clothes that tugged against oversensitive skin before flowing to just above my navel. The loose fabric was much like my outfit from last night. "Had it only been a day?" I wondered out loud.

I allowed myself a moment to run back through the day, through the memory of my temper slipping as I considered my odds of making this mission work in my favor as I headed down to the training levels. I was even more annoyed when I descended the stairs and Vance bowed slightly to me.

"Lady Lior," Vance had sighed as I entered the chamber that afternoon. His use of my title told me we weren't alone. He would never address me so formally otherwise. "Let me introduce Marli, our companion on this assignment." An eyebrow lifted toward his sandy blonde locks as he turned toward a shape in the corner. Had Vance not immediately introduced him, it would have taken me a moment to sense the slight shadow that stood at the edge of the far wall. Darkness seemed to emanate from him, covering the jet-black coloring of his eyes and hair. His leer gave me an oily feeling. He was opposite from Vance in every way possible, slight in frame and dark in every sense.

I didn't like being assigned partners. I don't do well in group projects, and I get annoyed when people slow me down. I thought of the way his size and appearance seemed to warp in time with smoky shadows that circled heavily at his wrists, shoulders, and feet and wondered if he would be a liability.

"Are you Marli, of the North." I asked with no preamble, my frustration from the last several days taking over common courtesy.

"Ma Lady, it is such a sweet pleasure to meet ya, officially," the Rogue bowed in mock awe.

"I doubt it," this earned a reprimand from Vance.

"Do ya now, but doubt is the playground of failure, aye!?" Marli responded in a voice I was already tired of.

Had we met prior to this moment I probably would have liked this guy. But today I was still tired from the morning, cold in my training gear, and he reminded me a little of the apothecarist from the market.

"It's just that I don't need a guide to help me to and from the ship. I don't need a guide in the North either if our party travels so far. I have completed many missions all across these lands, from the banks of bottomless lakes in the west to the churning seas south, and I do not need someone slowing me down now that I've finally gotten a workable lead," I challenged.

I shivered as the lights in the globes hanging from the roof began to lower, making if feel like my sight had dimmed, and casting Marli even further into the shadows.

"Shall I show you why I am not a liability, ma lady? Whenever you're ready, then," he taunted.

"Shall we dance for our first date, then," I gave a stilted bow in the same hesitant manor Vance had a moment ago.

I stepped lightly across the floor while locking shining aqua eyes with his dull black ones, wrapping bindings tightly about my hands and wrists. Everything about him seemed dull, from his eyes to the way he walked. Experience had taught me that a rogue allows you to see what they want you to see. This one set my teeth on edge and temper flaring with the blankly lethal stare he leveled me with. They always back down though, the ones that bark the loudest. His efforts at intimidating were wasted on me despite the pissing match we had prior to sparring.

The Rogue hadn't muttered a word during our session. His eyes never left me, training his gaze to catch my movements before I launched them. A few times I had him on the defensive before he would slip from my grip with deadly quiet and land a backhanded blow on my body. It was a move the Gentry taught everyone. It was important to have your own back sometimes, too.

The Rogue must have trained on the ship, yet I had never seen him. It should surprise me that Arike would send a stranger on a mission this important, but I still hadn't figured out why he is allowing the three of us alone to go first, so I didn't have the room to wonder over his motive for assigning this Rogue.

We lunged and danced about while Vance watched from the sides. We studied one another and bounced between footwork for half an hour before I began to create a full picture of his style. In that time I still wasn't able to grasp a fully clear image of him, his features beyond the veil of shadows.

I landed a blow to his thigh that made him buckle after several tries and began to taunt him while he straightened from the blow. I dashed to the side meaning to bring him down in a heap of loss, but he lashed out to bring his arm around my throat, with movements faster than I could completely counter. I leaned into the momentum to drive us to the ground and loosened my body to fall harder upon his. I bounced up and, brought my fists to the tops of his knees, pulling back at the last second. I jumped up and dashed a few feet out of his reach before he came completely into a crouching position.

Marli growled, though his eyes sparkled. We rushed one another from opposite sides of the arena; a cyclone of light and shadows and steel clashed in the middle. Genuine malice etched Vance's features for the moment it took him to gain control. He wasn't happy about the Rogue in attendance and our little clash had won him no favors with the Knight. Dismissing Marli with orders to meet on the bay half past sunset before I had any answers about why he had to be there at all, Vance spun and aimed straight for me. "Yes honey?" I purred.

I pulled bloodied wrappings back off my hands and fluttered my lashes at him. To my genuine surprise, he reached behind his head to pull off his training shirt and tossed it aside. His grin was the only warning before our fight began. Alone and in complete privacy, I poured as much as I could into ridding myself of the heat that ever plagued me as so much of my magic went unspent.

An hour later we both lay panting upon a cushioned ring. Ropes sectioned the room into designated spaces to keep Gentry from entering other fights accidentally while sparring.

"How long has it been Skarlet?" Vance propped his head onto a hand and looked down at my sweaty form, the shadow of wings flaring against the walls. Their dark gray color nearly overtook the bright white of the room. He didn't have to elaborate. "Four years since I came to the ship. Four years and a day since I saw my people, walked the paths of my Mountain."

I read the pity in his eyes and rage threatened to take over. "How long for you, Sky Knight? How long since you have been on unstained Tanirran soil?" Anger was easier to manage than regret and I poured every accusation into the question.

Vance smiled as he rose to his feet and repeated, "Four years since I came to the ship. Four years and a day since I saw my home, my plane." Pulling me to my feet with surprising tenderness, he added, "Pack with warmth in mind, Skarlet. This mission may lead to the beginning of new things. You will make it home, but without this kill it will only be the home your nightmares are made of."

My bath watered jetted and heated as my emotions rose; the ones that get you killed: regret and fear. They collided with excitement and a taste for the kill. Could I really take out the Prince and gain the favor of the Gentry this soon? One shot, one kill, and the worlds would be open to me.

I dragged my attention from the memory of the day and back to the warmth of the water lapping at my shoulders. I sank down to the tips of my ears and tried to clear the worry from my mind.

A sigh followed the thoughts as they were replaced with images. I reached for a different kind of release between my thighs just as the water began to rock back and forth, matching my breathing through the buildup. The boys could wait a few more moments.

X

"I could just trixxt us there, Commander." My playful gaze landed on Vance's face. The Rogue, Marli, was nowhere to be seen as I approached our flier.

He did not return my mirthful suggestion, instead replying with a growl, "You're late. Again. Fuck woman, do you think of nothing but your own needs?"

His words stung more than I liked. Swallowing a retort, I smiled, and the large leather satchels slung across my shoulders were carried by a soft flash into the world between. That is where I stepped into when using the magic of trixxt movement. So many things were kept hidden in that world between worlds; an existence amongst the gods if any truly remained.

A movement from the deep crimson nose of our flier caught my eye. Damn the Rogue. Had he been there the whole time? I made a note to keep an extra eye on him if that was even possible. I felt better about his presence on this expedition after our scuffle on the mats. He moved with grace and strength belying his trimmer frame. I scanned the vessel we were loaned to take us to ground. The Gentry meant to make a statement if we were caught. The grandeur and emblazoned emblems of nations gathering on its side and the rarity and quality of the ship would be as good as matching rings to tie us to the Gentry, if they wished it to be so.

This was a stealth fighter embellished with all the luxuries offered by our status. The command was clear: stay stealthy, stay hidden, and get home without revealing any Gentry knowledge or Secrets. The layered instructions for the execution of our plan had been nagging at me since training earlier.

Marli offered me a hand after swinging himself into the cabin and to the right of the loft housing our gunnery bay. If he meant to man the weaponry during the whole flight, he would find himself prone and awake for hours. My thoughts scrambled to read him and my hesitation gave me away, goading him into a grinning retort, "Ma Lady, I've been in the same position for hours at a time before, no harm has come of it, yet. No complaints either, aye!"

Before I could flip an obscene gesture towards the Rogue, strong hands wrapped around my waist as to lift me into the fight instead. I shoot a quick jab to Vance's ribs and trixxt myself in.

Marli did intend to man our weapons for the flight and made no complaints of it. What that meant was that this Rogue had more to offer than he liked to admit. Or at least, he enjoyed the thrill of a good surprise.

In general, Rogues were trained from very young ages by guilds placed all across Tanirra. Most were naturally in possession of some magic at birth. Theirs are often simple, like being able to command phantom hands and dark orbs to block out light. Some even speak to the shadows they shrink into, though the Veiliri wiped most of the Shadow Rogues out or brought them into their ranks. Any one of them with enough innate magi power to handle the ship's vast artillery of spells and alchemical explosion rounds were barely more than legend. No wonder he had been hiding in the dense, cold forests of the Northern King's sweeping lands. Marli had secrets to protect as well. He remained so quiet, I forgot he was on board as I drifted through the cabin.

Burgundy, white, and gold marked everything about the flier, from plush carpets coming out of the captain's pit all the way to a training room below where cargo was previously kept. Light darted between the linens draped across polished wooden alcoves marching along in large arcs around entries to sleeping areas. They were small, but with every possible luxury shoved in.

Candles glow from behind glass sconces set deep into the walls, gilding plush furs strewn across the single beds sectioned off down the corridor, all the way to the stairs. Wardrobes lined the wall set against the back of the flier, just above the tiny descent to the ship's bottom, and held a large cache of weapons behind the suits and coats hung among golden rods.

Personal effects were stored in the wardrobe provided with each cabin. That is where I now stood looking into an empty stand of polished wood with two golden rods fitted across and on top of each other, considering whether unpacking my bags on this ship was a good idea.

The boys carried on their gear but neither of them could travel the way I could, demanding the skies bend for me to walk across spaces. There was a dull thumping sound throughout the room when my extra supplies drop into the open wardrobe. My eyes shifted toward marbled sapphire handles of a Blue Mountain cottontail's pelt. I stared at the different shapes of white and blue piling in, considering for a moment the time it should take us to reach our drop. It wasn't long but there was no way to know how long we would use the space as sleeping accommodation throughout the assignment.

"Why not?" I muttered, and allowed my thoughts to wander toward bluer skies and warmer evenings than those in the north while I tried to convince myself to like this temporary home. Looking around I spotted the private bathing area half hidden behind a thin dressing mesh. Well, that was a plus. I hated to share something so important as a hot shower after a long, bloody day.

Holding up a fur lined set of long sleeves, I pushed against the fabric trying to feel the nearly weightless work of our smithies in the armor between fur and leather. Light hovered from around the loops at the end of the sleeves, meaning to wrap around my fingers all the way up to the armored chest.

Iridescent fingers of light came close but bounced back as though it feared drowning in the deep if any brightness were to accidentally flicker against the flat midnight black style that would cover me on this impending hunt. Before I could get the first of those uniforms on the hangers, Vance came to find me.

"We are on a travel current until we hit the Northern border. Did you pack your Gentry leathers?" Vance called toward me with the edge of thunder cutting through his voice. "We won't be grounded long, but this has to look like it's legit."

"Isn't it?" I asked. He just growled.

Vance had set the ship to self-navigate through the current and decided to find me immediately after. His voice set my body on edge as he barked orders at me from just outside the room. That man got off on trying to control me. He must for all the bravado he exhibited about my safety.

Annoyance boiled through me at the thought of being coddled as I tried to focus on the larger objective and hold my tongue. I failed as I pushed through the layered silks and velvets of the curtain to find him leaning against the wall; the candlelight playing against his fair skin and softening the glare that dared me to question him. The candlelight softened his features and soothed some of the anger from seconds ago.

"Oh honey, I brought the red dress you like," I breathed as I imitated his stance against the wall and added a lazy grin. "I haven't forgotten all of my manners. Just let me know when you want me in it. I can't wait to whip your ass with mine on display."

Vance scoffed, "Skarlet, did you unpack and check your gear?"

"Jealous of my infinite closet?" I teased, knowing I was pushing too far.

I just want to know if you will be disappearing for wardrobe changes while I am in charge of keeping you alive?" he countered.

The last of my patience burned away with the pool of magic gathering and boiling in my center. As much as he annoyed me, Vance should never think himself responsible for me. It was enough to get an idiot killed. Even a really strong one like Vance.

"They should have sent a divert and you know it, even if we are going in with stealth. Even if it's the last mapped island of the western sea, no matter how far we go or what the odds are. This is my kill, but it feels like our death," I hissed. I lashed out at the Gentry, not having it in me to really take my frustration out on Vance. I didn't really think we were on a death mission, but I didn't like how close we were to it either. I don't fear death, but I couldn't save the living world from the dead.

Confusion lit up his blue eyes before quickly falling away to a glare as Vance argued on the side of the Gentry. "The reason they did not send one is because we are boots on the ground for a quiet kill. A divert would be suspicious. If we need to be seen that's why the Flight Guild built these little beauties: Magic to hide us and magic to declare we are here if we are caught. We discussed this." His brows loosened as he took a long moment and a deep breath before continuing. "I know you need this. I know who this is for. I will do anything I can to make sure this kill is fast and clean, but I wanted to ask you something. I just need to know if you're okay?" Vance's face dropped as his voice did.

For a moment I could see past the stormy blue eyes and stoic positioning. Charcoal colored fabric moved as his body tensed, pulling the thin flight leathers tight and showing off his wide shoulders. Light shrinks from around him, leaving me with a smaller shadowed version of the Sky Knight. I never knew Vance as a boy, but I imagine this slip as his hidden visage; the place of vulnerability where his life changed, leaving him unsure of his rank and every title he held, including the title of friend.

Vance thought he knew something of my vulnerabilities. No one was left alive that could boast they truly knew what I continued to fight for or what each kill cost me. There would be no place left for me among the stars that guarded us when my soul was finished tearing itself apart all in the name of what Vance thinks I've lost.

Many fires now raged behind the aqua and silver of the stare I landed on Vance. Fires that burned as hot as the cities around Abruzi the night of the attack. The night I failed families, including my own family.

Magma sludged into my center causing a small gasp and a tear slipped to roll down the highlighting blush creeping across my face. I lifted my pale fingers quickly to smudge the wetness away and ran my damp fingers through my white curls. Vance was a friend, but I would never let anyone be close to me again. My heart couldn't take another break, and I was not ready to shatter myself for anyone.

I tilted my head up toward Vance, his blue eyes not leaving me. I allowed my features to slip smoothly into a look void of everything: the look of a Gentry Assasjine. "I can't guarantee what kind of venom will come out of my mouth, Vance, if you keep bringing up ghosts." He may be okay with that level of vulnerability between us, but the softness of it made my stomach sour.

Vance sighed and pushed off the wall. He made it to the stairs in a few strides. "I am not the one, Skarlet. Put the killer away or come down here and try to take me down." Vance didn't glance back to see the violence slip across the stone cold still features of my face. He was one step down when I pushed off the wall into a sprint.

"I got a whole pint says the girl wins this one, aye! And don't forget to wear the dress when you serve it up to me, Knight Commander, so I can decides which of ya has the better ass," Marli chuckled from above us.

How he had heard the exchange was something for me to mull over later. I seriously needed to remember to keep an eye on him. He couldn't be this good. If he were, what was he doing on this ship? More importantly, who exactly did I have on this mission with me?

XI

A phantom hand balanced a plate of cheeses while sliding two berry spritzers down the small bar with the other. Phantoms once served in the homes of a few ranking officers and almost all royals had them when Tanirra had thrived.

Mages that are capable of manifesting a golem did so with their elemental specialty. Mages who could bend the air and skies could create phantom servers. Few of them existed anymore and those who did served the Gentry for remote support. Phantoms that remained were just pieces of shattered sentient magic left behind by their makers.

"Mick, can we have some bread please?" I smiled toward the phantom in Gentry livery of burgundy and gold. The uniform slid around a form of smoke and shadows. "Making this one hit the ground so hard takes so much energy and I'm just starving!" The phantom shimmered with a low laugh as I leaned into Vance with a sharp elbow to his ribs. I shouldn't be here drinking and trading old stories with him, yet here we sat together waist deep in a blooming easiness that looked more like friendship than it ever had between us.

The sparring lasted way longer than either of us intended. So much could be said in the silences between the intense dance of the fight; my daggers swirling in rhythm against Vance's sword. Memories of a twisted past blurred white and fuzzy and all the unknowns of tomorrow faded away with the sweat that dripped and thinned the fresh blood under my feet.

We needed to be sleeping before our Northern landing. Instead we sat side by side with piles of cheeses, candied fruits, and dried meat platters stretched out on the low table suspended in front of its matching couch. Different hues of cream and white wrapped around the room, conflicting with the burgundy of the walls. A bit of ivy brightly provided a break in the Gentry colors of the room. Blooms of white winded down with the ivy and around the ropes connected to the table, keeping it level despite any movements of the ship.

Both of us situated the loose linen we changed into after quick showers. My hair fell almost to the floor as I put my head against the arm; the cushions sliding us into the backs of our end of the lounger. We sat laughing and drinking as though the success or failure of our mission didn't mean life or death for so many people.

"So that's why you didn't let her in?" I asked, the tears gathering in the corners of my eyes at the look of humility on Vance's face as I turned back to our conversation. The wine had made the glow of his skin brighter and his stature more relaxed. I stretch one foot out to poke his thigh when he turned to slip an arm over the back of our seat.

I am sure my face reflected his as we both faced one another under the biggest wall of flickering lights. His voice had no commanding bite to it as he spoke to me now. "That's the whole story, woman. I swear it." Vance waved his free hand at me and continued. "She just kept saying it over and over and over." He took a deep breath to imitate the female who still plagued him with offers of herself, despite Vance's complete dedication to avoiding her. "Reformed demon daddy! Let me break you!" He mimicked her pitch as he yelled the words that had gotten her banned from between his sheets.

Vance's laugh joined mine as I pictured the look he had worn each time I would catch him sneaking away from her through a crowded room. "So, she finally caught me entering my suite, saw me close the door and everything. I had to pretend I wasn't there. What was I supposed to do?" Vance shrugged.

"All I am saying is that trying to sneak out from behind the tapestries of our halls when you're the size of a mountain is not the brightest idea, no wonder she caught up with you." I pointed my empty glass towards him. "It would take a dedicated woman to sit outside your halls and track you down the way she did. She was committed, I will give her that."

"Ah," Vance answered, "but I was looking for you. I thought I heard your voice, so I opened the door and I was about to find out how you move across spaces like you do when you sneak away from my Knights. I was coming to let you rescue me."

I leaned my glass into his with a clink. "Just as there is no giant too large for the right stone, there is no Lady that can't be taken down by a bit of jealousy. Maybe a little humility, too. That's the real reason you were leading her to me. My beauty saved you again." I winked and our laughs mingled again before a distant bang sounded on the roof of where we sat, barely audible against our revelry.

"What do you know of humility, assasjine?" Vance's voice lowered to barely a vibration. "You have never missed a chance to shine under your own light. A glow from the heavens always bouncing around and highlighting your perfection."

Vance allowed his eyes to lower just a bit, dropping to where my red lips fell into a thoughtful pout. I had never seen this look from him. I didn't know how far to push a Vance that, for some reason, suddenly seemed to be deciding whether to disregard four years of his own rules about me.

Another series of tapping sounded, closer and louder this time.

"Did you hear that?" I didn't have a chance to debate over my reaction before Vance's tone lost its husky slow drawl. He silenced me with a hand up, fist out and in a ball. Vance turned his head to the right, his eyes on the floor, and listened to something I couldn't decipher. "What was that?"

Before I could put the pieces together, he was off toward the Captain's pit. The look on his face spoke louder than his words could have. No translation was needed to light a fire in my blood.

It was not possible! We couldn't have been taken off course by anyone outside of this cabin once the flier was set in a current. Not unless the whole carrier had been compromised.

"How long have we been off course?" My voice trembled as I pulled up beside Vance and took in the dark vista of night sky just outside the flier, all the joy from just moments before gone like a foggy memory.

We were beginning to slowly descend. Through the front glass of the cockpit, a forest reached up towards our ship as though it awaited our fall as reverently as it would a returning god. We were out of our travel current and headed straight for a forest void. We would soon be sapped of magic, nullifying it until we cleared the outer reaches of the dense woodland. If we could make it off this flyer before impact there, then our chances of surviving would only increase. I chanced a glance below the windows to confirm it, but a few more feet and none of the panels would register anything useful.

Dark descended upon us, reaching far into the cabin and wiping out the lights, leaving nothing but the candles dripping on the bar where Vance and I had just been sitting.

If there were any doubt of it a moment before, it was gone now. We were going into the blistering dark of the draining timberland. Vance looked up as he realized the same thing. We both spun toward the back of the flier toward our gear.

"How much time?" I asked. I pushed down my rising fear as Vance let his wings pull out of their mystic bindings behind him.

Before I could think of what I am doing, I began pulling as much magic as I could into my center. It was the only way I could try to hold on to any of it. Though the well within me was vast, it was not all powerful and would be turned off in just moments.

It felt like taking one last breath before jumping off of a ship just to feel the water cool and soothe you, filling up with as much air as you could before going under. I pushed in and thought of bright light wrapping itself around that piece and protecting it from the magic-snuffing void below us.

"I will grab as many weapons as I can, and you meet me here with the Rogue in less than a minute." Vance hid the fear from his voice by sheer will.

I didn't wait for him to finish before trixxting directly to my sleeping quarters. I grabbed the largest pack and waved my right hand to make my other items disappear.

"Alright you devil Rogue, don't make this hard on me," I whispered and shook my braid off a shoulder, closing my eyes and trying to picture the man who I had only registered shadowed glimpses of. A vision of Marli blinked in front of me, one of bright light with his features outlined clearly and all the malice of his grin gone.

He was behind the map lined door to the gunnery with bag in hand. I trixxt into the loft, coming in to focus barely more than a foot in front of the Rogue who stood waiting with bags strapped and weapons slung low. He held out a hand in silence and snatched up the staff he must have used to send the warning to us. It was he who had banged out a combination of an old system of communication which included intricate taps and hand signals, one that the Gentry taught us all the basics of. Whatever the Rogue had to say was not basic, evidenced by our sudden plunging as the ship picked up speed.

We landed a few steps in front of Vance right as the void dulled my magic, causing us to almost stumble into him. Marli tossed his staff from his hand and into a harness that crossed his back, under his gear.

Despite my constant pursuit of moments that drain the overlapping magic that plagues me, It was physically painful to feel the release of pressure when it was tempered. My chest expanded and fell rapidly under the loose linens I still wore.

I looked up at the wings pushed in front of Vance, his body completely still and eyes fixed above his head. There was nothing between the sitting area and the skies. The loft holding spells and offensive magic for the gunnery stopped short to allow the space for the drop to the training room. It is what made it hard to hear Marli's warning, and it is what Vance planned to use to save our lives.

A red satin bag appeared attached to each of our packs as Mick disappeared into the air with a quick nod to where we stood. I reached for Vance just as he pulled both Marli and me into him, tucking our bodies against his as tightly as his wings would let him.

A huge, muscled arm tightened around my middle before I could focus on the pain of more of my magic being ripped away like a flower petal in a summer storm and of the floor falling from our feet amidst the intense cold of night that cuts at our every edge.

Vance never lost the grip he had locked around our waists. He lifted dark wings in a circle again, shielding myself and the Rogue from the debris of the wreckage below. The Knight had pulled us straight up and out of the middle of the killing blow. Time seemed to stop for a moment as we were suspended above a silent explosion, as though the aircraft had been set to detonate like a mage's firelight show. All the sound was muffled by the skies where we hung amongst stars.

I could trixxt us out if we were far enough from the forest. Best I could do over a void forest though is to send out any icy blast that will slow our pummeling death descent.

"Vance," I tried to tell him to fly us further, but my voice was carried into the winds of the worlds. I wiggled a hand free to start the cast and the movement caused Vance to tilt, his wings affected by the loss of magic as much as the rest of us.

I felt the grip on my own magical well loosening and made to cast that which would give us precious more moments to reach the ground but which weakened with every second we hovered in the sky.

The whole sky erupted in ear piercing sounds all around. There were ship pieces flying dangerously close to where we were suspended. No, not hovering, but more like falling. We were falling, though not as rapidly as we would have, and those were not ship pieces flying near us. Ship pieces didn't have eyes of green in vertical strips that glowed as they flew on midnight wings birthed in the depths of Veill.

I didn't have time to think. Marli glanced my way only long enough to nod as he pulled out his staff and began fighting flying death from our ride's rear. Clearly, he had no plan that included going down without a fight. That didn't take long to settle then.

I banged on Vance's chest to get his attention. He was focusing on taking control of our flight down while also trying to keep us protected. I was still trying to reach Vance's weapon over his shoulder when Marli's foot planted into my side and grabbed my attention. I spied familiar blades in the Rogue's other hand and grabbed them greedily, silently thanking him for gathering them from supply before we jumped ship. The light of rainbow obsidian glimmered against my hand, casting colors of the sky in a warm glow upon my palm as I pulled my long daggers from the Rogue. His smile was as reassuring, and as dangerous, as any other monster would have been, if we had been sent with a Veiliri, and not Marli of the North.

Despite our unspoken rule to not question the past of our associates, unwarranted curiosity about the Rogue began to creep into my thoughts, and I pushed them back down, this was not the place to be concerned about his past with a future of deathly stillness waiting for us at the bottom of this drop.

The forest bottom seemed nearly inviting in contrast to the terror quickly filling the skies. A rancid smell assaulted me, and I pulled one dagger from the Veiliri I'd just killed and quickly skewed the other attacking Vance's legs.

The jerking movement of its death caught me by surprise, and I watched in fury as my blade dropped to the floor below, embedded in its shredded leathery wing.

Vance's own beautiful wings finally opened, and a warm wind rushed by us, teasing my freezing fingers as they tightened around my one dagger. I pulled another from the Knight's bandolier. A weapon from each guy, one for each hand. If I survived this, there was definitely a joke to be milked from that.

The wind gushed up and around us, turning our smiles into something terrifying, specifically for the huge green-eyed bastards sent as our welcoming party.

Dracothites would not have been my first choice of fodder, yet here we fell right into their poisonous, clawed fingers. They rose to usher us down faster, like a wind moving a storm across the sky.

Leafless tree branches crept into the sky as we continued to descend, roots grounded in the mires tossed about and surrounded each one. They awaited their prey, delighting in the bloodbath of the chase.

As our magic fed the Nymphs of the wood voids, so do they waken to feed their bodies with our own flesh. We must stay airborne, or we will likely die by their arboreal hands.

The rainbow and light mingling on my hand stuttered out under the blood from my last kill. A wing of black silk brushed against us as it fell with its venomous claws grasping for Vance's back as the dracothite's life blood stained my shirt.

Of course they weren't trying to kill him, just take us to ground, wearing on him until he could no longer withstand the bulk of us.

The weight of the moment washed over me, leaving me with few options for action.

I turned to the right in time to see Marli discharge two more dracothites off Vance's wings. The swirl of his staff flashed in his eyes each time the curved blades passed over the Knight's shoulder.

I took in kill after kill with my own blades, none of them working to stem the never-ending tide of flying beasts joining the skies now. There was no way that we could go up or even around. They surrounded us on all sides.

Air rushed into my lungs as Vance's grip loosened just a little. He was tiring, and we didn't have much time left. My dagger hand lowered to take out a smaller dracothite and caught a gilded cord. From the edge of the red satin bag that Mick had attached swung a chain with bits of ivy and flower still clinging to it.

I had no idea how the phantom did it, but I reached for the chain, pulling up a length way too long to have fit into the tiny satchel.

White petals clashed against the horror of the night and stained themselves in the palm of my hand. The fetter secured itself against my dagger, both hilt and chain now scratching the raw places where my own blood ran.

Red glimmered as the bag tightened back up after the last link was lifted. My arm flew out, pulling me from Vance as the length of metal and ivy soared above me, its weight no more than a light tug against my muscles.

The chain came down around Vance's shoulders and I climbed up before he had the chance to accidentally kill me. With one hand dispatching the danger from around us in bloody arcs, I had to pray that I could maintain the grip of the other hand now anchoring me to the Knight. I steadied myself on knees bent in protest against walls of wind and take a final measure of our situation.

We are almost to the edge of the first trees. The strain from dodging the grasping limbs of the nymphs and the immobilizing talons of the dracothites produced the agony imprinting into Vance's features.

I rocked a little off balance as a dark gray wing hit a branch and tried to right itself. We will be picking splinters from Vance's short hair for months if the amount of wood coming at me was any measure of the damage he was doing with his enormous body.

The branches were blending equally with the flying beasts now and I released the grip on the dagger in favor of tethering myself more securely. The ruby red hilt remained wrapped in verdant hues of ivy, not leaving my hand or the hitch holding it there.

All I needed was the dagger I still had left from Vance. Specifically, the tiny bit of chelcei that gave it color even in the emptiness of a void forest. My fingers warm against the carved handle and light began to swell beneath my palm; a gem of everlasting light. A dagger meant for someone else. All I had left was a choice to make.

I knew what my choice was; what hid beneath the swaggering assasjine. It was the one that would probably get me killed. I let go of the chain, knowing there was never really a choice, and gasp when it wrapped around my ankles.

An image is before me of perfectly still accommodations upon a swaying ship, all held by the same fetters. I jump from Vance's shoulders into the blackness where sky and forest blends.

"I am feeling so epic right now!" I screamed and grasped for a landing spot. It wasn't hard to find a tree in a forest if you are looking for it, even in an ancient, evil one. I swung into the top-most branch of an old nymph's limbs, wincing as chains tightened around my legs.

Trusting my balance and our lives on Mick's surprise grab bag gift, I planted my feet on the branch at my toes and reached into the cold of the night above me.

Flapping wings blew back white curls that were stuck to my face, leaving me with streaks of blood staining the wind whipped tips, but no attack came to rip us immediately from our perch.

I had one chance to get this right.

My palm met the blunt end of the dagger, pulling at every bit of light from the gems set in its hilt. I reached inside to feel for any magic that might still stir within, but what remained was too weak. The stone would have to be enough.

Power pulsing from the stone vibrated through every piece of me, straining the magic in my blood that tried to answer its call. The hilt of my dagger was no longer a rainbow against my skin. In its place the stone both burned at the touch and sank a chill right into my bones.

The feel of hands squeezing my thighs ignited a fire that burned away the fog of pain and weariness. The danger was always in what could be taken by using the fire of the chelcei if it was safely harnessed it will not cause harm to its owner. My skin glows a bright pink under the stone's pressure upon my bare hand.

I looked down to find Marli nearly crushing the winged Knight's chest between his legs, holding him against the tree despite the pull of the ground below, and holding me steady despite the weight of a mountain between him and a killer tree.

"Close your eyes," I yelled down to the Rogue.

Marli looked to Vance's slack face. I registered his closed eyes and the strain of his heaviness pulling on Marli's much slighter frame.

"Let's hope for light then," I mumbled, sincerely hoping Vance had only been rendered unconscious.

Words of prayer and invocation were lost in screams that blasted through the skies and began to fill in silences where just seconds ago the beat of hundreds of wings sounded.

Burning light, pure and made of the fire of the sun and the ferocity of the mother, burst across the night in an arc. I watched the tips of my fingers glow like a forge and pulse in tandem to the expanding web of death. Light and flame flew about and consumed the remaining fodder. Dracothites were creatures of the night, taking refuge under the darkened canopies of forests and rising to hunt when there was no light to burn them.

The fires of the chelcei sol buried into the very core of each beast, exploding them in bursts of light like falling stars. Dracothites cleared the sky completely and a few nymphs of the void woods fell, their frail bodies separated from their tree forms and strewn about the thickets below us. A blaze settled over the non-sentient woodland before burning itself out and circling back underneath where we dangled.

A lifetime of chances and mere seconds of choice rolled into one sharp exhale as I threw my head back. It was always about the choices we made when given the chance to choose. Those rare moments when we were defined by nothing more and nothing less than a moment of resolution.

I swayed a bit with the effort of holding the globe of light that dropped and wondered at the strength packed into Marli's body for him to still be steadying me while also keeping Vance from falling to his death.

Seconds. It had taken mere seconds to bring them down and I had one hope as we floated toward the ground under the last dredges of the magical breeze I'd created, light swirling about the three of us. I hoped that I timed that right and bought us a head start. We would need any help we could get if there was any hope of beating the forest at a game of the hunted and the hunters.

XII

Vance took hard hits from the claws of the nymphs on the way down and when we landed his head tilted back and he crumpled to the ground. It was chaos, wings flapped and talons struck the globe of the protection being cast above us by the sol light of the chelcei stone. Marli dislodged himself bodily from where he tangled with Vance and lay the unconscious Knight on the ground. He stood and disappeared into a blur of shaded blacks and greys toward the closest pile of dying dracos to send them back to the Veil hot lands from whence they came.

I cleared the rest on my side, gutted a dryad with wooden teeth and razor sharp claws at the end of her branched arms, and began to strip of cloths of my linens on my way back to my partner's prone body.

His wings were dropping feathers and both had small breaks jutting through the silken exterior, his knee swelled far past pushing the seams of his pants, some of them giving up under the pressure and busting. His left leg lay at an angle and he lay deathly still and I feared that I would never feel epic again if he died on me here in this forsaken land.

Looking around I take in the places in the ground where churning grounds had broken under the command of the woodland nymphs and then settled with muddy pools in their middles, dark limbs broken and pushing into the surfaces of the water like wooden ships. The rest of the ground lay littered with bodies or jagged rocks. I looked up to consider the beasts beating against the shield of the light and decided that we need to get Vance stable so we could drag him into a defendable position.

After a few tries, I finally woke Vance up with a slap to the face. He couldn't sleep yet, not with so many wounds open. His healing would be nearly instantaneous, but not until we were clear of the shithole of a forest.

"Fuck Skarlet, you didn't have to hit me that hard," he gasped. He tried to sit up but let a groan slip before his head was even off the ground. "Am I dead? I'm dead, aren't I?"

I followed Vance's eyes up to the arc of light pulsing around and above him. "It's just the chelcei sol," I reassured him with a nod. "Since this isn't magic, as long as we can keep the stone from sputtering out, the orb should hold. The fire will take a long while to recharge itself though and it may be a long time before we under the Abruzi sun again to do so."

That admission felt more like words of failure as I took a moment to consider that we may not make it home. Not me, not the boys, not even my blade would ever be whole again if we died here.

Vance took in the lit fires around where we settled him. His light brows drew in and wondered at the hard ground all about us where swamp land had been.

"Pretty sure I'm dead," Vance mumbled again.

"We couldn't be so lucky," Marli's voice echoed from the shadows where he emerged from a rock cropping on the edge of the darkness still rustling on the other side of our small world of light. He didn't bother with reassurances, but there was a lightness to his words.

"You've put them all down then? We need to find somewhere covered. The light will keep us alive but its got less than nothing against the cold wind blowing in." I say over Vance's body.

It took me a moment to register the drawl of his words, the clean crisp sound of his boots approaching as I turned to look at him. Those had been his first words since we left the bay in the Gentry's ship and they were soothing, clear, and empty of any trace of his previous accent. I tilted my head forward as I leaned into the wound I held at Vance's side.

It was hard to think straight but the next thoughts hit me so hard, I could barely draw air. I had to force my hands to relax so that I didn't open Vance's wound further. I looked for some kind of denial to lean on. "It couldn't have been them." My voice, low and raspy and raw from battle cries, still traveled well enough to be clearly heard in our small circle of borrowed time. I saw the looks from Marli and Vance indicating the need for me to elaborate.

"Marli, if that's actually your name, can I ask you something?"

He nodded and I continued to tend Vance's wounds, keeping my hands as I bought a moment to sort out the thoughts of betrayal assaulting me now.

Sweat formed beads upon my forehead as I struggled while choosing the best way to be diplomatic. Asking the Rogue if he was the one to nearly kill us might not be a good way to spend my time here. We would have to work together to get out, and we couldn't do that if he stabbed me for accusing him of treachery outright. Plus, Arike had said he was there to guide me. Maybe he still could.

"I was thinking that the last time you spoke was when we left the bay. The bay where we took a Gentry ship that was knocked off course. How many people had access to it before we left?" I asked.

The question was meant for the shadowed Rogue, but a small protest came from Vance's lips in response. It was all I needed to know about how secure the magic on our flight had been.

Vance's curse was low, and I couldn't make out whether he was cursing our situation, his own pain, or the idea of being directly sabotaged. Maybe it didn't matter, and we were screwed on so many fronts at the moment. Someone didn't want us to make our landing.

"Who didn't," Marli answered, echoing the sentiment of Vance's cursed mumble.

A tingle ran from my scalp down the length of my spine. Warmth from my chelcei sol tried to work itself into my bare skin. I had been so cold when we landed. Now, heat settled against the pale pink tattoo of double crescent moons coming together; A flaming star suspended in the middle of the crossing Illunas, the image situated perfectly between where my shoulders meet.

A roll of my neck releases some of the tension, but it gathers back up again as Marli approaches. I've torn most of my linens now to tend to Vance's dripping lacerations and send up a prayer of thanks to Asti that the sol is warming my body. I looked at Vance and wondered again how he had no talons stuck to him but my thoughts were interrupted by the Rogue's response.

"I spoke to you on the ship," Marli said. He stared at me with a curious look. I finally lifted my eyes to his and realized in that moment that he was beautiful. Muscles rippled over his slight frame which caught my eyes. Before I could help myself, I drank him in from the black hair braided over pierced ears, to the complete blackness of eyes, all made more vivid by the fullness of his white smile below to the corded details of his stacked but narrow chest.

The belt of weapons pulled against gray pants where a v cut in from the planes of his stomach. There were no shadows dancing about him now, as though he was allowing me a good look at him: an opportunity for him to build trust.

I sighed as reality came crashing in again. Maybe in some other lifetime

I could have taken the time to explore all the Rogue's tricks.

"You were in the loft the whole time," I nodded. Dark storms clouded his eyes as I held my stare steady, quietly encouraging him to confess to me. Even if he had done this to us, there was nothing to do about it until we got away from the torture trees waiting for us in the dark. I was too tired to fight, and he carried all of the weapons. I asked him quietly. "Did you have other orders to execute or were you in the loft, Marli?"

"Indeed," he answered with zero hesitation. "I am a lot of things, but disloyal is not one of them. My unfortunate duty is to follow this through at any cost to my life. However short it may be if the Gentry now want us dead" Marli's gaze shifted to Vance. "Did you manage to grab that red dress?" He asks me. "This situation would be much improved if we could make him wear it out of here."

I try to picture Vance as he was back on the ship, completely whole and laughing.

Images slammed back into me and memories from the evening began to blaze behind my eyes to clear some of the fog starting to settle there. Any type of casting took a lot of energy and keeping the chelcei sol circulating in its own light was draining mine. My mental acuity would slowly begin to follow. Actually, maybe it was going first this time because I was struggling to process the Rogue's words.

It took a few minutes for me to gather my thoughts.

"Marli, how did you actually hear that exchange? Haven't you been told that it's rude to listen to private conversations." The words felt stupid even as they left my mouth. Of course, he was listening. It was probably part of his literal job description. I hastened to add, "If you were in the loft, I mean?" There was no conviction behind my voice, and I was tired, but I had to see this through now.

Marli answered me in a calm voice. "Lady Lior, may I call you Skarlet?" The Rogue truly waited for the slight nod of my head before continuing. "Skarlet, what you did tonight was amazing. In my home we have only ever heard tales of your kind and not many traveled from the North to Blue Mountain for the opportunity to mine the chelcei in my time there before the fall, so it is extremely rare to even view a raw stone, let alone see its power firsthand. Watching you wield yours has given me cautious hope." Marli checked to make sure he had my attention before going on. "I am only here with instructions to protect you. Not only is it foolish to think me traitorous, but it is quite unlikely that I could ignore these orders even if I wanted to. Which I do not. You have my loyalty. For now."

"Clearly you are only sworn to protect one of us," Vance moaned from the ground, the rivers of his blood drying under him as new rivulets take shape slowly.

Any reservations about Marli would have to be stored away. For now, we only have each other and I would not wait for Grimm to wield death against me yet.

"Maybe you should have just given in and worn the dress for the man," I whispered. I leaned back among light chuckles, releasing Vance's wound to move to another. I was glad to hear the lightness in the tones of the voices with me in this moment, but the moment couldn't last.

"Ok, we have to get this mountain moved," I sigh. Vance is huge guy.

"How do we move a mountain?" Marli looked back toward the cliff at my question.

"Not that mountain, this one," I replied. I brought his attention back to the fallen Knight before us with a thump to Vance's bare chest. "We can't carry him. He can't fly us out and I can't trixxt from here."

"You should tell me, as I suppose you would know best, how to move a mountain." Marli winked and stood with a dismissive pat to my hand, his own palm coming away wet with Vance's blood. He did not wait for my reply before beginning a search of our area for any fallen limbs that had not caught fire.

There were few left for him to gather, but Marli made short work of it and soon approached with a roughly fashioned stretcher made of wood pieces and dracothite wings fastened with scraps of clothing.

Thin black wings had been stretched taught against four lengths of timber that were tied off at each overlapping corner and supported by poles of smaller limbs. Veins of pure silver ran through the dark leathery wings and Marli had trimmed them carefully to avoid any contact with the venom, leaving no claws on the edges to get caught on, but making the shimmer with movement. I was reminded of the Gentry's rule for owning furs of animals that were not also food. If their only purpose was beauty, then let them live and remain beautiful for all the worlds to see. All their ridiculous rules and boundaries didn't keep someone from trying to stall this effort to bring down the occupying Veiliri.

Despite their poetic contradictions, they weren't too far off with that one. Beauty could keep you alive and get you killed, yet so many people only have ideas of how to get more of it. The true beauty was in knowing that it ran so much deeper than a pretty face, or pretty wings.

The stretcher was large enough to accommodate Vance's whole injured frame, and I found myself both disgusted and impressed.

The chain from Mick's bag hung from Marli's belt like it had always belonged there. My pack was slung across one shoulder, leaving his hands free to maneuver the crude gurney toward Vance. Marli dropped my pack into the first dry area he could find near me and knelt to take my hands from Vance's last bleeding wound, the others having started to clot.

Surprise registered on his features when I pulled my fingers from his grip to place them back on Vance's sides. He didn't say anything, just gave the crusted gore on my hands a pointed look and lifted his hands palms up. His stare traveled down my face and heated my core when it dropped to the band about my breasts, then all the way down and back up. He held my stare and reached for Vance's wound again.

My eyes followed his hand to where strips of my clothes lay pressed against my friend. No shadow followed me as I stood and took in the mess around us; the mess on me.

What have I done?

A darkness passed in front of my face, soothing me. Marli still watched me. "You have done what you had to do." The Rogue nodded as though he could hear my thoughts exactly as I had. His eyes dropped to my pack again.

"You don't know that."

I leaned to pick up my bag, tilting too fast, and jumped when a golden hand grabbed me, the size of it wrapping all the way around my arm. Vance grunted and used his other hand to shield his face.

My breasts had broken free of their binding and assaulted Vance's bruised cheeks.

"Skarlet, this forest isn't the place to prance nude. I'll be fine while you clean up." Vance's voice was barely more than a whisper, gravelly and tired.

"Is that an order?"

I tried to pull my hand from his grip, but he let go before I even flinched. Annoyed when I should have been grateful that he was going to be alright, I turned away. Even severely injured, he was still worried about me. I started toward the rock wall of mountain a few feet away and looked back for a second, trying not to let the exhaustion take over my temper. The move cost me a few steady steps but I recovered quickly and picked up the pace, needing a few minutes alone.

Using the pale blue string that had held up the matching loose pants, I twisted my hair into a pile on top of my head. It still felt disgusting, and I imagined it looked even worse.

I threw the last dirtied rag into a fire burning just outside of the alcove holding our few provisions, rushing back behind the rock wall to avoid the rancid smoke.

It wasn't until I felt the shape of fighting leathers buried deep in my pack that I let out a breath of relief. At least I grabbed the right bag. With most of the bits washed or shaken from my hair now, I focused on the slight injuries to myself.

I closed my eyes and focused on each section of my body. No injuries worse than a few bruises marked me and the others were not visible at all.

Weight settled upon my shoulders as I slid my jacket over the dark and layered leather set. My cold fingers brushed against something coiled in my pocket. Clasping my hand around it, my mind went back to the day I went to the apothecarist vendor. I had tossed this jacket on after returning the Beezer.

Red and white combined in patterns that shimmered like satin against my emerging fist.

Poppima.

It was enough to ease Vance's pain and allow his body to heal itself faster.

The red parts would have to be picked out for it to work, but that left the white bits for me. For later, of course.

A tea would be best, but I decided that any delivery would work and began to dig for supplies.

A noise from just outside the cropping of rock wall interrupted the search. I slipped the piece back into my pocket and went to investigate.

Marli lumbered just outside, pulling the makeshift transport.

He gave a nod of approval toward the clothes now covering me as I approached. Warmth surrounded my body, relaxing some of the muscles and warming my freezing limbs. I wiggled my toes inside the boots I'd pulled on. They were made from the same material as the leathers I prefer, with thin black bottoms meant for complete stealth and fleece lining the inside.

It was getting colder despite the small fires still burning low around us and his breath gathered when Marli spoke.

"Feel better?" He asked.

I nodded. "Already daydreaming of my next real bath, though."

The light of my chelcei sol was moving alongside Marli toward our temporary shelter. Dark eyes smiled back at me, and my own anxiety began to settle until I took in the image he pulled with a length of the chain.

Vance's very still body lie on the carrier, wings leaving large tracks where they dragged underneath him. From this angle he looked completely broken. His light skin had paled in the moments since I'd stepped away. Fear ripped through before I could rationalize what I was seeing.

"Is he...?" A leaden fist pounded where my heart should be beating, and I couldn't finish my question.

"Skarlet," Marli jerked the carrier the last few feet with one hand and leaned toward me with the other. "He is too stubborn to die."

Laughter escapes me and starts to fill the cavern, low and hesitant at first, quickly rising from the humor between friends to levels of near hysterics as Marli's snicker rose in time with mine.

I looked to the stretcher to confirm that the Rogue wasn't lying and noticed that Vance's chest shook slightly with the absurdity of it all, indicating he still clung to life.

He really was a stubborn ass. I sat down to avoid falling over, still laughing against the wall. The chain rattled and weapons clanged with the rhythm of Vance and Marli's lingering hoots. The tears that wet our faces as we all laughed could have been from realizing how completely fucked we were, or realizing how completely fucked we are. Either way, I was glad for the knife of humor that diced up the tension lingering between us.

The Lady Lior and her warriors two? I suppose we would have to make it work. It was this thought that grounded me into our reality. I suddenly had a lead after years of searching and someone wanted to make sure I didn't succeed in following it. The odds were stacking against us at an incredible pace, but this mission was important for all of us. We had to back each other up to get it done.

Terrifying and soothing, the thought of having anyone in my corner caused me to drop my head, weariness rushing in, eyes dropping of their own accord. Wrapped in a temporary sense of safety and pulled down by the weight of our night, I found a moment of rest.

XIII

Cradling the watered down white poppima tea Marli made and served using some of the cave's discarded hollow rocks, I paced about the small space to think.

Asking Marli personal questions had gotten me nowhere, and it seemed he wouldn't give up much on his career either. I paced and thought of the most obvious reasons this could have happened. With rebel groups missing and strange activities around the last of the closed Gates, there'd been plenty of rumor circling about the next surge. Nothing hinted at the Gentry being behind them, though.

My thoughts wander back to the last few hours, looking for something I may have missed when I spun to Marli again.

"Can you control a phantom?" My question doesn't take him by surprise. Instead, he gave me a look of appreciation. "Your shadows, are they your own magic or someone else's? Mick disappeared right before you started your little tap dance. He came back in just enough time to send us off with these crazy magic bags."

I placed my empty cup aside and hoisted up the red satchel. I had never seen someone take a piece of the heavens and shove it into a bag. There was no other explanation to how it could hold so much stuff.

"I cannot control a phantom, nor can I make one," Marli answered. "My shadows, as you call them, are mostly my own. They communicate in a very similar manner as a phantom. The shadows engage with other sentient elementals. Most of my information comes from the things people pay little attention to."

I tucked that knowledge away as I huffed and walked toward where our lambskins sit, having left them to fill from the mountain water trickling down a slab of swirling granite. Frustration was useless in the moment. Despite that fact, it was the only thing I was feeling as I grabbed the water supplies to be packed.

"Hey woman, need another nap? Seem kind of on edge," Vance taunted me from his spot against the wall. He must have balls of steel to tease me in his condition.

They let me sleep for a few hours before I had to take a watch, and I would never hear the end of it.

I glanced up at the edge of light creeping closer, essentially locking us in a small cave a few feet away from the temporary location we were at the night we crashed. Vance wasn't wrong, I was definitely feeling the pressure of our limited time. Soon we would have to move, and Vance still had drag marks where he sat, his wings mixing in with the dusty cave floor making small, careful movements. There was no way he could fly right now.

The forest was home to creatures of chaos long before the dracothites decided to nest here. I just needed to buy us a little more time. I glanced toward the barren lands where every manner of death surrounded the orb waiting for us. Looking out of the cave entrance I tried to think. Time. Just a little time.

I stood huddling in the entryway, my hands rubbing warmth into my arms against the increasing chill. The answer was just beyond my reach, in the disorienting faded places in my logic.

"The answer is just beyond my reach," I say in a voice heavy with frustration.

"I don't think you will find any answers by just standing there." Vance's wings moved slowly up and down as he winced and tested their strength, hoping for a miracle. His features were cloaked in bravado as he fought against the pain. "Skarlet, come here and take my hand for a moment. Take a break from trying to track down a time dealer," he begged.

The poppima we convinced Vance to take had helped his healing, but he refused to touch any more of it. Only a sadist would refuse relief from the pain he had to be in on principal alone.

"Why would I take your hand?" Genuine confusion blanketed the look I gave him.

"Because I need to stand up and I can't without your hand." He waved me over, one leg already underneath his massive body. His other was still swollen from around the knee but he straightened it indicating no fractures were hidden beneath the odd angle he'd landed.

"You do not need to stand up, Vance." I stalked over to him and he jumped to his feet before I could push him back down.

"It was a trick to get you to come closer and to take a break. If I ever ask for your hand, it would not be from a position of weakness," he replied.

"You are the biggest pain in my ass," I huffed and pushed a palm into his chest. I immediately regretted it when Vance wheezed and wrapped an arm around his ribs.

"Shit, honey, I'm sorry," I apologized.

Shadows danced upon the planes of his face, smothering the low laugh that escaped him. There were always shadows upon his face from light and dark mixing. Because one cannot exist without the other.

I spun away from where Vance stood, now trying for quicker movements and testing his weapon handling. He appeared to be moving with some of his normal finesse, though blood still oozed from open lacerations.

Staring at the burgundy colored stains splashed across his torso, the fog lifted from my mind enough for something to finally click. The nagging thought that had been there since I thought of how Mick seemed to serve the ship but not be obligated to stay as it went down. He was free to leave, existing in the place he was spelled to serve but with certain liberties.

Images of light and dark circled with the speed of my thoughts. So different yet one cannot be known without the other. And then it hit me, the answer.

"Marli! Where are they? The phantoms, the shadows, where do they go when the light drowns them out?" I tried to keep my voice neutral. I knew how phantoms were made, but my knowledge of anything more about them was extremely lacking. The way mystery herself seemed to obey Marli was suddenly, enormously, interesting.

"They go back into the darkness from which they are born and they wait." He didn't hesitate to answer.

I swing my gaze to Vance.

"Can you do more than cheap tricks with that blade, or was that the best you've got right now?" I found Vance grinning my way, straightening and lifting his wings weakly out of the dust, gripping a long blade with both hands.

"I believe I can fight, but I doubt that I can fly. Despite that temporary hindrance, I will follow you into whatever carnage you have in mind." Vance pulled a red pack that we discovered spare leathers in it toward him as emphasis. I didn't have time to grab everything from the ship, but Mick managed to slip them in. Mick managed to slip in a whole lot that he shouldn't have had time to conjure.

Marli was considering the weapons laid out in front of him and getting our gear ready to move.

"Skarlet, your sol is keeping all shadows away, but we have to face the darkness soon. Since there's nowhere else to go, I will follow you to whatever death you have in mind." His teasing grin seemed to land on both me and Vance.

I angled myself so that they could both see me, silken strands of cord from where I held the phantom bag for Vance falling through my fingers while I thought.

I lifted my head with an air of confidence. The empty look of an assassjine taking over delicate features and hardening them.

"They will come though." A nod of my head helped me to convince myself of my own words. "I have to believe that your shadows are not far from us and if they can communicate with other shades, then they can find ways to lead us through the mountain where the forest's horrors can't trail us."

"I have searched every inch of this cave, even if the shades return with directions out, we won't be able to enter the mountain from here." The Rogue moved to help Vance get holstered into his bandolier and coat, hanging it in a shredded mess upon his shoulders and wings.

Both males stood looking to me as though any idea I had would not be questioned, despite Marli's candid assessment from seconds ago. Just hours ago I wasn't sure one of them hadn't tried to kill us but friendships have been found in more unlikely places. I took inventory of those faces and committed to memory the unexpected gazes of expectation and loyalty that crossed them. The crack in my features betrayed my hope for all of us to finish this together. I offered a small smile of assurance before looking around, whispering a desperate prayer to the mother.

My eyes glowed softly against the light swirling around the cave, accenting the water trickling down from tiny crevices. The pockets of amethyst and pink quartz backing tiny pools made me think of the lakes of home. Breathtaking sunsets the same shades of pinks and purples shining with rivulets of water here were identical to the dusk-laden skies we revered as the gods' own paintings. For me, the brilliant sunrise waking up the valleys in colors of the season was the only time the land felt alive. I would spend so many mornings choosing between lakes or eddies to play in. The pebbled shores of each would shine like the jewels of the mother's crown, reflecting the mountains and the sol in mirrored perfection.

I looked at neither companion as I indulged pleasant thoughts of the past for a moment before continuing to explain the plan coming together in my strained thoughts. This may be the last moment I will have to think of home if we are killed here, our bones left for the scavengers to pick dry.

"I have always loved the water and submersed myself in any I could, whenever I could." I began and my voice softly drifted toward them. "As a child I would play in the shallows of lakes dotting Blue Mountain. I played with my magic by casting light in shapes of mermaids and water pixens into the lagoons. Then I would sit back against the softness of the bank and watch as they would dive to the deepest, stillest waters, disappearing into obscured caves where the water met the mountains." I lifted my eyes to the dull ceiling of the mountain alcove, its look nothing like the wildness of Blue Mountain. "The shapes would emerge in blasts of firelight above a cliff or against the side of a rock wall by finding shafts to follow out."

My eyes were hazy with the memory of sun on my skin and wisteria on the wind. I still didn't look at either male to see if they thought I had completely lost my mind yet.

"I always loved to play with making new shapes and having them dance upon the waters. When the mists lifted and the sun's rays grew hot, I released them. The light always aimed straight for the dark, where it could re-emerge brighter, more powerful." I swallowed back emotions and buried them deep, hoping there would be time to face them soon.

My focus sharpened and the memories cleared when I heard the loud intake of breaths from Vance and Marli.

"The light. It's the way out," Vance reflected. Marli tilted his head in agreement.

"The light and magic here are strangled, but I could bend the sol into something smaller and send it out to search. There will be many places in the rock that pieces will branch off into, but the first opening illuminated by a large swirling of light will be where we enter. There may be no way out from there and that will use all of what is left of the stone powering the chelcei sol, so we will either be free to find our way out, or we will die in the arms of the mountain."

I didn't even realize my eyes were closed until a weight settling on my back startled me. Marli stood to my right, staff in hand, while Vance reached to tighten the straps of my pack as he placed it on me. Neither of them said a word until I opened my hand scarred by the chelcei stone during our fall. A tiny star shaped marking adorned the area where the stone burned into my flesh, linking me to it.

Marli's eyes glanced from the sunburst shape of the star marking to Vance, who was eyeing the spot with open curiosity.

"Even with the stone drained, I should be able to use it for this. I had no reason to believe it probable until I felt the light begin to speak to me. Very softly whispering around the fear I have harbored while here. At first all I could feel was the drain of energy," I offered my explanation for keeping the possibility of this from them. "Then I had to wait to see if the linking would settle before there was any chance of a controlled connection without the stones being charged. In a land where magic had not been sucked dry from even the grounds about us, I would have healed and connected with the sol within a moment or two at most. I was as surprised as you are now at discovering the new tattoo shimmering against my palm after finishing the poppima tea." I gave them my honest and embarrassing answer to their unspoken questions. "I still don't know how far the mark will take us, or if the innate bindings of my magic to the chelcei's power will remain with me." Placing my tattooed palm face up for them to see better, I clarified, "The heat of the skies pushes just beyond my reach, I have never been bound this way and wouldn't risk your lives' on the glow of a pretty scar."

It was Vance who broke the silence first. "When you direct the light, as you say, to go play within the mountain's private places, will that leave us in complete darkness?"

"Not completely, though with so little power left to work with, the most I can do for us is a glow so that we can see where the danger gathers as we move against the rock wall." I stared down at my palm and willed every spark of my power to that spot. I sent up a fervent prayer meant for the ears of Asti, straight from my trembling lips.

"Well, what is the point of death if you can't see where it's coming from, right?" Vance tried to laugh.

"How can you fight Grimm when he comes swift on the winds of time and smites you down with a weapon fashioned from your own sense of invincibility." I tore my eyes from the linking mark and laughed at the absurdity of it all.

Marli's hands fell to his side, his freshly braided hair tumbling along his back and shoulders. "I will take the fight to Grimm when he comes for me, but that will not be today. Death must wait, for Lady Lior needs her escorts." Marli joined Vance in a strained attempt at humor.

The shuffle of feet and a deep sigh break up the silence that oppresses the room. Black gloves groaned against the fractured hilt of my blade as Marli passed it to me to be holstered into the long sheath fitted into my stealth leathers. The other side of the leathers had an identical sheath, though I had only had one blade to fill it with. I bent to grab throwing knives and another blade before Marli packed them away.

"We will still have to run for our lives, fighting as we go, but when your light begins to focus itself on whatever it finds, I will call for the darkness. Vance, you flank to the outside while I bring up the back, where the least of the light will be." Marli's voice was low and now devoid of any humor at the thought of moving in darkness on a wild hope that the lights would keep us alive and find our way to the shades who may guide us out.

"They will come, Skarlet. I share in your belief because the darkness is always there waiting." Marli added tenderly.

"Hey, you two come finish binding my wings. Be gentle, they're sensitive." Vance cut through another moment heavy with tension. "They are too heavy to lift with one hand and wrap with the other, and I won't fit through any mountains with them dragging behind me." Vance's shoulders straightened with pride at the mention of his wingspan.

"I don't know that we will fit you through a mountain at all, even with your wings secured." Marli leaned against the wall, weapons already strapped on. Again, following Vance's lead and matching his lighter tone.

"Maybe we should have you try to plow a way through the rock before risking the movement of the light," the Rogue suggested.

"In my red dress," I suggested with a smile.

A small crease lined Vance's mouth when he answered, turning as we made quick work of securing his injured wings. "I can't plow a mountain any more than you can become one, but I will wager you a dance in that red dress that I plow more dracos and nymphs than you before the dark even reaches us." Both massive golden hands wrapped around daggers from his bandolier in open challenge.

"Oh, but I can become the mountain, as soon as the light fades you will not see me, brother. Neither will these void annoyances, which is why I will take that wager. They will not even see their own deaths when the darkness binds to me again." Marli's staff extended into double blades; the same staff he used during our descent to slice heads off and tear wings with the smooth and serrated edges.

"Well, if that's true, maybe there is one mountain I could plow through." Vance's laugh echoed as he dashed toward the dark side of the rock face with Marli barely a step behind.

Ok. So, we're doing this now. Like right now. Fuck it. A smile slipped through where the terror was edging in, and insanity took its place.

"To death or glory we run!" I shouted. Opening and closing my marked hand, I breathed in and out, focusing purely on the light as I ran.

I followed the boys to the edge of the dome of light and began the swirl of a painted red nail along the mark on my palm, feeling the heat answer me had unbelievable relief almost dropping me to my knees. Galaxies and the colors of all seasons spun above, matching the tempo of my hand's movements. Opaque hues of white appeared where the light was separating, answering my call.

In those spaces opening to the darkness, all the horrors of the forest waited to attack. If I took down the orb, we wouldn't have a chance to even turn before a talon or tooth had us bleeding out where we stand. The reality of my error in judgment knocked the breath from me.

I had seconds to make a decision that would keep us alive. Fuck death, I was here until glory was mine. Glory and revenge.

The light of the stars shining from my palm flared, blurring my vision. I felt it stirring, the sol in me, so I called to stop Marli and Vance with renewed plans.

"Marli, take this and tie it to your staff," I whispered, handing him a chunk of my broken hilt. "It's possible that I can still use it as a conduit when I light this place up."

Both warriors stood completely still, eyes averted, weapons held in white knuckled grips. A nod from each of them was their only acknowledgment that I was speaking.

"Vance, you're up to my left. When we see our mark, then do whatever it takes to get to it." A foul smell broke through, carried on warm winds from the beat of silken wings, and we all knew it was time.

Gripping a borrowed dagger in the hand with the starburst tattoo, I pulled my thoughts in and focused on the connection. All at once darkness fell and light speared out in front of and behind us, projected by the dagger as sharp as it's blades. Pieces of light broke off and headed into a hundred different directions, and we began the hail mother run of our lives looking every bit the image of a kaleidoscope's mechanism, casting lights about, sliced images of horror taking the place of colored patterns.

Warmth fell from above, streaking down my hair and face from the kills Vance landed. I heard absolutely nothing of Marli from behind me, his movements silent upon the forest floor, but I knew that the Rogue followed by the continuous thuds and vibrations from bodies hitting the ground behind me.

Hours or moments passed; I couldn't tell. The bursting of lights coming from the rock faces we ran past were becoming dimmer and smaller. No entry made itself known to us and the only thing I knew at this moment was that there was no way we could keep this up. Here, right now, we were basically nothing more than a few mortals fighting against swarms of magic creatures.

The warmth of courage that flooded me as the mother guided me earlier was morphing into an icy feeling of failure. What had I done? I fucked up; I shouldn't be in charge. When I led, I got my people killed! I didn't know how we got here, fighting a demon legion of hundreds with a simple trick of the chelcei and a few weapons as our only hope. I had no doubt that this was my fault, though.

Light spun about me so fast it appeared as though portals followed us in our mad sprint down the mountain face. Keeping my connection while slicing into a dozen dracos at a time was draining and still no call from the sparks searching the mountains.

Up ahead a few feet I spotted movement along the ground and turned to see if Marli had gotten past me without my notice. He stood just a few feet to my rear now, shooting me a brief, blank, look before another beast hit the ground at his muddied feet.

Before I could turn back to Vance, the large shadow of the beast appeared, knocking into me with solid force.

The breath left my chest on a wince, and the dagger bounced out of hands that spasmed against the force of the hit. Slowly I turned to see Marli pick up the glowing staff and turn his back on me.

I called for Vance, but he was gone. I couldn't find him anywhere on the ground or within the sol still swirling in areas around us. A loud screeching from above drew my eyes to the dark sky, but all I could make out was an enormous mass falling to the ground.

The dracothite's body thudded to the ground at my feet but I couldn't jump away, something had hold of me and I was being dragged into a small space I hadn't noticed open in the rock wall.

Rock and bramble scratched and pushed against the matte black leather of my pants while I screamed and thrashed against the invisible force pulling me away. The sound of bone and bodies breaking against boulders in the dark shattered me.

Something pierced my shoulder in a burst of pain and my legs went numb instantly. I spun to dislodge the creature against the rock, but the damage was done. I'd taken my eye off the fight for a moment and the beasts recognized the opportunity.

I couldn't move.

"Marli!" I barely recognized the emotion in my own voice as I called to him. If he left me trapped here, I'd be dead in seconds.

He turned back to look but didn't focus on me, instead looking over my shoulders and giving a small nod before wielding the light in front of him like a shield.

"Marli, please." My own sob was the last thing I heard before darkness took me.

XIV

Lights swirled behind my closed eyes and voices echoed around me. Voices that I didn't recognize in a language I didn't understand swirled around me. I tried to pry my eyes open, but they were leaden and all I could manage were broken images.

I reminded myself to breathe as I registered the pain of an unfamiliar weight on my chest. A weight like rocks, and at least the size of a tree. The wind shifted and with it a faint scent like a summer rainstorm floated towards me. A frantic hope filled me as my mind became clearer and the image of a Knight with wings the color of storm clouds formed before my broken vision.

"Vance?" I called in a strangled voice. Fear and anger battled within me while I waited for an answer.

"Skarlet?" I couldn't try to lift my trapped arms to feel for him, but his strained response confirmed he was there. The weight nearly smothering me was my Knight. He was alive and really fucking heavy.

Under his weight, it was impossible to tell if my legs were still immobilized by the venom in my shoulder either.

"Stop talking," a voice growled from above my head. Marli stood looking down at us, light from his staff barely illuminating the area. My light. My sol.

"Not possible" I whisper.

"A lot of things are possible if you know how to ask for them." Marli's eyes followed mine to where the broken stone was tied then to where I lay smothered beneath the weight of my friend. He lifted a leg to kick Vance off of me then turned again to the dark.

A single voice remained in the space we were trapped in, calling to Marli in a huffing, growling sort of dialogue.

"Grab him. I have her. Run with the force of midnight winds and stop for nothing. You know where to meet." I couldn't see what Marli was speaking to, but he did so in our trade tongue. No response or objection sounded from the dark as Vance was pulled from me. Before either of us could protest, the Rogue tossed me over a shoulder, going straight into a full sprint and collapsing his staff.

"Do not make a single sound, Skarlet, or you're dead." Marli said.

I tried to protest, but my voice was raw, and my body buzzed from the sting of venom still making its way through my limbs. I dropped my head against his back and opened my eyes again some time later.

Wind blew the loose pieces of my hair about so harshly that it felt like flying. No one moved this fast, not even a traitorous Rogue who clearly had many, many secrets.

Complete and unending darkness surrounded us, the change in temperature and Marli's mad flight my only indicator we even moved.

Awareness crept into me as we sped further into the abyss and my senses returned. Awareness, fear, anger, and questions. So many questions.

Warm tears stung new cuts opening on my face and I felt betrayed. My limbs felt leaden but functional, nothing permanently damaged. I didn't want to be this close to the Rogue but demanding to be put down would have meant death in an unknown tunnel somewhere.

Still, the only thought I had was how he'd looked before I passed out. Like this was the outcome he'd hoped for all along. His stony face had looked past me as though I were nothing more than dirt when I fell.

Despite everything he's said and done to prove his case, I couldn't help the swell of anger rising inside of me. I raise my weak fists to bang on his back, deciding I'd rather attempt walking, or dying here, if it meant getting myself upright to face off with him.

He put me down and I began to drill him, anger boiling just under the surface.

"Stop it, Skarlet!" His command landed like a whisper upon my ears.

"You're a bastard, Rogue. Was this your plan? To use us and then leave us for dead. What have you done with my partner?."

Before I could raise my voice above an angry whisper, he stopped and slammed me forward against a wall with a hand over my mouth. My head bounced off the jagged rock when he released me and the smell of blood settled in the still air around me as I heard a blade slide out of the body of something Marli must have seen in the dark before tossing me aside. A heavy thud suggested it was a large something.

I felt Marli approach rather than see him, his cool breath against my cheek surprising me.

"I said stay quiet." His whisper chilled me to my core, the reality of my situation settled uncomfortably around me.

"I can't hide you in darkness if you refuse to stay tethered to me and every noise you make calls another of these demons to our location." He turned my face gently towards where the slain mountain dweller must have fallen. "Do you want me to carry you, or will you behave and let me protect you?"

"Protect me? Is that what this is? What about Vance, is he being protected?" A scratching and scuffling noise above us silenced my accusations.

Blood slid down the wall next to my face, and Marli tossed another unseen monster down from above and finished it. He pushed further into me while he made sure his kill was complete.

"I gave you, my word. You have to trust it." His response was quiet and clipped.

His hand wrapped around my wrist, and I submitted to him. There was no other choice left for me to make. I accepted that I would be bound to him through the darkness, fully dependent on Marli despite my current mistrust of him. His guidance was the only thing I had to hold on to if I hoped to see the sunshine again. I could accept that I needed help, but I was not naïve enough to think he could handle the denizens of this pass and still keep me from being skewered completely. I needed to be able to respond to threats, to cover his back and my own.

I lifted my loose arm, and the dirty blade of my own dagger came up between us, the tiniest flecks of light floating out of its hilt. I could barely make out his face with the tiny bits of light, but he didn't seem concerned. Pulling it from his waist had been simple once I'd spotted the specks of color pushing through the darkness. Cold sweat beads formed upon my forehead as I bunched my brows with fear and anticipation. Killing me here would be pointless now, anyway.

Marli considered me briefly then pulled my unarmed arm forward, silently wrapping one of my hands around the hilt of my other blade. Relief flooded like water over fire through my body. He was arming me willingly, but against what?

Once my blade was gripped firmly in cold fingers, he moved his fingers again to my wrist to pull me a few inches, no distance between his chest and mine. A flicker of curiosity surfaced seconds before Marli pressed his full lips against mine.

It was a kiss completely devoid of any passion, though it was deep and consuming. My lips cooled beneath his, as the heat rising in me was snuffed like night falling upon an evening landscape. A scent of autumn evenings and heady smoke mingled with my own blooming jasmine florals. A feeling of smoothness like the wind against a black lake mixing with the shattered light of my own sol.

Both of my wrists fell to the side as he pulled back, staring into my eyes. I didn't know what he saw in mine, but his black ones began to glow and he looked around us in a small gesture, indicating that I should take in the space we stood in.

Marli had taken my light and brought me into his darkness, giving a piece of himself to me. The awe of this new night sight made me forget we still stood chest to chest. The Rogue watched me as I discovered what the dark had hidden. Around us I now saw what he did as my eyes adjusted to the blackness. Mountain walls were lined with sparkling veins of unbelievable beauty and its crevices held monsters I had never even heard of.

"How?" I began to ask, but his fingers pressed against my mouth. He pointed to a corner where a serpent with layered horns and dripping fangs began to uncoil toward the sound.

They couldn't see us. His shadows were deeper than even the mountain's.

I still had so many questions, but now was not the time. I noticed the slain demons piled behind us, littering the path he had carried me down. I looked up at Marli and allowed him to take my hand. My only option was to run like hell with him into whatever depths he was leading us to.

XV

The deeper we went into the heart of the mountain, the colder it got. Our breaths came in gasps from the pace we were keeping. Little blasts of cold air filled the bubble of darkness, appearing as spirits in the snow as we moved silently down tunnels and up through tiny crevices.

I started to feel small tingles of fire deep inside of me. Little bursts of magic were trying to come back to life, and I knew we must be almost out of reach of the forest completely. How long would a void have to exist for its grip to leach magic from grounds this far away from the Nymphs?

I wondered constantly about Vance. I hadn't been able to see him clearly in the dimming light, but he'd spoken to me and I felt him moving slightly before being snatched away. I couldn't ask until we cleared the tunnels, unless I wanted to risk waking any manner of trouble slithering about in the dark.

While I thought of my partner and tried to ignore the pain in my shoulder, Marli slowed his pace, still silently commanding me to follow him around bends and crevices that no one should have been able to navigate. Then, Marli was something no one else was.

I was not even sure I wanted to know. Honest answers sometimes made you wish you hadn't even asked questions, but actions that questioned loyalties could never be overlooked.

We began to ascend a path and my legs began to scream in protest, the paralysis in the venom still weighing me down a bit. As soon as we clear this path, I will be able to catch my breath.

My feet were nearly still at the sites suddenly before us as we crested and continued into wider tunnels. Gone were the rough walls and dangerous creatures and in their place there were etchings in the likeness of enormous flowers and winding circles that knotted together in infinite movement. Citrine glowed brightly over arches to branching tunnels off the one we moved along. The sunshine shapes of the doorway adornments drew an eye to my palm. The swirl of the golden tattoo lit up immediately upon my command.

Thoughts of my partner and dracothites and throbbing legs drained from me.

I looked to Marli to see if it was safe enough to light it up. I needed to inspect the art within the mountain, the images calling to me against even the feelings of fear and abandonment uncoiling in me.

The Rogue's shoulders were surrounded by gray mists that lightly curled around the lines of braids above each ear before disappearing for another shade to take its place. Information from the things most people never notice from shadows.

"Her beauty was meant to be seen when people still traveled through the temple. Please enlighten us." Marli answered and his mists faded before I even began to glow.

"And Skarlet, you will see Vance shortly. We get through the last of this and you'll meet my partner. You were right, the shades responded in full."

I stared for a moment before allowing myself to trust him and turning to take in the details around me.

The light pulled beauty from the mountain that settled pangs of memory upon my pounding heart. Carvings of the Constellations of the Asti, Goddess of the Moon, and her dragon companion stretched entirely down the length of our passage. At the end a final soaring piece in the shape of Rhaegar, the Asti's Dragon, his golden wings shaped to emulate him in flight and sparkling with diamonds and golden quartz signals the exit onto an overlapping series of walkways and bridges. The Guardian Asti's rock form stood under him, blades of chelcei in hand and ready to protect the South as she did in her last battle.

Marli took my hand to lead me under the deity's depiction onto a soaring foot bridge, crossing a cavern large enough to hold many courts at once. Pillars help hold up the sides and top of the mountain room, reaching all the way to the opening at the top where sunshine filters in, bouncing off stones set in replica constellations, some that I didn't recognize.

A single tunnel was situated between two pillars, ancient symbols of a compass embedded into the middle of each, giving entry to the East, West, North and South. Looking down I saw that the general direction we came from was the nearest the southern tunnel, marked by a downward pointing arrow and surrounded by images of the phases of the moons.

I looked to my left where Marli leaned against the edge of the bridge, a staircase led downward behind him to branch off into different areas within the walls and landings and then finally to the floor.

His dark eyes, lined lightly in a silver glow, never left my face as I turned fully to him and finally asked, "Why?"

His head dropped a fraction, his eyes still upon mine, and he seemed to fade into shadow just a bit before he answered. "Duty." He turned to lean his elbows against the banister, facing the room then settling his view on the Eastern tunnel entrance.

"I need to wait on the Knight to join us with his own escort here. There are things he will be needing to tell you, too. No one betrayed you because we were never here just for you." He held no weapon to me, and no hate laced his words. He spoke just facts. "Join me for a chat down there," he nodded down the spiraling stairs. "I will begin to try to explain."

I felt for my dagger, sheathed to my right thigh, thoughts of what Vance could possibly have to say raced through my mind along with images of his body being kicked off of mine and dragged away. I thought through the claim that he would arrive with his own escort when no one else could have known how we would get out of that forest or even that we went into it.

The Gentry would not have sent a team in, surely assuming us gone, our ashes mixed in among the wreckage of the flyer.

"Fuck it, you go first though." I thought Chof the kiss and the many chances he had to leave my lifeless body in any of the many pools or dens we passed on the way here. "If you don't make it to the bottom before I decide to no longer trust you, then I imagine your fall would save me from burying my blade in your heart."

I realized that my own heart wasn't behind the threat, even as the words left me. Many things the last few years of my life were put on me that left so many questions. The dead don't give answers though. Marli's death may well come at the end of my blade or by the fire of my light, but the need to know about Vance, about this place, even about Marli's story took over as I gripped the rock banister and descended behind him.

XVI

"The Gentry have long been a thorn in my boot, but when Arike sent for me, I knew I had to answer. His missive was short and clipped. I located him on the ship after we sparred in the training rooms and his answers were no more forthcoming in person," Marli began.

"Are you protecting someone, Marli?" His answers seemed to come from somewhere unsure and I pushed against the training that tells me to allow others their secrets in hopes of discovering even a small truth.

"Yes, Madam Lior. You," he sighed.

I gave Marli a pointed stare and leaned, exhausted, against a dais carved from the wall. I rolled my jacket behind my head and my arms reached for the milky light shining from above. "So you decided to come on this mission as part of a more super-secret mission to babysit me? I thought Arike chose you for an assist on a stealth kill. It can't be both," I pointed out. Gemstones and trinkets and gilded scenes glowed around and behind us. My magic was humming strongly through me, and I let off bits of it to keep the heat of it from overwhelming me as it returned.

"Can't it be?" Marli sank down on the bed of moss at my feet, his shining black locks spilling over the crossed arms stretching behind his head. He was completely confident in our safety while we remained in this nook in the cavernous temple.

"I protect you and you make the kill. Is that what he told you?"

He still stared toward the Eastern wall. We had been talking long enough to eat a small amount of cheese and dried meats from Mick's packs while we waited for Vance and the ghost guiding him. I glanced at the dagger supplied to me by the Rogue now settled in the left sheath of my leathers and I knew I would not be killing Marli, at least for now. If there was anything I loved more than good sex, it was a true rebellion. Marli seemed to know exactly where the fighting was, and I needed to be a part of that.

He probably could have led with that. I would have made me a lot less cranky with him.

"Marli, I know as little about you as I do this temple, and I know that Arike told me nothing more than your name. Not even your full name, just Marli of the North. I am here for a shot at my honor kill. You are my escort. I tried to find out more but was shut down."

I knew from my own meetings that there were a few still standing against the Veill. Marli had given me hope, ever so thin as it may be, that there were far more than I had been told. Not all of Tanirra completely trusted The Old Order of the Gentry, and despite my many precautions to not be recognized, I had been told that I was known almost equally in clandestine circles for my kills and my beauty. I had no problem believing either of those things. According to the Rogue, leaders did not want to tell their secrets to an assasjine grunt though, no matter how stunning she was.

Keeping Marli close would help move that agenda along if his words were true. I hoped that they were because losing him now would not sit right with my spirit, as fractured as it may be.

He sat up to lean on one elbow, glancing at me and downing more fluids. The malevolence of the void did nothing to taint the mountain waters we gathered there; they were the sweetest I have ever tasted. His lips glistened and his throat bobbed with the gulps of the liquid he took in.

His lips were cold when he kissed me. Was that a kiss or something else? The dread settling in me didn't allow me to articulate the question.

"You are here as one of my escorts." I followed his gaze toward the Eastern wall. The silence spoke what we couldn't vocalize of our anxieties about where the other escort could be. How hard must it be to get a mountain sized man through an actual mountain?

"Who leads the rebel groups in the North, or do they answer to their own law? Tanirra is a vast world where so many could hide." I felt about for more information from him.

"They have a leader," He replied softly. "They do Skarlet, but you do not, even though you search for a way to power your own cause because your heart is too wrapped up in the Gentry's directive." Marli leaned back to take in my features. He had a way of saying things that stung and soothed at the same time. "You will never know anything of uprising and retribution if you continue to pursue this honor kill for your own glory and try to cloak it in avenging righteousness."

"I know of vengeance and pain. That is enough," I replied. My voice edged with bitterness at his vague response and the judgment of my motives. "It was my leader that sent you on this errant adventure."

"It was, but Arike and the Gentry have reasons behind their actions, with more selfish motivation fueling each desperate plan as they have begun to run out of ideas for winning Tannira back. And sadly, hope," he grumbled.

"Look, I don't want to argue with you. I want to know what you know. I want to understand where the leaders are so that I can make them an offer. All I want is to see Tanirra rise again."

"Skarlet, rest please. I know that this will all be fine, and you will be where you are needed when the time is right. Time is a fickle bitch though and seems it has stopped for now, dragging out the wait for our Knight to emerge so that you can get us out of here." Marli pointed upward to the open top of the range where light drifts of snow gathered at the edges.

I pointed a finger toward one of the slanting rays falling from above and shaped it into a tiny, cloaked version of Marli. "I will not be taking us through the top of the mountain so stop pointing at it. I am tired and dirty. I plan to have us settled in front of a fire within two blinks. Just not by going up like a winged Veiliri."

Using the palm with the sunburst tattoo, I pushed the command to dance slowly toward the tiny figure and mimicked Marli's voice. "I can't tell you things, Skarlet, I am an enigma, and you don't deserve the darkness that saved you. No secrets shall pass my lips, and I am immune to your charms, silly girl." I gave the tiny glowing replica a twirl and a mock bow. "Choose to serve your allies or service yourself, but choose you must." The tiny light puppet shot Marli an obscene gesture before swirling away.

Marli shook lightly with laughter, one side of his lips turned up and his face settled in a look of mock indignation. "I don't shake my ass like that, and I surely know how to bow before a Queen or King. The only right way is on your knees. Aye!" Marli's humor surfaced with the return of his rough, roguish façade.

I shook my head in mock despair, I would get no more information from him until Vance arrived. We both busied ourselves in the silence by checking our packs and weapons. The thoughts ambushing me tricked me into believing I truly may never see Vance again, and the thought of continuing without the Knight rendered my heart still. He had been my day one hero.

I looked about and tried to slow the thoughts by picturing the vast variety of deities carved about the cavern as I imagined they would have appeared amongst the living. Beauty, power, wisdom and fun, they were each known for contributions to our worlds.

I searched the cave for more distractions. Engaging ones were like poppima and music; they took you away from the things you couldn't afford to feel. I could use more of either one right now.

A sudden thought turned my head sharply back towards Marli. "You kissed me?" How could I have not come back to ask about that already? Maybe sitting in a cave waiting on fate had something to do with that slip.

"Did I?" His laugh rumbled around where we now sat, and I couldn't help my own grin.

"This is madness, Rogue, all of it. How can we sit and laugh away the moments also spent worrying over the fate of a friend?"

"I am not worried, I am waiting," he answered. "I was bringing you into the dark with the kiss" He sighed quietly in a softened tone. "I knew you were upset, and I had no time to explain anything to you. I had seconds to make decisions for all of us. My life is irrevocably entwined in the rebellion, but I also made a promise to you." Marli leaned a shoulder into mine and looked down at me with a face full of emotion. The glow still hovered against the walls highlighting the blue center of his black eyes. "What I did could have been done in other ways, but the quickest is often the most intimate. I never meant to put that on you. You're my girl, the one who gets naked to save friends and fights with the fury of Asti against incredible odds." He knocked a knuckle under my chin, and I swat his hand away with a scowl. "I told you why I took this assignment, but I haven't told you that Arike mentioned you in his summons specifically, and not unkindly. He wrote that he would accept my appearance in the training rooms prior to this mission as agreement that I did solemnly swear to protect you, so now I find you are a part of my quest in ways I hoped to handle without you. Things won't be easy for you as the next few hours unfold, but remember that feeling of our connection when you start to feel confused about things." Marli's chest rose and fell with deep breaths before he continued. "We may not have been here for you in the way that you thought, but you have been here for us despite all of this."

"Oh honey, you can kiss me any time we need to connect. I don't need an excuse to have a little good, dirty fun together," I grinned.

"You are incorrigible," he shook his head but lit up with his answering grin. "What is true companionship though if you can't journey into a friend's darkness when they need you most, even if you do nothing but sit with them there?"

"I will forever be grateful that you made the hard choices that got us here. We can sit together anytime, though I do prefer the light, that of both the sun and moon. I love them all, so maybe we can spend a little time there, too." I cast an array of crawling yellow vines heavy with blooming blue jasmines and black orchids, making the area look like transitions in colors of dawn to dusk. Marli took in the scene with a small smile.

"In lightness and darkness, Skarlet, there are no limits to the places you could shine. The strength you wield is in the way that you don't hold back. Live life with beauty and your heart full, my girl, and fill the world's cracks is what you will do," Marli mused.

My insides felt warm as I took in the serious planes of the Rogue's face. "What about your world? Is it so different from the one I am so pushed to fix? Do you exist outside of that possibility or..." My words trailed off and Marli and I jumped at the same time, both catching a noise coming from the Western wall. The wrong wall.

The entrance we had our backs to while watching for Vance to emerge filled with clamoring voices and the sounds of fighting. Vance's voice rose above the crescendo trailing him, yelling for us. Marli and I looked at one another and aimed for the middle of the temple. The only other clear way out was to fly up from the center if I couldn't trixxt us fast enough.

Vance was not supposed to come from the paths headed west. That tunnel was on the opposite side of where we waited, too far away to cover him using our blades.

Judging by the masses of darkness bouncing against walls and screeches echoing, Vance had attracted a horde of demons for us to play with on the way out as well.

My legs burned with the challenge of keeping up with Marli's sprint toward the temple's epicenter. Boots slid silently on blue floors while our palms filled with weapons, our shoulders pressed together, and we readied our stance to fight back-to-back. We had no idea what may follow Vance into the last murky rays of the setting sun, so we waited.

Boots splashed through blood that ran in rivers from the opening of the western tunnels. Wings appeared, unbound and unharmed before the Knight's face and body came out, bending at the waist, and barreled into the temple. It was clear enough to see he was focused directly on me. His fingers moved rapidly, mimicking the words he yelled for us. All I could gather through the tremors of seeing him like this was the word "GO!"

Marli spun me back toward the Northern exit into the Andele mountain range, pointing at our contingency plan and dispatching the first yelping dracothite with his staff. He paused and slipped the sleeves of his tunic up on one arm and tiny blades gleamed as he tossed one after another, each one a killing shot, taking out the monsters closest to Vance.

The demons slowed their chase of the Knight, though one shape kept pace with him, and a few others flew above, despite the rays of a fading sun now burning through their skin. Some dracothites didn't make it past the first mezzanine or breezeway before being blinded and turning on their own, leaving the fallen in piles, their deaths staining this sacred place with malevolent decrement.

I had to get them close enough to trixxt out, which would be a lot harder with flying death swarming all around. I pulled my weapons up, bringing the dagger down into the skull of a winged mountain dweller.

Gold glimmered from the palm of my left hand, the busted dagger balancing upon my fingers as pure fire emitted from the tattoo. Light and heat incinerated the flying bastards around us. My fingers erupted with the fire of a thousand southern nights while flames danced along the edge of the blade, cleaving demons and darkness in droves.

Vance was almost to me, but Marli was against the wall running to intercept a few stragglers on his side. A massive shadow moved beside him, hurtling toward Vance's back.

I lowered the flaming blade for Vance to get close to me and felt Marli's cool breath beside me. The mass of black still sprinted toward Vance, and I aimed to blast it when both males grabbed my hand. The barreling weight behind the jaw that gripped onto the armor of Vance's right hand nearly upends me. All of Vance's strength pulled the beast towards us with that arm, the same one grasping my own. I pulled the heat into me and began to think of the stars that marked our destination, making to move before this went from an adventure to a funeral.

A jerk and a growl startled me right as I entered the casting, unsure if that was Marli or his staff that vibrated off the floor as I pulled us out. I truly hoped we were all together. I could live with losing a staff, but losing Marli would be unbearable.

I struggled to be heard against the chaos. I contorted my face and opened the raw space inside of me to voice warnings to my companions to hold on. Nothing came from my throat but fiery anguish heavy with unknowns. Pain tore through my body from what felt like a hundred different slices. Wings of the dracothis beat heavily against the tearing between worlds where I hauled us through and away. The fighting from seconds ago faded into the background and a wind heavy with the scent of honeysuckle and gardenia wrapped around the weight I clung to, desperate to get away from a skirmish we couldn't win.

I tried to step through the fold on the other side, but my feet were heavy, sludging through the tapestry of realms and I couldn't make the full jump. Magic bled from me like the drip of a fresh, fatal slice. I aimed to take us to a northern home of the Lord Drake at the tip of the Andele mountains and give my last drop to get us close.

XVII

The smell of pine surrounded me, and I knew something had gone terribly wrong. Cedar trees grew around the area of the northern fortress, with no pine forests around for miles. Thuds and the slide of weapons accompanied the gasp torn from me as I materialized against the prickly bark of a tree and slid down.

Paws of impenetrable black landed on either side of my head. I stared up into the scruff of a shadowed panther. I registered the pain in my head and tried to roll off the rock it lay upon, pulling for my dagger. A stiff growl from the giant cat stilled me and a paw swiped up to cradle my face, stopping the movement. Honey golden eyes stared down at me, then back at the dead dracothite lying just under my back with a poisoned talon not two inches from my skull.

Pain contorted my limbs pinned under the body of the panther, and images blurred between when we left the mountain temple and how we landed here. The panther's body moved, and an unobstructed view of the sunset off to the western horizon welcomed me. We had made it out, but it seemed we had some last minute additions to our caravan.

A feeling of numbness crept back into my legs just below the throbbing behind my knee. I tried to move but found myself stuck. Before I could begin to panic from the stillness taking over my system, the panther gently moved me, and I felt something being ripped from my leg. Two black dracothite talons were tossed to the side of where I lay under the beautiful pines. The irony struck me that a pine box for my body wouldn't be hard to find here.

I tried to endure the fire shoving into me from everywhere now as the poison coursed through my veins and made its way to my heart. The thought of how we got here played across my mind again in the moments of lucidity between waves of agonizing pain.

When we were leaving the temple, my vision was blocked by massive bodies and a dark that fell consuming everything around us. The pressure pushing against my body could have been from the hands of friends or foes. The memory of an intense stabbing pain to my shoulder and calf pushed through. It is what caused me to waiver, bringing us here, wherever here was. We could possibly be miles from where we needed to be.

I do remember the panther prowling nervously around my legs. I nearly pissed my pants when this monster of a shadow shaped like a feline female materialized with us, taking down a swarm of dracothites with sites on my exposed rear flank. Not quickly enough though. Whoever, or whatever, she was she didn't hesitate to assist my companions. Absolute exhaustion overtook me, and I fought to keep my eyes open. I saw Marli sitting under a tree with Vance hunching over him to patch up a few rough spots where jagged tears of skin bled.

Their eyes moved to me at the same time, watching the enormous cat and making no move to be rid of her. Neither made an effort to come to me either. A soft sensation nuzzled at the side of my face in an effort to bring me comfort. I tried to thank my nameless hero, but an unfamiliar voice interrupted my thoughts. The melodic, heady, and demanding voice was accompanied by strong arms that lifted me upwards.

Pine needles stuck to the blood of my tunic, and I stared at the claw that dropped from my leg to the ground beneath, I took in the scene from the height of the stranger and tried to make sense of the scene.

I looked up after a moment and into the most beautiful eyes with sparkling verdant hues. I have never seen beauty set so perfectly, mixing between delicate eyes and chiseled jaw, perfectly setting off lips with full curves despite the frown he held there. The pieces of my brain would not put together the words being said, but the voice of the male soothed me, drawing fire from my body. It felt like being wrapped in a tapestry of night, soft as velvet and safe from any nightmares. His voice was a song my magic recognized, and those eyes, those sea glass green eyes, felt like a home I always knew waited for me on the other side of sacrifice.

I had no idea who the fuck he was, though.

"All good then?" the melodic voice asked. The gorgeous male tucked me in tight and spoke to my crew whose mumbled confirmations of welfare seemed to satisfy him. "This one won't make it all the way to the northern border as she is. The Lady of the lake house has offered her hospitality, and her home is about halfway between here and the regional divide. A few extra faces among those already gathering for the feast will prove no more a threat than the season already brings. Her recovery can be completed in privacy there."

"Skarlet will likely stand out amongst any crowd if we bring her in dead. Her regeneration will remain nullified until the paralytic is siphoned from her. Is there somewhere closer for her recovery? Maybe outside of the villa until we're sure she's stabilizing." Vance's voice was threaded with concern, but not mistrust.

I clenched my teeth and tried to take a deep breath, to ground myself to this world while an unheralded dalliance was rapidly fortified around me, our next steps decided, and directions vocalized. My lungs burned with the effort of expanding and I was denied any great inhalation. No air rushed in to surround me in a wicking embrace, no breath to cool the heat of pain or cleanse redolence before it festered. I could smell the demons on me, the stench of decay wrapping my body in a pungent blanket. Choking on the sickly scent of my own approaching demise made my heart lurch and twist into a profound ache.

Choppy black and white images were all I could see where moments ago the colors of life still painted this area brightly. Warm blood trickled easily into hair already stained the color of rust throughout.

A clanging, shrieking shrill ripped through my head, the sound echoed for only me as though the venom was trying to break me into tiny pieces, denying any chance at grounding myself or finding comfort, fucking with me before making the final push to take my life. The ravishing of my senses left me with little capacity to process those moments fully. I only just realized how no one moved to aid my prone body before the stranger arrived. My crew should have done something, anything to ease the pain I was in.

Vance's wings looked perfectly healed when I chanced a glance at him. Marli had little more than flesh wounds. Both appeared to be fully functional, so why was a stranger cradling me and giving out orders?

Bile fought its way up my throat that was still closed to any sound. I tried to fight against the male holding me, but it was like trying to pound against marble floors. My hands barely moved, doing nothing more than sliding against the hard planes of his stomach. A purring vibration sounded near my feet, and I saw waves of onyx fall against the stranger's face as he looked down past me. Strands of deep burgundy entwined through the black hair, highlighting the coastal pallet sparkling in his eyes.

I couldn't make out his joking words to the others, but I didn't miss his glance to where my hand hovered over the muted shine of a line of black buttons holding his pants up. "You are a hard Lady to track down, Skarlet.

Even so, you will have to wait until you can stand before we can play."

The prowling night beast stopped at a command from him and shifted into a humanara form. I heard her introduce herself as Castilen. Her eyes of gold lined with emerald hues peered down at me. When I looked at her a familiar feeling fought its way through the pain but never became a full thought.

"You're indeed a cute little thing. I hope you were worth all of this," she winked before moving out of my limited vision.

The heat continued to recede from my body, clearing my field of vision further, but I still missed the sight of shaded wings behind the beautiful face until they lift, shooting us straight into the night sky above. I heard Vance grunt under the weight of Marli and Castilen as he took flight behind us. The chill of the air filled my lungs and each star blinking to life in the night sky pushed a little more magic back to my core. A feeling of safety wrapped itself more tightly around me before I let the weight of the last few days break me.

XVIII

"Be still, woman," Vance fussed as he used rags to help wash away the poison that drained from my back. He was sopping it up and burning the rags in a fire blazing beside the warm pool I floated in.

Scratches on my hands drug up the memory of the winged male that dropped me here and left. The futile banging of limp fists against his chest forced him to pull me tighter and his shifting exposed the daggers lining the inside of his jacket before he fully secured me and aimed for the clouds. I thought of the black buckles falling from the sides of his open coat where a simple flat tunic peeked through, the top forming a deep v against defined muscles.

I squirmed again, my hands gripping the rough edges where mossy rocks led into the spring. My shiftiness had nothing to do with the death leaking out of me.

A pile of black glistened against the rage of the fire. Claws pulled from my back, legs and torso tossed about as Vance and Marli worked to remove them all from me.

Castilen prowled up to the edge of the pool, black spotted fur glistening in the spray where she plopped down to nuzzle my hands. The barreling mass of midnight that came for Vance in the temple was Castilen in her panther form. She escorted him through the mountain while I was wrapped in the darkness of the Rogue.

"This," I gestured to her relaxed form, "is a good look." I was immensely thankful for the shadow cat that brought my friend through that mountain. I took in the golden and emerald eyes and stilled myself in an effort to further appreciate her raw beauty. "If you are not a Veill cat, then what are you?"

A prickly tongue lashed out to nurse the slashes along the top of my hand. I watched as the wounds began to close before Castilen moved to inspect Marli's work on the wounds along my backside.

I stared at my chipped nails and frowned at how slowly I was healing. The toxins were working diligently against my ability to regenerate.

The splash to my left surprised me and black lashes fanned against dark golden skin when Castilen laughed. I forgot about the poisoned talons as she moved through the water with unfaltering grace. She was mesmerizing. Wild thick hair of deep chestnut fell across bare shoulders, covering breasts not quite immersed in the warm waters. Copper and gold tattoos of varied paw prints stretched from the middle of her back and stalked upward and over both shoulders.

"Who am I? Who says I am not a Veil cat?" Castilen tucked her hands into the insides of her elbows and leaned back perching on a shelf submerged in the water. "Or what am I?" The pop of peach that brightened her cheeks as she mocked modesty and humility would make any beating heart skip. "I am a shifter known as a Sranvaal Shade." She looked at me with a look of curiosity. "Which doesn't help you because you have no idea what we do, clearly."

"I know what a Shade does," I answered quickly, feeling Vance wrap his hand around my hip, pressing a forearm across my lower back. Castilen moved closer and my skin heated under her smile.

"Of course, you do. You are not a stupid girl." She moved matted locks of white curls from my face.

"Not stupid. Foolish and damn near reckless? Yes. Without good sense? Sure. I could go on about Skarlet's wits and inability to refrain from danger, but she is not stupid, which almost makes it worse," Vance grumbled from behind me, drawing a small laugh from Marli. I looked up at him and his clothes were soaked from the splashes of warm water. He was wrapping his hands around my wrists in an effort to steady me against the spring's rough edge.

"Next time I save your life, I expect a little gratitude, sir. A parade maybe? Let me go or I take it all back," I responded. I closed my eyes and anticipated a fun retort but none were forthcoming. Silence settled around us as no one spoke for several long seconds.

"I can't, Skarlet," I felt Vance look down and I tried to twist to see behind me. The only site I was rewarded was that of the water now turning murky with blood.

"Fine. You saved my life, too. We both get parades," I winked at Vance and tried to pull my wrists free, but the right wrist wouldn't move. I looked at Marli for answers as his hands slid further into the water, further up my body toward where tense shoulders bobbed in the warm spring. My stomach churned and I started to kick as panic settled in. Vance pushed himself against my back and wrapped an arm around the front of my stomach, pulling me closely and tucking me against his body.

"Hey," he whispered. "Hey, you're going to be fine. We have one more to go. The claw of a dracothite that got very close to taking off your pretty little head is lodged just here at the base of your neck where it meets your shoulder. Its toxins are sinking in and making it where you cannot move that arm."

Vance's hand touched on an area that must be where the slim talon was lodged. I didn't feel it. The weight of the last few days came crashing in around me and shallow breaths rocked me as I thought of all the ways I could have and should have died.

"No. No, no, no. This is not how the story goes," I dropped my head and muttered.

I understood the futility of fighting my friends, but that didn't stop the irrational dread sinking in and demanding that I move or die. They all sat there with nothing but looks of patience pointed toward me as I struggled against the iron hold Vance had on me. Each one looked weary and edged with their own grief. That they were willing to sit in a cave and tend my wounds was not lost on me.

Still, I couldn't admit that I was scared.

"Skarlet," Castilen called quietly, but not weakly. "Let your friend remove the last piece. The dracothites are a breed of draken very much like, well, very much like beasts we have back home, and I've been pierced by them before. The injury is in a critical place but the claw has to come out. I am surprised that you can still move your legs to kick this brute right now. You must heal very quickly indeed." A glint of curiosity lit her face, and a hand landed against Vance's back with a loud smack.

"I have reason to suspect that your beasties and my beasties are not the same Castilen," I replied. I tilted my head towards the right hand that Marli quietly sat massaging, waiting on my next move.

My sour mood did not reflect in the smile she gave me. There was something comforting in it. Something more than a stranger showing up in a dark forest to drag us through a mountain. It was instant kinship. A sisterhood of genuine empathy and likeness lie just behind that smile. I took a breath and steadied myself, placing my feet on top of the boots Vance still wore.

I heard a clink and saw embers float by as the cavern and the faces that filled it started to waiver. Nausea slammed me and my legs went weak. I could do nothing but lean back into Vance and try to hold my eyes open.

A hundred questions suddenly came to mind. Why couldn't I keep my eyes open? Where were we? I was so weak. This was unacceptable. When did I become incapable? Why weren't any of the others hurt? It was the last one that I managed to ask.

"How am I the only one floating in this pool?" I scanned the bodies I could see and didn't find any remarkable damage. "Who else has talons in the fire?"

Marli and Castilen both turned toward Vance as he finally lifted me out of the waters, and I began to calm. The silence lingered while I regained my footing, and my whit's.

"No one, Skarlet," Marli answered as I was settled into a place nearest the small fire with no claws burning inside of it.

"How," I questioned.

"Do you remember Kalein?" Vance sniffed and shook the water from blonde hair.

"Of course, you got us roped into an extraction for a Rogue elitist that had gotten himself caught up with a group of mercenaries deep inside the mountain, and then stuck there when they were all killed in an ambush. In Kalein Keep." Castilen wrapped my cloak around my shoulders before Vance continued, then took one for herself. "We were on mission with orders to bring the Rogue in unharmed and not to come back until we had him," I continued.

"Arike was so pissed when I turned up, dragging you behind me on feet that could barely hold you. He just kept yelling for us to give him the Rogue." The dance of the fire highlighted his smile directly across from me while the others sat, flanking my left and right.

"He was," I laughed, and a small pain bloomed where no feeling had been moments ago. "It's the only retrieval we ever failed. It was not for lack of trying though. Once you got us into that mountain and the dark took over, I didn't know up from down, I didn't have Marli's unique abilities guiding me that day."

"No, but you made do. There wasn't a Gentry in the group that didn't piss himself a little when you decided your patience with their methods had been exhausted and you began to plow through the caverns, the heat of your light burning through creatures and darkness and announcing our arrival to anyone who might stand against us," Vance laughed.

"The Veiliri dropped their weapons and fled, so I would have to say things were going well for a while," I cleared my throat and leaned further into the warmth of the fire.

"Arike was angry with you for this failure?" Marli asked. "That is interesting."

"Not really." Vance responds. "He stays angry at Skarlet."

"That's ridiculous. Who could be angry at a face like this?" Castilen laughed and cupped my face, squishing it just a bit.

"It's true, I am not the belle of the ball by Arike's standards. He is often quite frustrated with me."

Marli crosses his arms, leaning away from the fire, and his face is obscured in shadows. "What happened to the Rogue? Who was it?"

"No idea, we only had a cover name for him" Vance answered. "The Veiliri ran, Skarlet speaks true on that, too, and on their way out they released a particularly annoying cage full of leira. Bastards are only the size of my hand, but the pincers are razor sharp, and there were hundreds of them. They wasted no time flying into the tunnel where we waited for the clear to move."

"I still can't sleep on silken leira sheets without being annoyed because of that night," I sighed.

"A small price to pay, considering," Vance shrugged. Vance's look lingered on me for a moment, assessing. "We barely got out. They came down on us so fast. Skarlet gave the order to retreat but we weren't fast enough. We were caught up in a cave and about to die a miserable death by silk weaving bugs. I had barely pulled my daggers out, prepared to fight and fall in a tiny tunnel deep under Kalein Keep, when a circle of light dropped around us. All of us."

Vance's jaw worked, his tone flattening and losing its mirth. "Skarlet's light, of course. It blazed outward, flames dancing about like she was the sun and they her worshipers. A few Veiliri had snuck back in during the chaos and they planned to run us all through. They did not count on her, though. We ran a race against Grimm and his waiting hands of death with Skarlet scorching anything that got near."

"That was the first time Vance and I had the chance to utilize that particular skill of mine. We got out, though. Down to the last male, most still shaking in their boots," I continued. I looked past Vance into the black of night just outside the caverns where we sat. "Do you think that event has something to do with this mission?"

"No," Castilen answered for the Knight. "He thinks it is how you were the only one seriously wounded. That is the question you asked, is it not?"

"She did what she does," he answered with a small shrug, "She stood there, back straight, chin up and took a breath, pulling that light back into herself. The light of the gods flowed around her and when the last dropped swirled from her ankles and disappeared, she began to bleed. A thousand tiny cuts began to appear on her face, her hands and linens of her Gentry uniform ran red with her own blood. She just looked at me, her mouth moving but no sound coming out."

"Actually," I interrupted. "I was saying for you to thank me later, after we made it home. I also threatened to stab you a few times for getting us into those tunnels." Smiles lit the planes of their faces and I continued, "You got me to the ship and if I have never thanked you for that then consider this my official offer of gratitude."

"So, when she pulled the light's power back into its center, the cuts just appeared?" Marli asked. He slowly sat forward and cut his eyes at Vance.

"That is exactly how it happened," Vance confirmed.

"It's a gift that I could even get us all out of there, for sure, but my magic has a very strict policy on balance and exchange. I exchanged a few moments of discomfort for the lives of many. There will never be room for regret for that and if needed, I would do it again. Now. For any of you," I explained.

"You did do it for us, Skarlet. That is why you are the only one with these marks tonight," Castilen explained. Her warmth infused the space we took up, now sitting shoulder to shoulder. She ran a thumb across a small gash remaining on my leg where the cloak fell short just above my ankle.

I looked up at her face, taken by the kindness there. She smiled and smoothed her hands over my own, rubbing life back into my right side, mimicking the movements of Marli from earlier in the evening.

"Thank you, Castilen," I said as I squeezed one of her hands. "When you found us at the edge of the forest, I wasn't using that same power, though. No magic survives amongst the rot of the trees there. I used a chelcei stone from within my own curved blade to power our run. It's a small known detail of the properties of the chelcei stone."

"I don't think you were, Skarlet," Vance interjected. "I think you used your power before you should have been able to. Whether I am right or wrong doesn't matter, I suppose. I doubt any of us want to return to test the theory, but I would be willing to wager a bottle of my oldest liquor that you were able to call the light by your own innate abilities."

I opened my mouth to answer, true confusion settling in at the idea of that being possible, but the Rogue cut me off. "Ah, leave the girl alone. We all have secrets, aye?! Secrets make the sex better and the kill sweeter." He gave a small laugh and stood.

"Here here," Vance stood and decided to let the conversation fade. He looked to where Castilen and I sat. "If you have decided to live, Skarlet, then perhaps we can get out of this wet place and find something to eat?"

"Skarlet told me you don't get laid enough, Knight. Not accustomed to wet places, aye?" Marli winked. He had made his way to the cavern's entrance.

"Marli, leave him alone. Vance is sensitive," I winced a bit but found it comforting knowing my legs were holding me on steady feet upon standing.

"Sensitivity is sexy in a man," Castilen whispered and grasped my packs and pulled me forward. "Are you ok to travel?"

"Absolutely," I responded, having not processed anything the flying stranger actually said earlier, I had no idea where she planned to take us but agreed anyway. No one said I was the sensitive one.

XIX

My fingers trailed up and down Castilen's back, leaving her glistening black fur in disarray. She had taken this form at the mouth of the cave and led us into the night. Since we have been walking quietly, her by my side and the boys following closely behind.

I had asked about the male who'd flown me in, but the crew begged off answering until we got somewhere more secure, leaving me with my own imagination to answer those questions as we trekked toward our destination.

I offered to get us there faster, but I couldn't transport somewhere I've never been. It was one of those stupid rules of balance, so I teetered on with tired legs.

I had never fallen so easily into companionship with anyone the way that I had with the shifter. She traveled at my side, making no complaints, and often nudged me and huffed in time to a light jab from one of the boys. Her huge paws made no sound against the grassy rolling hills as our companions followed her through the few remaining moments of night.

When we left the springs, I was surprised to find a heavily wooded area circling the cavern. Enormous old trees towered over the lands, their roots gnarled and reflecting dew off its covering of moss. Their branches were heavy and full of birds that sang a song as sweet as any I heard growing up in the shadowed valleys around Blue Mountain. There were no gigantic rock faces on the other side of the tree line though. While the birds may sing a like song, the land beneath my boots bore no further resemblance.

Eventually, Sun cleared away the mists blocking our views and warmed the lands. After a time, the proud oaks began to mix with willow trees. The grass still rustled under where the willows parted, unbothered by the cooler weather.

Limbs bent by many seasons curved aside so that the sparkling lands just beyond the foliage lines could be seen. Bridges of worn stone appear held together in some areas by little more than the vines woven in through the gaps of rock. Narrow foot paths scurry through the overgrown flora, peeking out between blooming flowers and running back through vibrant liana. Water gushed and gurgled all around, reverberating off the trails and trestles. A dozen pools sat just beside the main tributary, sloping upward in gigantic, hopscotched steps. Each perfect pool reflected equally perfect images of the sky. Small whirlpools appear in the main river, swirling ferociously before dumping water down the waterfalls at the edge of each eddy.

I was mistaken in my earlier assessment of the flat, forested lands. The path we climbed now was so familiar though I knew I had never been here before. It was the feeling of comfort after a long ordeal. A place that hummed in peace and joyful celebration like the smell of grass warmed under the early sun wrapped around.

Floral aromas clinging to the last days of summer hung in the breeze. Pieces of my hair danced around to touch my face on winds peppered with the perfume of overripe summer berries. The combination had me closing my eyes in remembrance of how that moment took me back to memories of a happy home in a beautiful mountaintop.

A small smooth hand wrapped around my fingers and squeezed. The memories were lost when I opened my eyes to see Castilen looking down at me with a patience I envied.

I studied her perfect profile lit by the smile of a thousand happy days. She pulled the sides of her cloak tighter, the dark green linen falling lightly across her deeply tanned hand. The linen was too light for the turn of the season, especially toward the north and west of Tanirra.

"Castilen, honey, where is your heavy cover?" I tried to relax the worry in my brow. "Have you been on the road for a very long time?"

"I have, actually. And when I left my rooms, summer was just waking up, the evenings were warm and the days were bright and long," she answered sadly and leaned into me.

The smile of light and beauty faded from her face, replaced by a rocky look of fatigue and dejection. Her eyes clouded with a look I knew. She had lost a home too and now she was doing whatever it took to find it again. She had been on this mission for too long, though. The truth of it was written in the way she had to shake herself before blinking tired tears back. She had been on the road for too long and her efforts had equaled the expectations set upon her, but the results were less than hopeful. I nodded my head, smiling up into her face and giving my full attention to her.

We stood like that under the dappling light for a moment, both taking the other in.

"Do you know what my favorite time of the year is, Skarlet?" she asked.

"I don't, but I'd like to," I smiled.

"It's right now at the beginning of autumn when the air still holds the stories of summer in its warmth but promises new stories of adventure. There is so much opportunity. Every day the wind grows a little colder, washing away the sins of the heat," she detailed.

"Some summers linger though, don't you think? The ones you want to remember?" I encouraged.

"Indeed, we all make a little room for years and friends we simply can't let go of. It would betray who we are to the core to lock them from memory. But the cold touch of the season is welcoming to cool the racing burn of summer triumphs, and failures," she nodded.

"Indeed," I agreed. "This one is letting go quickly it seems, the biting winds of autumn continue to nip at the spaces between my shredded leathers and I must say I'm sad to see the long days end."

The daytime temperatures were teetering on unseasonably cold, even in the sunlight.

I caught the tilt of her chin right before she began to smile and drag me along behind her, giving me little chance to protest. We neared the last incline and looked down at the path below that led into the woods. The wind was blowing freely, tilting the world about it in images of blooming arches above and the river below. The drop off was too far away to hear, but I imagined it was the sound of the small ones that danced around us, only far louder, roaring its dominance from across the wooded lands.

"Where does the river go? Past the last waterfall?" I greeted the boys with my question, all eyes drifting behind me.

"Underground," Castilen smiled when she answered. "You will get to see it if we cross the lake. If you don't want to magic yourself over there will be small boats that can be used to get across."

"Have we missed the beginning celebrations?"

"Not if we hurry," she smiled.

"Ok," I laughed, "but what are we hurrying for? Will we be tumbling into the middle of a wild sacrifice, or perhaps the cleansing smoke of a Shaman's totem."

Castilen tensed briefly at that before clarifying, "The casting of dreams is the opening ceremony celebrating the transition into the cool season, in much the same way it is done at Blue Mountain."

I didn't know how she knew that, but what bothered me was the deflation in her tone. Of course we celebrated the equinox, but celebrations were sometimes as varied as the lands were. It was the specificities that made each region unique.

"How do you cast your dreams?" I asked, curious about what the details were that clearly gave her much joy.

"The elementals," she smiled. She dropped my hand to cup hers together, reproducing the image of a caster controlling his element. In this case I would guess water. "We are all given a piece of sugar parchment to write our wishes on. After the sun began to drop in the sky, the drummers began their beating. Sometimes you can hear your neighbor's beats from miles away, they all carry and become one in the valleys." She lifted a finger to point behind her. "The drummers stop, and silence drops right before the first voice is lifted from the hosting family's Lord or Lady. The whole house and everyone in attendance sings with the happiest moments of summer in their minds. We gather around the small waterfalls and wait for an elemental to come and take our wishes. The water shines with light of the lighting moon as the first globe of water is lifted to float down the river where it bursts upon the rocks at the bottom. The paper dissolves into a glowing rainbow of light and color against the clear water. I will save the details of the finale for you to see yourself." Her smile grew as she began to turn back toward the path.

"All of that takes place here. With the drums and the chorus?" I asked, observing the colorful garden.

"Not anymore," Marli answered for her. "The occupancy of Tanirra has stripped us of many old customs, but smaller events still take place, outside of the eye of the Veiliri."

"We will see our dreams delivered to the ears of the Asti, without the beacon of noise to draw attention to the family hosting us." Castilen didn't look back, the memory of life before was in the details and I smiled knowing that she had chosen to share hers with me.

I followed Castilen forward until we came to a stop at the top of a small set of mossy steps, their incline almost vertical. I saw the brightly painted doors before noticing the stone wall. The ramparts hovered above us, eyes peering from holes in the stone that snaked around to the left and right, its ending obscured by dense forest. The doors reflected the sun's muted rays, the golden patterns twinkling brightly under the light and bouncing softly against painted stone doors.

"Castilen, how many more strays you gonna bring through our back door before you get tired and join us here?" A guard called down from where he stood on the balcony, one of the four doors opening below him.

"Progress never tires, Barry," she smiled up at him before ushering us through and into unexpected shade.

I reached out to touch the ivy choking out the sun where it had long overgrown the lattice on either side of the walkway.

Light filtered through the top, increasing in intensity as it passed through thickened honeysuckle. The smell would have been overwhelming had not a strong gust swept in as soon as the guard closed the door behind us.

"Elementals are truly a blessing from Asti." Castilen murmured. Warm blasts of air circled around us, created by currents the elementals could manipulate.

"Yes, a goddess who knew that humidity is not beauty's friend. The Lord or Lady here, are they the elemental that created the conditioned air?" I asked.

I secretly hoped they were. Like calls to like and it's no less true with the scarcity of free elementals that I would want to imagine that life is as it was before the coup. The time and freedom to sit and enjoy the company of others like me.

"No. Not exactly," Castilen shook her head and dashed the bit of me that had begun to hope.

I couldn't see anything beyond the ceiling of scented vines but wasn't surprised when the path opened to an outdoor receiving patio. The ivy continued upwards above the door we entered, forcing my eyes forward. The door opening in front of us matched the glowing blue of the heavy doors in the wall. The grey stones of the home and battlement garishly clashed against its brightness.

I followed the others in, bringing up the rear. My sight was focused completely on the details in the doors as they seemed to tell a story.

"Mi Lady," a young guard attempted a warning, but he wasn't fast enough. The sound of bodies crashing filled the hallway as I ran shoulder first into Vance's legs. My intense study of the doors caused me to miss the long steps where my companions had stopped to wait on me.

A thunderous noise clashed through the open glass doors leading into the home. My companions went down like a line of totems with Vance bouncing into Castilen and she into Marli. I should be embarrassed as I stared at them, eyes wide, but it was a pretty door.

"Well, I never thought this would be how it happened. Not very private, unceremoniously piled against one another, and smelling like the road." I squeezed my hand where Vance's ass had landed, closing on a handful. "I'm all in."

"Stop it, woman," Vance barked. "Leash the freak please, at least until we are introduced to the host."

"And Help me up," he added.

I ignored him.

Marli was the first one back on his feet. His staff in hand before he figured out what happened. A cough of suppressed laughter escaped him.

"Where is your hero spirit?," Marli responded, a half-smile lifting his face.

I was cut off from responding by a deep voice. Familiarity rang in my ears when he spoke.

The voice came from the other side of sheer silk curtains painted with a stunning scene of distant mountains and a lake large enough for ships to sail it. "Marli Burlescci?"

Large hands lifted the glimmering panels and two thoughts assaulted me, hitching my breath still in my chest. The first was that the view we were greeted with, the view that was not a painting on silks but a perfectly created vista through a wall full of open windows that stretched from floor to ceiling, was incredibly peaceful. I took in the lake to my right, its waterfalls centering the landscape and perfectly framed against sloping valleys. Just on the other side of the glass and nestled around the manor were more gardens, all full like those we had just walked through. To my left stood the other assailant.

The voice belonged to the man who flew me to the caverns. His green eyes pinned me in place. The smile on his face not quite reaching the sea glass eyes. I couldn't move or tear my face away as he approached. A fire awoke low in my belly. Magic, lust, and curiosity rolling together to make being me very uncomfortable. I still didn't move.

He didn't stop until our breaths mingled, and he peered down at me. His lips full and topped in a bowtie, stretched into a soft smile. I felt his hand on my face and didn't protest when he gripped my chin harshly and turned my face side to side.

"A fast healer," he mused. There was a bit of venom laced with the question in his voice.

With my face tilted up I could see his wings were gone, his shoulders broad enough to block out the sun now fully streaming through the walls of windows. The gorgeous man dropped his hand, and the cool air came rushing back in between us.

Castilen suddenly appeared in the cool void between us, smiling. The male didn't drop his stare from mine when dipped his head to place a kiss on her temple.

"Thank you," he whispered before pulling away from her.

Tilting her head and smiling toward me was her only response.

The male's eyes narrowed and any heat from a moment ago evaporated. His eyes flickered briefly to my hands. His face cleared of any feeling when he focused his eyes back on mine. I was determined to not wither under his scrutiny. He was just a man. A gorgeous man, possibly the most gorgeous man I had ever seen, but still just a man.

My hand reached for a dagger, but I came up empty, realizing too late what the male had just assessed. Mine were broken and lost during the portal out of the mountain and I had not had time to retrieve any bags I stashed before the ship went down. I was unarmed outside of my magic, and I didn't want to kill him despite the growling, prowling step he took toward me.

He leveled me with a stony look, before straightening and tilting his head toward me. "I've been looking for you," He mumbles, the fire in his glare cooling to something different, something that made my heart beat just a little faster than it should be.

Marli slipped past Castilen and blocked my view of the male, holding up his hands to pat the air, backing him up and putting space between us again.

"Easy now, Ki." I felt the air shift from behind Marli as he spoke. "A glass of whiskey while these girls get bathed up and I'll tell all that my shadows have shared, friend."

Friend? This guy?

I wasn't sure if the exhaustion pulling at me had muddled my hearing, too.

"You two know each other?" I asked Marli. Suspicions creeping their way back in.

"Obviously, Skarlet." He responded.

"Now would be a good time to tell me why that is." I barked.

"No, it wouldn't." He gave a pointed look around to all the people traveling through the center of the estate.

I chanced a look at Vance and he acknowledged the area with the same nod as Marli, his eyebrows lifting in a way that he knows I hate.

I growled low but turned to follow Castilen, having far more trust in my new friend than I did the man staring me down as I left the room.

XX

I dried my hair and rubbed orchid oil into the ends, weighing the curl down and into large twists where it hung around my chest. I had taken entirely too long in the bath but couldn't bring myself to feel bad about it.

Elementals had been good to the Lord and Lady of this manor, warming several thousand square feet of the main house and infinitely heating the water pumped into the baths. From the glow rising as the sun sets, I saw that elementals were not the only friends of the family. Fae lights in every shape and color illuminated the grounds. A line of the candle soft lighting glowed behind the balcony where I stood, lighting up my room as well.

The breeze, both elemental and natural, swept in to shake the heavy drapes around, spreading the scents of the season about the room. Inhaling, I closed my eyes and let the feelings wash over me. The peacefulness this land was saturated in eased the near constant burn of my insides, like unspent energy and white-hot elemental flame.

We'd been summoned to an evening feast. It was an activity that was low on my agenda after the last few days we'd had, but our host requested that everyone attend and there was no real reason why I couldn't. My injuries were minor now and I had no way to leave, anyway. Borrowing a dress from Castilen's room she apparently kept in the manor, I quietly agreed.

I heard my bedroom door open and Castilen joined me to watch the sunset over the lake before it was time to leave for the supper. I had many questions for her, but they had lost their priority within moments of her climbing into that warm spring with me, a girl she didn't know but needed to comfort.

"You are flawless." Her voice broke into my reverie, drawing my gaze to her.

"If I am flawless, honey, you are perfection." The dark green dress she wore was light and nearly sheer. Dark skin set off the glittering gold in her necklace, the end dropping against her bare stomach and disappearing beneath the dress right above the apex of her thighs.

The air in the room was suddenly heavy. I looked up to find her judging my own dress that was light in fabric and split all the way to my hips. Delicate silver loops flattened against my hips, holding the navy gossamer panels together on each side. The same tiny pieces were linked together to form the back of the dress. A chill ran down my exposed back, and the wind lifted white tresses from the front of the dress, exposing my body's natural reaction to her beauty for anyone to see. She gently moved the strands back to their place. White against blue like clouds against a late evening sky.

The sound of footsteps drew our attention to the bedroom door. Someone banged a few times to be let in and Castilen opened it slowly. A look of happy surprise fixed on her features.

"Grace. Casi," the deep male voice called out.

"Who is Grace," I demanded at the same time Castilen protested. I peered around her to see the caller.

"I hate that nickname, Ki," she growled.

The man I now assumed was called Ki grinned, his smile burning through me. His eyes captured mine and held me there, animosity temporarily forgotten. There was no reason for him to have been rude to me anyway, he didn't even know me.

"Grace," he smiled and slid an arm around my waist. "Never has anyone taken down three warriors as quickly as your graceful feet did. It humored me greatly."

I didn't laugh as he slid his other arm around Castilen's waist, eyeing the chains with appreciation. She sighed and leaned into his shoulder. I wondered what their relationship was. A throbbing in my center began at the thought and I resolved to take another, much cooler bath after our introduction to the hosting family. I shook my head and focused on the lights beyond the open door and worked to battle the heat back down. The tiniest light escaped from my hand before I could reign in the need for release.

I need a fight, or a few climaxes, maybe both, to settle the raging fires of unspent magic that pushes through when I got excited. My body had always mistaken excitement with fear, mixing reactions of the body with reactions of power. Stepping out of his embrace I looked up into green eyes right as they finished devouring me in a way that scorched from the inside out. Seeing the satisfaction cross his face, I smiled and asked him something I had been burning to find out.

"What's your name, Sir?" It was almost a whisper.

He pushed us toward the exit with him.

"Call me Kian," he smiled.

Stopping, he asked Castilen to meet us at the tables and turned his attention fully to me.

Warm callused fingers snagged in the silver draped across my back briefly. Kian ran his hand up the center and grasped the back of my neck, demanding my gaze meet his again by pulling my head back. "I am regretful of the way we met."

No excuses were forthcoming. Instead, he nodded once to indicate that was the end of that. He slid his hand back down to rest lightly at the small of my back while I focused on collecting myself completely before we entered the receiving hall at the bottom of the largest staircase.

XXI

I woke to a knock on my door as the sun was rising the next morning, having fallen quickly to sleep after returning from both a delicious meal and fantastic evening on the edge of the lake where large groups of people wrapped in cloaks cast small boats filled with sugar papers that were intricately folded and placed to hover neatly above. I thought about how We stood watching as the water lifted in tiny fluid hands and welcomed the dreams into the home of the mother of lake, who weaves dreams as gently as the waves for those who send her a request.

I hoped it was true. That was the only thought I focused on as the lights of candles the revelers carried were put out one at a time, then in a swooshing wave of darkness.

I turned to follow the line of trailing cloaks up the embankment and stopped when Kian appeared to block my way.

"All of my apologies," he said, but made no move to clear my path.

"No need at all," I said with feigned courtesy.

Kian popped the building tension by laughing lowly before moving just off to the side. He slid his hands in his pockets and tilted his head to regard me.

"May we start over, Skarlet," he quietly asked.

I considered him for a moment and in the cool winds of the night I found a calm place to rest my racing heart. He stood over my tall frame and peered down a face full of chiseled art.

"Maybe we should," I responded. "Do you have a plan?"

"I thought we could start with a walk in the morning, just the two of us."

I nodded silently, giving in but only barely.

"I know where to find you," he backed away from me and turned before disappearing into the dark.

Now the sun is fighting the night for its place in the sky outside of my window and there is a tall, dark, gorgeous man at my door requesting my company before I could well and truly open my eyes.

He laughed at me as I struggled to get my bearings and I pushed him out of the room to dress once the night began to return to me. When we met at the front doors, he carried a small cup of steaming chocolate with him and I forgot to be mad.

We walked for a few moments without talking, taking in the peaceful way the lake lapped against its pretty sandy shore some distance on the outside of the little village. We were approaching a small stone building with four large arches breaking up its circular shape. Inside sat a forge, its fires smoking up the sky alongside the kitchen fires that sprung up in the small chimneys of painted cabins on either side of the pathway.

The fog of the morning was dense and it mixed in with the smoke, giving the basin a distant feel. When I sighed, a puff of air billowed in front of my face. The first freeze is going to be here early this year. I wondered as we walked about where I would be when the snows fell and covered the sins of our cities.

I turned to Kian and studied his face for motive behind his invitation. Before I could voice my curiosity he cut me off and announced that we had arrived at the forge of a friend that Lady Cyneil had suggested may have a set of blades that I am welcome to use for as long as I fight for Tanirra.

I looked around for this friend and spotted a small female with her arms extended above her fire and her face covered in a mask far too big for her tiny frame. She looked up and considered Kian and then the metal in her hand and waved him on, deciding to continue with the blade she worked rather than walk him to the available weapons.

He grasped my elbow gently and led me outside of the room and around to a small annex that had several displays of weapons placed upon its shelves. I wanted to spend the entire morning getting to know the blades here, but my leathers will only hold a long dagger, not a sword or scimitars, so my choice was really only between two sets of knives sitting coldly on a middle shelf. I grasped one of each set and tested the balance and weight and swung a few times at Kian to test their speed. He took it in kind spirits and soon I had selected a set of simple daggers with roughened leather hilts.

As I carried them back in my arms, wrapped in a leather satchel to protect the blades, I asked Kian if the smithie was in servitude.

"Absolutely not. Cyneil would never hear of it. Her guests are all treated as equally as she can manage, even if they are in between battles."

At the top of the hill, where the path from the village narrowed into paths around the manor, Marli appeared from a connecting walkway and insisted on inspecting my blades before allowing me to return to my rooms. I agreed to allow it and thanked Kian for arranging this.

He replied nonchalantly and left me to continue on with only Marli to walk me back.

XXII

That night, I had to borrow another dress from Castilen for the evening's events. I was able to retrieve my bags from the place where I conveniently kept them, stashed between the realms, but I hadn't anticipated the need for so much formal wear. I had assumed I would need exactly no formal wear to be exact. Being able to use a glamour for short periods of times had often been enough to get me in and out when I wasn't hunting. The hospitality the Countess offered was worth more than a weak mirage of my best efforts. So I selected a dress nearly identical to last night's and Castilen selected one a shade off from yesterdays and adorned with more dainty silver rings.

We had walked arm in arm to meet the others in a room best described as a theater with seating that encouraged every guest to be on the same level as the performers on the stage that was set nearly flush with the gleaming floor. Only inches separated its edges from the floor, its intent to identify a clear mark for the actors to hit.

Platters of food were set out on small tables barely above the height of the floor. Plates and utensils were served to all of the guests and we were encouraged to choose from the many offerings like a buffet. I chose to sample many of the items including the local honey mead before moving to wine.

"Vance." I turned to look up at him from where I lay propped against his side. His eyes remained closed, the vices of the evening working to relax him as well.

His answer was a grunt that I barely heard under the swaying, hypnotic sound of lore set to the soft strum of guitars. Bards gathered to tell tales of heroism and misadventures for the changing of the seasons and all the Lady's guests piled into the theater after introductions and a decadent dinner. The guests are scattered about the cavernous room, lounging against thick furs and satin pillows. The Lady had not bothered with the stiffness of traditional seating for such a sacred place. She divulged over dinner that music and performance are of the greatest delight to her.

Fae lights that danced like flickering flames floated about the room freely, highlighting the gray stone and reflecting in the white wine, gilding each equally. I was working on my second bottle of Notre Vino, and it was fucking with me. I took another big sip before I responded with my question. "We will leave for the northern border in the morning?"

Castilen looked up at us from where she lay in my lap, hands stretched above her and tucked under her head. I had hoped to have time to talk to the boys about asking her to join us, but we didn't need to stay long enough to let the Gentry take my kill. Listening to the tales of giant slayers and dragon riders was a gentle reminder that we did make it off that sabotaged craft and safely to the home of the Lady hosting us without asking questions. Any piece of that would make a great little ditty, but only if the hero gets the job done. If they fail, it's a different tune they'll be singing.

Vance didn't bother lowering his voice when he responded. "We can't leave in the morning, Skarlet."

I felt Kian's stare land on me again, as though he could hear our conversation from across the room where he lounged next to Lady Cyneil, talking softly to her, and smiling down gently at her when she spoke. I met his challenging glare with my own heated gaze.

"Brief me, Knight." I didn't challenge Vance's admission about our safety, or his methods for gathering the intelligence we needed to make our next move, but I expected a thorough report updating me on the level and type of threat we faced if he had that information.

He lifted his head and cleared his throat. I did not take my eyes off Kian, appreciating the view.

"Skarlet, as soon as our ship went down, the Gentry should have been notified. They would have sent out our backup team before the ash even settled in the dryad forest. Arike is lobbying for a team to go in for body recovery, and he has promised not to issue an official loss statement without it. Right now, we are ghosts. Dead to anyone who doesn't look too closely."

I fully expected to hear that the Gentry was apprised of our ship's failure, but I did not expect to be dead.

Castilen's hair pulled across my lap, dropping to mix with furs of the same dark shades. Her cheek pressed into my thigh when she angled her head to look up at us.

"Being dead means no one is looking for you or expecting you." Castilen's pointed gaze bounced between me and Vance.

Marli leaned his head forward, his dark lashes fanned out against his smooth cheek, and his eyes closed. He contributed softly, "It is much harder to catch ghosts, assassjine, than it is to bring them back to the living. Give Arike a little time to consider all of his options."

"You have been briefed and there is but one safe, viable option. Allow our hostess to provide the offered respite for a few days while we wait to hear of the kill confirm or a loss statement," Vance said.

Wait? Until someone told me if I could move or not? Those words didn't settle well with me.

He and Marli both rested their heads back against the satin patterns of their tall pillows, done with the conversation. A wave of Vance's hand further confirmed that my plan had been dismissed on the basis of plain fucking common sense. I felt the heavy weight of eyes upon me as I battled reason with my selfish desire to get our mission done, to get my kill, and win the Gentry's alliance.

Kian smiled at me as soon as I found his face again. My cheeks burned, but I tempered that fear and excitement far down and slid a little further down Vance's side. I gently adjusted Castilen's head a little further up my thigh. Her silken sepia hair caught briefly in the tiny silver chains holding my lovely dress together. I won a full smile when I loosened the strands gently for her.

Kian's attention didn't waiver until the Lady requested his company on the walk to her rooms. No one stood as Kian and Lady Cyneil walked by, instead they bowed their heads and knees in honor before settling back to wrap up their nights, talking in hushed and reverent tones to one another.

I chanced a look at the elegant picture they created together as they approached.

Lady Cyneil was older, but not delicate. She had been running this manor alone since her husband died and stood with the confidence of all the years of strength she had cultivated. I was told she suffered no shortage of lovers, and she moved now like she demanded the air of old royalty with her every step.

A translucent mass of yellow skirts slowed before my slightly bowed head, nothing more than bare feet swathed in the panels of a gown much like my own. A diamond shape was woven into the corset styled bodice, just under the lay of heavy breasts and large enough to show the top half of her navel. The high neck highlighted the slender slope of her petite frame. The smell of oak and sunshine mingled with notes of a rose heavy perfume.

Kian's voice was even and cool when he stopped the Lady in front of me so that he could bid us good evening. "I will see you each for lunch tomorrow. We hope that you rest at least until then."

Lady Cyneil straightened a bit, her shimmering train fell evenly down from her shoulders, across her exposed back, mixing in with the wave of skirts nipping at her heels. "Tomorrow we gather to celebrate the shifting of the seasons and to welcome the cool winds of change and forgiveness into our lands. You will find instructions and basic items we use in celebration so that you may follow along or join us if that is to your preference." Her voice was light and softened by her own gift of glittering wine.

"I don't think Castilen will be as forgiving as you, my Lady, if we dare prefer to not celebrate her favorite season," I teased without lifting from my hastily bowed, kneeling position.

Kian gently urged our hostess away with a flat order for us to follow immediately to our own rooms. "If you do need anything, I am at your service." He paused before fully stepping away, catching my eyes for a far too brief second.

"Yes, sir." I lifted my head to match his stare, catching the grin he displayed before escorting the countess through tall blue doors.

XXIII

A soft gold dusting of sunlight drifted through closed terrace doors heavily inlaid with images in painted glass. Delicate, warm rainbow rays swirled across hardwood floors in a silent ballet, hope brightening all spaces as the morning's star performer. Bits of muted warm sunshine caressed my back where I slowly woke myself, content and wrapped in nothing more than a large, brightly colored, feather-filled blanket.

Chirping sounds filter in on the breeze of bloom laden winds, past sills that nearly touch the floors and the lifted windows, many feet above them. Soon enough the warm air of the elemental that swirled around the chateau would settle into a winter lull and the large fireplaces dotting the manor would be lit, welcoming the weary travelers and the children of war and the story tellers all.

I pushed blonde and strands out of my face and sat up, bunching pillows behind my bare back to lean against. The position allow for unobstructed views of the morning's greeting. A single bright red cardinal sits staring back at me, its tiny claws stretched across the thick banister around the small balcony, and the images splintering through the light of the doors into a kaleidoscope of replicas. My thoughts shift immediately to the last few days and the others I traveled with whom I seem to be bound to now. Confusion clouds the process that should be clear. I should leave them and continue to pursue my mark, make use of the time until someone discovers we lived through that crash. Every bit of training and every part of my history says I need to focus. But instead, I lean back further into the pillows and think of the strings of fate working to bring us together.

It's been no more than a few days since our team went down over that wretched forest and, while my pride is hurt, my emotions are running rampantly towards a rare level of organic happiness. Of all the things I have seen, experienced and survived, I know not to doubt the truth of the bonds that have been so tightly and rapidly bound between Castilen, Marli, Vance, and reflected in myself.

Simply put, I couldn't leave my companions and they couldn't leave without risking their own safety. I had lived for years now with one goal in mind, and in less than a week, all those things seemed to be pressing upon my soul with a little less force.

Fate was a mysterious mistress, always swaying to a haunting melody we can never hear. I could feel each shift of her symphony with the arrival of those down the hall. A motley grouping that seemed to want to know my burdens and unload some of their own. I felt the childlike pull of innocent connection and desperately longed for relationships so easy as those built under the skies of youth. The world burned around me, yet with emotions raging like a child, I wanted to ignore the fires that scorched my name into destiny's hands and run with abandon toward a safe life of star filled nights laden with laughter.

Perhaps as Marli suggested, being perceived ghosts will buy me, at minimum, a few hours of peace to find out about the dark nights that haunt my companions while we navigate our next moves. The secrets and purposes of each perch upon their shoulders appearing dark and heavy. Their own deeds and demons dance in the sun with mine, making us strange but inevitable partners. I am bursting with a burning light and raw infatuation for each of them. If they are determined to see my own darkness and embrace it then I will add my fires to the world that burns if only to offer a little support, for as long as we are meant to entertain the seemingly fated twists of this dying summer.

The truth of this world bites back with the opening of my door and the pop of meandering daydreams. Bitterness wastes little time on me once the smell of fresh flowers and strong tea embrace my body nearly as delightedly as the blanket covering my cool skin. The tray trembles slightly in the hands of a dark skinned, horned and slightly hunched gentleman. His thick hair, long turned white, hangs loosely about a crisp tunic. A toothy grin mistaken for a snarl gives me a brief moment of hesitation before he fully enters with my breakfast.

Upon his hips are swung long swords that gleam as brightly as the day they were forged and while his hands sloshed slightly the tray, causing toasted scones to soften in places, his walk was sure. Confident even. A sway only earned by time in true and bloody battle. A soldier forced into the routine of a household for whatever reason.

"Lady." His voice rattled with gravel nearly as violently as his hands shook, pulling me from racing, mixing thoughts.

Moments ago, I felt a rare happiness and I desperately try to hold onto it now, to keep it from slipping into something darker. I wanted nothing to ruin this bubble I had found with the countess, however short it was meant to be, I never thought the needle to be that in the shape of a future of loneliness and servitude staring at me from under rust-colored horns and eyes the dark black of too many years.

"May I?" he cast a look toward me and lifted a finger towards the stained glass doors. Each part of his finger seems to go in a different direction as though they had been many times broken and never properly reset, perhaps causing the tremble in his hold far more than age would have. A warrior with a bit of true grit was always something I could celebrate.

"Of course, Sir." I shot him an award-winning smile, forgetting my near nakedness for a moment. I leaned toward the steaming cup sitting a few feet away, slipping discreetly into a robe the color of an indigo sunset.

"Name's Sigari," he announced. A quick bow makes the moment official. "You got a tray there, but those on the road for a while always gets a second bit to catch ya up if you want it. Lady's orders." His instructions were as committed and final as a last rite's prayer.

"Yes, I see that." The scone on my plate was nearly gone when a mix of fruit and pile of eggs took its place on the plate. "A Lady could get used to this kind of treatment, good Sir. My ever flowing gratitude to your Countess and Cook."

The gentleman smiled with satisfaction and nods, job well done, no doubt.

"Flowers came with a note for ya too." Another bent finger points toward the bouquet he'd placed neatly in my room. Its blooms flowed down the wall from where it propped against the mantle. Winds circling through the windows and out of the open balcony doors stir the flat black ribbon attached to black roses and pale pink peonies.

"Anything else you'll be needing then?" he asked. He bowed low, but this time his deep bow wasn't a formality as much as a goodbye, with no option to extend his time with me.

"Thank you, Sigari," I tilted my head with a smile. "May the blessings of that wildest life and honorable death chase ever at your feet."

The door shut quietly behind him, the only noise the clanging of weapons that didn't quite match the wear of their owner. A few more bites in the room alone and my curiosity does its job on me. I abandon my ever-full plate to inspect the huge bundle of blood-black roses and bleeding violets mixing in with large white and blush peonies.

Dew still clung to each of the buds, the ground they were just dug from still scenting the stems. This manor was surrounded by gardens and hothouses. It was also the brightest home I'd ever been in. Those things were nothing if not opposite of this bunch of flowers. Darkness and beauty bled together in an achingly natural cycle of all things and sat there tied together with simple soft ribbon.

Different.

Beautiful.

The envelope attached is simple but elegant and opened on a thought once in my palm. In keeping with the elegance of its presentation and matching collection of blooms, the handwriting is strong, without frill or formalities, no crinkling or rustling broke the silence of the room as I read.

Grace,

Drinks in the eastern garden. I will meet you when you arrive.

Yours,

Kian

I stared at the note a bit longer, noticing the thin slant of his "s" disappearing into the letter beside it, making the postscript appear as "Your, Kian." I quickly folded the letter back in its envelope and gasped as it disintegrated into the sunlight making its way across the room. I could not help the budding smile that plastered itself to my face, growing ridiculous over the next few moments. My Kian. What an absurd thought.

A steaming bath fills while I happily pull items from my bags. I sorted out my pack with my provisions and leathers and slipped my new daggers carefully underneath the bag and returned to monitor the tub. A mix of oils and flowers swirl around when I finally lower myself into the water, the light of a smile still brightening poppy-colored lips. The smells and oils work their way into my hair and mind to stimulate and relax.

I reached a hand down and slid an oiled nail over a peaked nipple, the water heating and igniting magic and need as soon as I submerge fully. I take a moment to appreciate the warmth and move another red tipped finger slowly over a different peak.

Fire starts to take over the moment I release small bits of magic and mixes with the thrumming under where my own fingers work toward climax. The convergence of vibrancies has taken years of practiced self-control and timed releases, magic and manual, to manage the constant quake of might and need that seem to play flint and tinder to one another. I knew exactly how I like my magic taken care of.

Bubbles popped and swirled to the tempest of magic and cresting pleasure. Closing my eyes I focused on expelling bits of power with each wave of climax, careful not to put too much of either in the mix. Steam circled around the tub and dashed out into the room like a vine taking over a trellis. Its heat grasped the whole room, creeping into the cooled air, pushing against the invisible walls of it. It is hot, thick, sweet, and it is mine, mimicking the movements of fires within my pinnacle.

My body settled into a rhythm and my eyes closed tighter. Allowing my mind to wander during a release is a euphorically healing way to also cleanse myself and boost mental clarity. Once I let myself relax, I did not expect green eyes to invade so easily, locked onto mine intensely.

Eyes the color of shifting grass, lightened by a beating sun during long summer days. Darkness surrounds his image, giving just the smallest bit of him to me.

Kian.

"Skarlet," I heard him speak my name, his voice thick with need.

Imaginary Kian speaking my name sent me over the edge, and before I could pull any of it back, water evaporated and light filled the room, now shadowed by an intensely dense fog. My body still shaking from that expulsion, I pried my eyes open and for the second time today reality comes crashing in.

Eyes of blue pierce through the shrouded room, the heat quickly being devoured by the cooler, drier air. Eyes of blue? Wait, that's not right.

Blue and gray steel instead of warm sea glass green. I have seriously got to get my shit together.

"Skarlet," the voice rang out again, closer now and much louder.

I waved a hand to clear the space of more heavy steam. A feather ticked in Vance's sharp jaw. Yeah, I know that voice and it does not belong to a gorgeous stranger. How he could be pissed at me when he sidled into my room is beyond comprehension right now.

"What the fuck Vance? You just stood there watching? That's creepy, even by my standards," I hissed.

"I called your name," he shrugged. He slowly tossed the navy-blue robe and matching towel my way before backing towards the bed.

"And some have called my name many times in a day. Was once enough for you?" I fumed as I stood up in the steaming tub, the heat drying most of the remaining water. There was no way I would ever admit I heard him, intensifying my climax. Even if it wasn't his face speaking my name.

"Cover up." He pointed toward the proffered items.

I scoffed and leaned towards the towel. "Must have missed the announcement of your arrival then. I have been known to miss the obvious from time to time, especially during private times." I piled the towel on my head and gave him a pointed look. "You would know that by now, no?"

I regarded him from across the room.

"No, I guess you've never been able to commit to making a move on me. Is that why you were watching me? Curious?" I poked at his resolve.

A hunger flashed across his hardened features changing his eyes to a harder steely gray. The air of the room felt heavier, and I stood without moving, allowing him this scrutiny. The robe hangs loosely, open and untied, showcasing a gleaming, pale strip of body from my collarbone to the edges of my bare feet. The fabric darkens briefly with its contact with water, reflecting off of the shining white of the large tub. Recently licked lips pressed into thin lines under the scrutiny of his stare. A few seconds more and a hand stretched toward me. I stepped over the edge of the tub, unsure of his intentions. For all the teasing I've done over the years, his stoicism is rock solid. Almost unnaturally so. I never have worried about where I stood with him, though I have wondered many times if he ever thought of our time together as being anything other than repetitive assignments.

The bubble of tension bursts when his hand touches mine, assisting me in a manner of gentleness, with none of the hunger from seconds ago.

"I like your hair when you don't have hidden. Did you finally get the draco's blood completely out?" Vance didn't let go of my hand as he lifted his other to finger the ends of my wet hair.

A complete turn in demeanor.

"It came out easily enough once I was able to properly attend to it, but I may try pink extensions eventually, I quite liked the dusky shade the blood made when it faded into the white," I explained.

Vance's hands dropped and his smile lit up the room. "Never thought I'd like you in anything but that weird natural blonde color, but the mix is cute. Especially the pink. Can I escort you to the terrace? I understand we are to join the others there."

I gave him a quick nod, swearing to myself that I would mull over his mercurial mood later. I also give myself a hard mental smack for thinking the invitation from Kian was anything more than a summons, polite though it was.

What a handsome bastard.

"A few minutes to get dressed and I will be ready." I didn't care if he stayed to watch, and I told him as much, but I knew he would decline. He chose to wait outside my door, just out of reach.

XXIV

Staff bustled in and out of the many courtyards, sweeping lime rock walkways and hanging lights. Our guide, a young shimmering Pixen with delicate features and long reedy limbs, led Vance and I gracefully through the different gardens. The paths were as varied as the flora and I tripped a few times while admiring the changing beauty of it all as we walked.

"Do you spend every year here celebrating the season, Linora?" Vance asked as we passed hedges and arches leading to endless gardens.

"I live here on the estate with the Contessa, Lady Cyneil. I oversee the summer gardens mostly and help with lighting during events." Linora crossed her hands in front of her slim frame, tips of each finger shimmering slightly with the colors of her magic.

"You're the pix who keeps the manor glowing?" I asked.

"That's my mentor, but anything outside of the manor is my design." She slowed to give us a moment to really look around. Lights strung across the trellis running from one stone arch to the other are glowing and moving in the breeze.

A lush sitting area hidden by bush and tucked into a corner up a few steps of moss-covered cobblestone suddenly came into view. An outdoor kitchen sat like a stacked brick sentry across the diagonal corner of the right of the courtyard. A dark table in a violin shape sat decorated with fresh cuttings and a long runner of flattened wildflowers with a dark center and violet purple leaves. Despite the intense activity of everyone on the grounds in preparation for the summer's end celebration, inside this oasis, it was as though we were the only guests that mattered. The silence grew thick as we approached the table. I realized my heart sank when I didn't see Kian sitting with Castilen and Marli. Linora took a bow and told us that the spell will let us in and that no one will hear as long as we want to lunch there. Sliding a ball of milky white and gold into my palm, she leans in to look me squarely in the eyes and whispered, "We hope you make the best of your recovery here. Some places are safer than others, but nowhere is impenetrable. The spell to silence a space the size of this courtyard is in this." She squeezed the palm with the gifted charm. "Your magic will keep it well charged. Use it frequently." She surprised me with a hug before dropping her eyes and nervously shimmering to the edge of the courtyard, leaving with the briefest wave.

I'm still not sure what happened when I turned back to the table and watched Vance take his seat, though I couldn't say it wasn't a nice moment.

"Did you give the poor Pix a scare, assassin? I wouldn't advise doing so." The chill of Kian's voice so close cost me my sanity for a moment. He had appeared from nowhere to stand blocking my path.

A shadow lengthened in front of me when he took a step forward. His mouth was at my ear and the heat started to build as soon as he spoke again. "Did you know that Pixens have a drop of all the magic lines?"

I turned slowly to my left, our noses aligning. When I lifted my eyes to his green, I saw timid humor there waiting.

"Since the Pixen, the Alastar, and the Tanniran Priestesses are all races with a drop of each magic line, I would say even an assassin isn't stupid enough to cross one. I'm afraid her rapid exit is all your doing, Sir."

"By simply existing?" he mused.

"Yes, unfortunately it seems that is the only thing I have seen you do. Breathe air, be in the way, and break poor little hearts like the one in our Pix. I only told her that you enjoy extravagant black flower bouquets and long walks under the stars. Maybe she has a chance?" I teased.

"I knew you would love the invitation I sent." His tone deepened with mirth and he pulled away, teasing, "Black like your little heart, even the red canna lily will fade to a deep scarlet when the sun sets."

"The satin violets?" I asked, curious at his open attention. And because they were blush pink, making his point only half valid.

"They were available." He shrugged and pulled away. The heat left me cold and oddly empty when he stoically offered me his arm.

The oversized sleeve of my loose, deeply bronzed romper draped across the tan forearm of my escort. The cool in my center thawed and I took a deep breath when Kian pulled a deeply padded, high back chair from a table already laden with delicacies. The smells of intensely sweet strawberry fritters and chopped veggie frittata almost distracted me from the storms of emotion whirring in Vance's features. Glasses of honey lavender lemonade and honeydew sorbet being served provided a needed distraction from the sudden tension around the elegant garden table.

After such a large breakfast, I was surprised at the hunger rumbling through me now.

"The Countess sure knows how to help a crew relax. This spread looks delicious," I mentioned.

"It is indeed built for entertaining. Her husband was the biggest producer of crystal projectors in the continent. Many scenes were filmed here, lending the whole property a poetically eclectic feel," Kian said while taking his own chair to my right.

"That explains a lot of questions I've been harboring about the grounds actually," I laughed.

"Don't let me confuse you, the Countess is an eclectic character herself, don't discredit her delightfulness by ignoring it's particularity." Kian's chuckle broke the seriousness of Vance's gaze that now bored into the side of my face as I continued to stare into sea foam eyes, ignoring the Sky Knight.

A cool breeze lifted Kian's deep black hair, the sun showing auburn pieces tucked into the black in alternating patterns of natural beauty. His hair and beard were neat though, long and scruffy, but in a way that screamed aristocratic gruff.

"I'm not so easily confused, sir. The Countess has been more than kind and I have never met anyone quite like her. The hospitality she has shown while we are keeping dark has been unlimited," I replied.

Vance grumbled from across the table. "The Countess has earned our gratitude for this reprieve, but it is not enough to bury our heads in the sands and daydream." His eyes simmered as they cut toward Kian. "I came for new information, not idle chatter. What do you have?"

I wasn't sure what the personal problem was that Vance seemed to have with the gorgeous stranger, but the animosity was palpable. Kian, however, seemed to be amused. His smile only grew larger as Vance's face flushed from their stare off.

"If you two are done comparing dicks, I have some information to share that you may actually find useful." Marli announced.

Kian dropped his stare to look toward an archway on the other end of where we were sitting with a look of concern darkening his features.

"It is no new information that my dick is by far the largest," Marli smiled.

A sneer and more than a few chuckles rose above the quiet of the gardens.

"This is so peaceful," I sighed happily.

"Most of the time, my Grace," Kian's tone fell lower, mincing his words.

There was no time to wonder over his abrupt change in demeanor. I'd known this male less than a full moon cycle and already he vexed me, leaving me with questions I know led to nothing but more questions. His seaside eyes locked with mine and I realized he was still speaking, but there was a moment where no sound existed in the garden, then it erupted.

XXV

I found myself surrounded by noise and movement as a portal opened on top of the bed of daisies and eggplant ivy that were placed along the table as a runner. Castilen growled low from somewhere behind me and Marli blocked my front. Vance had two daggers pulled ready for action, but Kian seemed unfazed. His green eyes were nearly twinkling at the man attached to a large, white-booted foot that emerged a fraction of a second before the twinkling tip of his staff did, still spinning in time to the whirling shades of the portal.

The party crasher's staff cut through the haze of his portal like the tip of a tall building bursting through an overcast day. The magic spinning around the handle shot streaks down each line of the staff.

The stranger made a move straight at Kian as though no one else in the garden existed. Was this his lover? That would absolutely be my luck, to catch feelings so fast for a stranger and him to turn out gay. I supposed I could get them a really nice commitment gift to say sorry for lusting over your new husband. There was a place on Tankan that did excellent sets of sheets that were modified to always be the perfect temperature. I would have to travel off-world to get them but....I was snapped out of my ramblings by the stranger's announcement.

"We lost the gate." He said simply.

There was no pretense or grief in his tone, though there was anger boiling behind green eyes like the kind of moss found deep inside of a damp, quiet forest. His appearance was not so calming. Earrings lined each ear and tattoos peeked out from every surface not covered by the most ostentatious suit I had ever seen. The suit itself was nice enough with flowing organza sleeves and slim fitted pants over boots a shade darker that were edged in gold trim.

A flash of danger across the eyes of the Sky Knight drew my attention back to him and off of the stranger. Vance's face settled into an impassive granite stare with the features of a demi-god. I leaned to the side to see past Kian who was still blocking me with his body.

"Come on Ki, nothing? Castilen got your tongue?" The white pirate stepped off the table and shoved bacon in his mouth, as though he hadn't landed in the middle of the table to announce that the Veiliri had broken through another Gate, threatening Tanirra with another surge from Veil.

"Seriously Safamir? Do you take nothing seriously?" Kian's frustration and humor mangled his statement.

"I certainly hope I never have to, darling," Safamir smiled again. His blonde hair was cut short to his boyish face, and I noticed the beautiful red of his nails when he waved his greeting to me "Who are you?" His question was merely a simple curiosity.

"Skarlet." I reached a hand out to shake his, still not sure that I should, but assuming that Kian would stop me if this Safamir was truly a danger.

"Mhm," he breathed as he kissed my hand lightly looking to where Marli sat with his feet propped on the table that Safamir had tossed about during his entrance.

"But who are you?" Instant desire filled his features and he openly drank in the Rogue. I could tell instantly that this man feared nothing.

The rogue dropped his feet from the table, truly grinning back at the beastly male.

"No. No, no." Kian finally moved, signaling Castilen that it was ok to do the same. He turned slightly towards the right and glared at Marli and Safamir.

"Which Gate?" He nearly yelled over their greeting and the tension rolled from one male to the next in a wave around our table. I felt a pressure building inside and an uncomfortable tingle from the magic being leaked from each male in the circle of ego I was stuck in.

"THE Gate, Key. The gate we have all spent weeks and weeks holding against the Veiliri and their fodder. We lost THE gate." A look between the two ruined any hope left that this destroyed gate held back nothing more than weeds and bunnies.

"You're not nearly as funny as you think you are. There are still many gates, and you've come all this way just to ruin all of your aunt's hard work preparing the flowers for this table with your big ugly boots. You're an idiot," Kian scoffed.

"Your face is big and ugly, and these boots are fabulous," Safamir scrunched his nose and continued. "Alas, I can agree that I am the number one idiot in charge, and we have lost the gate. I will go and let the Countess know that her nephew is home, and she will need to prepare a room for meeting and I will brief all at once." All humor dropped from his face as he added, "There are many things that need to be discussed." His tone harbored no option of negotiation.

I still had no idea who he was.

A cut of dark mossy green eyes flashed from Kian toward me before Safamir took a step backwards and was gone again, snapping himself directly to the manor and out of the garden the same way he entered.

"Bastard makes the most absurd entrances," Kian sighed with a note of friendly melancholy. "Let's go let Safi show off before he does anything even more dramatic while we stand here talking about him."

Dramatic show-off.

I followed his gaze toward the direction of the southern entrance to the doors of the welcoming home and didn't take time to think about my next move before grabbing Kian's hand. One blink and I would have us standing on the same patio the mage portalled to. Kian gave a slight glance and nodded as he wrapped his hand around mine tightly. There was a sense of trust in his grip as if I had just passed a threshold I didn't know to aim for.

I did know how to aim for an over-decorated foyer though. I pictured the mage and tapped into his location, along with the general direction of Kian's glare, and blinked us out of the previously peaceful garden.

There was no need to do the physical act of blinking. It in no way contributed to my abilities, but I found the antic satisfying and ritualistic. Wind blew both warm and cold breezes from every direction for a split second when time was frozen as I moved the two of us bodily through the cosmos. If you could wrangle one star, then you could walk among them. Just throw a bit of magic on a hearthstone and aim for the sky, quite literally.

We landed two feet in front of Safamir, rather awkwardly with hands clasped and mirrored looks of intrigue toward the mage.

"Do you have a spell for that? A way to share it and transport it like a portal, perhaps," Safamir purred, completely unfazed that we appeared as abruptly as he did in our garden of delights. "I'd offer you advice on those terrible shoes in exchange for that secret."

"Nice," Kian's look lingered on our clasped hands for a few extra heartbeats before letting go. We both turned to look back toward the door where the others entered.

The annoyance rolled off of Vance in waves cutting through any mirth starting to fill the room.

"Sky Knight, is there a problem?" I asked as he huffed past us toward a room with doors just thrown open to show a table the size of a small lake with maps adorning the bits of visible wall.

"It makes me very uncomfortable when you do that, Skarlet," Vance's glare burned the back of my blonde head as we walked toward the assumed meeting location.

"And I have little concern for your comfort concerning my safety," I hissed. I swung around to face him. "Yes, I know that sounded ridiculous, but you know what I mean. You cannot keep moping and storming about this home because you don't like something I've done, again. It's simply poor manners, my love." I placed a placating hand against his rough cheek.

A darkness clouded his eyes, but he relaxed the hard lines of his mouth, allowing them to fill back out to a perfect pout. Just before his hand landed on mine to cover it in an intimate moment, I pulled back with a slight drop of the chin.

Vance didn't fight back but instead followed me toward a seat at the other end of a large, dark, and classically decorated office space that had been expanded for recording a scene about fictional war crimes. A more perfect cover for a rebel base had not been built yet.

With my feet landing lightly on the dark hardwood floor, I quickly walked toward the head of the table. Honestly, I didn't know why or where the hubris to do so came from. The look coming from Safamir as he mirrored my steps along the opposite side of the room should have been warning enough for me to learn my place, but I have never been accused of having too much common sense, so I walked faster, beating him to the chair at the head of the table.

"Skarlet darling, you are not wanted or necessary for this discussion. Please vacate my seat," Safamir sneered. His lips pressed into a line did nothing to distract from his beauty.

"No, I like this one," I shrugged. For absolutely no reason I gave my rump a little wiggle in the chair. With no undergarments and just the satin finish of the deep bronze romper separating me from the dense burgundy fabric of the chair, I nearly regretted the move when my magic threatened a tsunami of power. Release was needed, soon.

Sea green eyes the color of every happy summer memory ever snapped to mine. Kian's smile was dazzling and distracting. His long dark hair and scruffy beard hid the quick glimpse of a grin just before I blocked Safamir's staff with a gust of light magic, without moving my focus from the solution to my magic problem standing right in front of us. First, I had to piss off the stranger a little more.

"Choosing violence first is a true sign of weakness. Is this your answer? I should definitely run this discussion then. All in favor of making love, not war, say aye!" I lifted my hand as if voting and flicked it, pulling his staff from his grip to mine. The shock of his magic silenced any further fuckery.

"You're not a mage!" Standing, I looked up into his deep forest eyes and was close enough to see the specks there, like the bark of an ancient tree, sparkling with long lines of magic.

Shaman magic.

It wasn't so rare to meet a Shaman anymore, but it was uncommon to meet one with such blatant power in Tanirra. Normally, it's the Mages that control the magic in the field with great power, but this guy stepped through a portal like it was a strip of grass, indicating he had great power indeed.

"Tanirran Shamans aren't common." I said, distracted by Castilen's retreating frame when Safamir took the chair and sat with a delighted smile. "Who are you, though." I looked down intently at him.

The heavy doors slammed closed to give us privacy and he rolled his shoulders before responding.

"I'm a Shaman, but that's not the most important issue in front of us, so I won't be answering any personal questions, now." Safamir growled, dismissing me before settling into his seat and commanding the room back to the fallen gate. My curiosity would have to wait. Safamir wasted no time giving a play by play of every action he took to stem the tide of Veiliri that rushed the gate before they could be temporarily closed again. Most of the Veil fell before getting past the southern marshes and the others were driven into the thrashing currents of the sea. Help was needed to find a way to stop this from happening again.

Turned out Kian was right and Saf is a bit dramatic. We have long inferred that small breaches in the magic of the gates is behind the fresh soldiers that seem to show up in waves across the continent. I tucked the Shaman's words away for later though, unsure of where this alliance was going to lead me.

XXVI

I couldn't get many personal questions answered before Lady Cyneil had appeared to commandeer her nephew for something outside of our meeting. While my curiosity still burned I was satisfied that I'd gotten the intelligence from him, as slight as it was. Leaving the room left me with an annoying list of new questions that I'd have to circle back to later, though.

I left the meeting room and aimed for my quarters to change and collect my chaotic thoughts.

I heard Kian call my name from behind and picked up speed. Since arriving at the estate, my objectives had been altered for me and I was annoyed that he was part of that, even indirectly.

I suppressed a huff when he caught me turning the corner to our quarters. The gate hadn't fallen completely, but they needed our help to hold it. I knew without deciding anything for fact that my mission would be on hold until answers were found, though the next pieces hadn't been placed yet and there was no way to know what they were. For a better world than the one I have been handed, we make the choices we have to make. I put all personal feelings aside as well as possible and leaned in to hear his question.

"I'd love a walk around the lake while we wait on the Countess to release her nephew to us. Until then, there is nothing left to do except wait," he whispered.

Not what I was expecting, considering we only had hours to plan our next moves.

We needed Safamir and his small band of rebels to combine might with our group to get quickly to the gate after dark fall. I could trixxt and he could portal the entire group in a few short trips, though that left everyone here at a high risk for discovery. The Veiliri did not kill their rebel leaders. They chose instead to do much, much worse to them.

I looked up into his handsome face and heard myself agree.

"Sure, since there is nothing else to do, for now." I responded.

His eyes dragged down to the breasts swelling under jumper, and back up. Slowly.

"We can find something to do, if it so pleases you."

I stepped back and around to him, continuing my way to change. I didn't tell him that the idea pleased me very much.

Several moments later, we stepped arm in arm into the cool sunshine.

Surrounding villages were already gathering to celebrate with the hostess, the Countess, tonight. Baskets and woven carts pulled by small wheels and motors run by the same magic powering our ships whipped by, hauling goods from tiny row boats lined up on the docks by the lake.

We walked for a bit, speaking to others we'd seen about the manor over the last few days. The whole area seemed wrapped in peace, and I began to relax as the sun started to set.

The chill started to blanket the area as soon as the sun dipped on the horizon. Hues of pinks and purples shot across the darkening sky like stars dipped in candy that were tossed about, leaving trails of beauty wherever they may fly.

We climbed to the top of a small mountain top across from the docks on the lake. The smells blowing in from Lake Cyneil reminded me of Vance's. His scent was masculine, deep, and full of something bright that you couldn't see. I breathed in heavily to wrap myself in the idea of such serenity before willingly walking away from what had been offered here to throw myself back against a force that will likely kill us all. Even the immortals could be killed if you try hard enough.

I took another breath in and stopped, almost choking myself when Kian's warm scent filled my nose. Everything about this male set me on fire. His eyes melted me from the inside and the smile hiding under the messy warrior exterior started a drum beat inside that swelled with my own magic.

"Is this why you brought me way out here?" I asked.

"Why did I bring you way out here, my grace?" Kian asked quietly, his stare lit with desire.

While I changed and packed, he had shaved and trimmed his long hair to shoulder length. A dimple peaked out from under the weight of his shimmering smile. I could barely stand under the onslaught of magic and emotion; one and the same so often.

I stood for several seconds, reconciling my need for him against the absurdity of needing a stranger at all. I considered him for a moment, his dark hair shining in the setting sun, before making a choice.

"I don't care, actually." I took a step forward, putting us but three feet apart.

"What?" His look still sizzled under a moment of confusion.

"I don't care about your why. I care only of my own," I replied.

It only took seconds for our mouths to connect. A sizzle cracked the air and I stopped to take a breath. My body shook and the seams running the length of my ass pushed in under his rough hands. Suddenly I'm lifted against him and already screaming for release. The sky darkened and his kiss deepened under a sky swirling with our connection. The sky was swirling with lights and sound.

So much sound.

Too many lights in a sky just ripe with setting sunshine and dusk a moment before.

I instantly froze, my legs still wrapped tightly around the white undershirt Kian wore.

"Where's your armor?" I worried out loud.

He placed me on the ground in front of him and snapped himself back into the black piece and matching boots from our first meeting.

We waited for moments to make sense of the sounds coming from the skies around the mountain peaks.

The evening air was cooling the sweat saturating me but not fast enough for my clothes to slide on smoothly. I've got to stop trying to hook up in random places, this shit never ends well. I feel my stomach drop and all complaints are silenced when I take in the formations appearing in flight above us.

"They've come for the village, Kian," I whispered the acknowledgment before jumping to my feet and spinning to take in the lake and rolling hills beyond. There was no way to spot a beezer fleet against a sunset like this, but there were not supposed to be enough of the golden flight beetles to have built any armory out of them. Either way I didn't believe the Countess would have planned anything this ostentatious with so many here under her care recovering from post trauma injuries.

"The interruption at the end of the meeting, did she mention anything about this?" I asked.

Lady Cyneil had swooped in and taken Safamir not long after our briefing started without explanation.

"No, she had a conversation with him concerning his quickly waning window of opportunity to do literally anything with his life. Nothing about having flyers come in," Kian shook his head.

His expression matched my own dark and confused one. A few seconds passed and it was suddenly clear that the Countess had not orchestrated this event. The Veiliri were attacking.

It all came quickly rushing back as I stood glued to my spot beside Kian: the night of the Veill attack. When they came for Blue Mountain, I was outside, too far away. It wasn't until after my caretaker and sister in magic were killed that I could trixxt. Having been stuck here on Tannira, she couldn't return to the skies which birthed her, leaving her magic vulnerable. I took it on as she gasped for air as she died, siphoning to me that which should not have been mine for many years yet.

I still hadn't learned to fully control it. I had to shut the fear down to a point where reaction would be possible.

I needed to move. I needed to get into a position to strike the first wave just as they had reached the shores of the lake, I needed to land as much debris away from the clusters of villagers that could be seen pulling shields and blades from hiding places all over the grounds.

I looked to Kian to relay my plan when he stopped me with a question.

"What do you want to do?"

"What do you mean? There is only one thing to be done isn't there," I asked.

"Indeed. Do you want to fly with me or will you be jumping to the middle of the fight on your own," he questioned." His shoulders rolled in a stretch and he shook gently as wings in every shade of blue unfolded in a leathery snap.

"Why would I go to the middle, maybe I'll jump to the side and join the Rogue."

"His laugh barely registered before he shot into the air to meet the oncoming fleet on the other side of my blast. I let him clear the lake before I drew up blasts of fire from the well of magic deep inside and sent a blast out in a pulse of heat to bring down those beautifully dangerous flyers.

The lights began to fade from the sky and I got my first good glimpse of the attacking front line: Veiliri soldiers followed closely by a small fleet of armed beezer-like flyers

Fear choked me again and I blinked quickly to get myself into the fight from here, but it was too late. I was hit.

Blood gurgled from the wound on my left thigh from the missile I took right as I entered the mists of space and time and I had to grasp for a thread to pull myself back out on the other side but the time in there had worked to heal the wound completely. I stumbled and ducked into a roll coming out the closing doorway.

I concentrated again and when my eyes opened, back on corporeal ground.

I pulled up using a tree glowing in the sunset colors of a sky full of flame. We would have to fight before we could meet at the gate. We couldn't leave these people to clean up our mess.

There was a flash of confusion as I thought about these words. For once, I didn't think I had done anything messy here. We still weren't leaving the civilians to pay for harboring fugitives and dead bloodlines there. I took a deep breath in and held it to calm my racing heart.

It was time to act.

XXVII

The mist cleared from my mind a split second after I landed. I could see that many men, women, and even a few young teenagers were fighting the flying Veill soldiers. Each one a winged artillery in himself. No women flew with the Veiliri. I had heard once that it was because they have to steal their women and couldn't afford to have them killed in the battles they were always waging. That was a bard's tale from a backwater western village though, so maybe they're just racist, sexist pigs.

Marli appeared a few feet from where I landed, fulfilling the prophecy of my joke from earlier. I made to angle myself into his path to fight as near him as possible and thought of our best options.

I took a steadying breath and smiled at the rush of release I knew to be coming. It had been one long day after another since our last assignment before the hunt and I needed an organic relief; the kind that drained you.

I waited and held my breath with the whoosh of wind rustling the white tips of my long braid. Nearby, Kian fought with a soldier that knocked an elder butler out right above where I'd landed. He landed a knockout blow seconds before seeing my meeting my eyes in a welcoming smile.

I watched him move with the grace of kingdoms in his blood amongst the Veil crowding into the gardens. He slashed bodies with a long blade that glimmered in the dark, as though the night were guiding its strokes. His wings rustled as he lifted himself into the air and dropped Veiliri from the skies with absolute confidence.

I nearly forgot myself watching his movements. A gust of air across my ear brought me back to the soldier barreling at me with his bow raised. I shot blast after blast to bring down the squirming line of warriors advancing me from all angles. The sun's last rays were still grasping the skies when the next wave arrived. I looked around for answers but came up with only one option to stop what would be a massacre if they made it to mingle with the forces already encroaching on the families holding the manor.

I saw Kian dash into the horizon and meet the leading Veil at the opposite edge of the lake. The met in a tangle of muscled arms and snarls and jetted up above the tailing squadron. Kian screeched and thrashed against the male for several seconds before I saw their bodies falling back to the surface of the water. Right before they made impact, Kian released the body and allowed it to be lost below the churning depths before turning back to land in a heap in front of me. Looking up through the blood leaking for a gash in his forehead Kian breathed a single command.

"Skarlet."

In the next second, I heard his voice in my head like the echo of a large horn announcement. He meant to help me clear the field for a blast to end this surprise onslaught. Now I knew why it felt like I could hear his voice in my thoughts. I saved that bit of information for later and followed his eyes to the sea of friendlies watching with one eye on the clearing courtyard and another to the Veil starting to clear the shore. All eyes turned to Kian when he spoke and after a few seconds they all dropped at the same time and I unleashed the power of a thousand stars on our enemies. Many fell dead instantly, the others pounced upon by villagers.

The quiet following my blast was eerie, no other flyers filled the skies. No other winged Veiliri hung in the twilight above for me to fight. The force of the attack was too slight, too fast for it to be over, but the silence was absolute. The skies empty now.

I was nearly spent. There was coolness filling spaces in my body that magic had burned for days. I sunk to the ground as small pebbles dug lightly into the leather of my leggings.

Quiet falls like darkness. I released another loud breath and shifted to sit on my rear. Kian walked toward me, but his eyes were focused on something else, rather someone else.

Safamir was approaching from where he was speaking in hushed tones with Castilen and Vance. Marli stood off to the side, face tilted to the clouds in anticipation.

Safamir's white suit was now a white and cream leather tunic over breeches with a cape and hood that cover from the tip of his six foot two inch frame to the matching deep blue boots. He wasn't conspicuous at all. I rolled my eyes which gave me an instant headache. I was weak, but I loved it. My magic was already replenishing, so I dropped my head to enjoy the feeling for a few more moments.

I stared at the ground under my thighs until it all blended into one solid color between a grey and beige. The natural beauty of the place was hard to deny. A sense of healing settled over the chill bumps running the length of both of my forearms.

The skies shone a deep crimson in the last few moments of sunset. The only wings for miles now were those of the birds drifting on a dark evening breeze and Kian's injured ones being babied as he surveyed the damage.

Is that it? A few waves of Veiliri seemed like barely enough to frighten the town, not take it over. With another gate recently damaged, there could have been thousands of Veil pouring into Tanirra, and there should have been a lot more to this attack.

Did the Gentry have something to do with this? No, those were Veil soldiers in the sky.

I shook my head to focus my thoughts and try to place the nagging anxiety that plagued me. This shouldn't be the end. I looked at the rocky paths around the village and thought of our walk through it in the sunset the morning before. There were plenty of places for an attack to come from underground here. If they knew of the emergency tunnels dug deep into the packed dirt ran all the way under the mountain passes directly to the waterfalls and beyond.

The thought had barely been completed before Safamir gestured at us. His blazing blue cloak reflected the twinkle of each star. He was the epitome of power and elegance.

"How is she?" Safamir angled his head toward me to emphasize his question.

"She can answer for herself. Skarlet, are you alright?" Kian asked.

I couldn't help the small laugh that escaped my mouth at his look of expectation. "I am quite well, sir."

Before a reply could be made the land quaked and a rumble of boots rushed us from all sides. Women could be seen ushering their young out of their hiding places leading into the tunnels and out behind a human web they formed to protect them while they scattered into the mountains to hide.

"Duck, Skarlet!" Safamir yelled before his staff produced a bright pink shield to block a ball of lightning barreling toward us. I was thrown to the ground and the breath was stolen from me immediately. Lightning hit the shield and shattered it into dozens of smaller fingers of light that reached around, encircling the shielded circle we sheltered in, trying to find a way to attack.

A scrambling Safamir jumped back up and looked down at Kian and his twisted wing.

"You clearly won't be flying back into this, Ki. Skarlet, can you jump?" he asked between breaths.

"I can," I answered quickly. It was the best I could whoosh out with the suddenness of the ground units descending upon us.

"Good, find a spot to drop me at the edge of the village where I can stand with the parents while you gather their children to me," Kian requested. He squeezed the hand he held under his own as small rocks pushed into my wrist. "I'll be back, Saf," he yelled to Safamir.

Kian rolled to his feet and lifted me with his outstretched hand.

"Don't come back until everyone is cleared of these blasts," Safamir shouted back at us. He pushed us with his free hand before casting a blinding ball of bright white light out of a tiny opening in the shield to give me time to blink.

I did blink, but not before I saw another missile aim for our Shaman from somewhere in the dark.

I didn't hesitate or bother to think my next steps through. It was a character flaw of mine I had come to accept at this point in my life as being mostly positive in its alterations of common plans. I stepped through the mists of time and space and dropped Kian a few miles outside of the homestead.

The small village home shone with candles in the tall windows and thatched roofs rustled in a light breeze giving the landing an extra eerie feeling. I didn't have a choice. There was no time for looking for a better, safer place. We performed a fast sweep of the area to check for soldiers and injured villagers or guests. The town proved to be completely empty, with most citizens having gathered down at the manor of the Countess that guided this region, much like a monarch would in the human continent.

Kian tried to grab my arm, knowing my intent without a word, but I blinked before he got any closer. The lakeside retreat that I admired just hours before was nothing like the burning shit show I walked back into when I stepped away from Kian. In the few moments it took to cement our plan, the garden had nearly been overrun. Oily smoke wafted from hay bales lining a field of wildflowers where the fireworks were set to be displayed. Safamir stood in a glade opposite where I left him on the other side of a gigantic opponent.

Drops of fog rolled off of a portal and dripped in a steady, nauseating beat. Silence strolled in with the flog, blanketing the area like a heady scent on hot night. The scene unfolded in slow motion as I took it all in.

The drip of condensation from the cold of the portal was the only sound now, the scene surrounding me surreal. Men and women fought winged soldiers hand to hand with weapons pulled from anywhere. There were no children in sight as a strong wind lifted pale blonde strands off my shoulders, pushing me to move; forcing me to make a choice. I could leave and go back to Kian and hope that they all lived to fight another day, but that wasn't who I was at my core. Nahnni didn't raise me to run from a fight ever.

I faced Safamir on the other side of the tiny beach, casting and holding the blasts coming from the portal on his own. Blasts of fire hit the portal, shaking it and casting cool droplets into the air to turn them to steam. He spied me and dropped the offensive to yell for me, waving his arm franticly in a shooing motion.

I thought back to the moments before my jump to the village with Kian. It had only been moments ago. How did we get to this point so fast? There had been no time to encourage families to return home or to get everyone safely inside. Now the children were in trouble. Children were our most precious and important assets, and they were only protected by those fighting up the embankments, trying desperately to keep the danger from reaching their babies.

The Veiliri would likely not kill them, rather they would keep them hostage to keep the parents in line. There were dozens of camps full of families that had been displaced since the incursion full hostages and slaves to the Veill.

The weight of the initial attack hit me again. I was exhausted and shouldn't have spent so much energy at once to dispel the attack from the sky in the beginning. A chill ran down the back of my neck and I realized that I may not be able to save both Saf and the children. There wasn't enough magic left for me to save everyone without help.

Suddenly another portal opened in front of me. Black boots hit the sand within a flurry of movement as I took off towards the embankment away from the Shaman. I looked back long enough to throw a prayer up that he could hold whatever was coming out of that portal for long enough. I needed enough time to find the children and keep them safe.

Saf yelled in my direction as a means to stop me. His hand stopped at the bottom of a large chopping motion and he moved them rapidly before starting the onslaught again. He was indicating that the children would be up in the caves above.

Well, shit. I changed directions and sent a mound of sand cascading over the bottom of a large, tan boot poking out of the portal to join its twin on the ground a few feet to my left. Darkness had fallen and the night breeze cooled me as I made a mad sprint for the entrance to the caves that Kian and I stood at less than an hour prior. It took too many sticky moments to run the distance and I slowed to catch my breath in front of a slit between two rocks marking the downward entrance to the cave. Two tiny girls in celebration gowns and swords stepped forward from the entrance with perfect precision. I dodged an unexpected sword strike and grabbed the first girl by the wrist to stop a second strike, pulling them both into the dark interior at the same time.

Nothing could have prepared me for the attack of rocks and tiny fists that came. There had to be two dozen adolescents here. This jump won't be easy, but time for thinking came to an end the moment I saw this place under attack.

"Stop!" I yelled while blocking my pretty face from the flying, slicing rocks. "STOP it! I am here to help you and I don't have time for this shit." The outburst settled nothing, and the hits kept coming.

I blocked the hits coming from the front while an organized attack of snack-breathed-heathens ensued from behind. Their weapons were barely more than sticks, but the wielding of the weapon appeared to be an art form in the way the fourth local adolescent appeared from around the corner of a tiny entrance. Arcing it high over her head, she whacked my ankles with the other end. I bit my cheek at the sharp pain and stared at the newcomer; the image of grace containing the true shaking of her frame, she stood barely above four feet. I appreciated her effort and tenacity. Though appreciation, like flattery, only could carry one so far.

I needed to create a diversion from their diversion. With just a draw of breath and slide of fingers, the rocks situated at the edge of the bluff behind her began to slide at my command. This did little to faze her and I quickly lost patience.

"Ok, let's go!" I grabbed the girl guard, knowing the others would follow her, and blinked straight to Kian.

Our appearance almost knocked him backwards when we landed. I thrust the girl's tiny hand into his and gave him a brief rundown, but he shook his head. "You have to get them all," he insisted. His face darkened as anger threatened the surface.

The girl let out a tiny whimper at our exchange and cringed from both of us, no longer feeling any safer than she was in the cave.

"Try to calm her. I will return with the rest, I promise," I continued. My softer tone seemed to relax the girl a bit, but Kian's face was still a mix of hard resignation and confusion.

Before he could retort, I blinked again and returned twice more to the cave and back to Kian, bringing no less than two dozen bodies with me to the safest location I could find away from the surprise onslaught of the villa. On the third return I received sincere platitudes from the tiny leader, the first to arrive, and assured her that the safety of each youth was in excellent hands. No appreciation was necessary.

I looked back toward the colors erupting in the distance. Was it a battle or just a random attack? Did the underhandedness the attackers exhibited by assailing a civilian stronghold with no resources to flee have a directive dictating this maneuver?

Kian approached from where he watched me land and unload children. The fear on his face was gone before it fully registered. "Are you tired?" he asked me.

"Exhausted, but they are all here," I replied weakly.

"Is your magic inexhaustible?" Kian asked with a tilt of his head.

"Not at all," I smiled.

His eyes glowed green as they studied me. "Skarlet, I must go back for Safamir and Castilen. You for Vance and Marli. We can't leave them there. Can you do that for me without hurting yourself?"

"We can't leave them here, either," I replied. I gestured at the children who were watching us keenly.

The look of helplessness and frustration darkening Kian's features were the only answer I received when I gently touched his injured wings in a reminder of why I had to be the one to do this. I took a step back from him, nearly toppling over a tiny blonde child. There was only one choice to make yet again.

So, I blinked and jumped right back into battle, leaving Kian to protect the children.

XXVIII

The fighting around the hold had picked up with Veiliri coming in from paths all around the lake through the same caves we used just days before. I took to the ground as soon as I stopped moving, dodging an array of castings. I blinked again and slowly opened my eyes. The terrain had changed from flying shrapnel and rocky caves to shattered wood frames and bright glistening glass from busted vases. Walking between space and time took power, and mine had been drained nearly twice today, not to mention the still unfamiliar magical nuances inherited along with my newest ability. The tight fabric of my battle suit pulled even closer under heavy breaths as I tried to orient myself.

After many head-spinning moments, I walked away from warm stone lining the balcony of my room and blinked to the ground rather than risk climbing. The courtyard was filled with bodies, but there didn't seem to be a lot of fighting still going on. Lady Cyneil's people obviously had their own secrets. The organization against the scourge was fast and efficient.

A winged soldier kicked up dirt and took off in a vertical lift. A movement in the corner caught my eye and Safamir emerged from a skirmish with four Veiliri. Marli could be seen darting between the shadows of the tall trees and in the distance, Vance and Castilen fought back to back against the stragglers appearing around the lake.

I spotted Safamir and saw his face drop at the image I made standing across the strewn, pebbled grounds. There were lines of worry etched through his brows. He finished off a soldier emerging from his right and ran towards me. He was nearly to me when I noticed that he was not alone.

Dirt and petals flew at his heels and people scattered and limped out of the way of blue electric spheres coming from the shaman chasing Safamir. A full suit of armor on the pursuer slowed him slightly, giving our shaman the break in battle he needed to drop an offensive totem. Sparks flew from the small carved piece in rapid successions behind Safamir as he turned to me with wild eyes.

The air sizzled with fire and lightning as shadows ebbed and danced against the busted white wood fencing and colored glass shards as the battle between the shamans raged on.

Two Shamans. The thought clanged around before I could focus on it. This was an attack planned with mindfulness. Did they have a mage? I chanced a look around for evidence of one but nothing stood out.

Pushing the question aside I looked around for a place to gain ground on the attacker. That is when I thought of how he had arrived. He had dropped a portal and simply stepped right through. He was connected to it and if I could get to it I could end this fight in seconds.

The circular gate glowed and grew in front of me, dragging our eyes toward the lime rock wall it was spreading against. It stopped at the edges of the courtyard wall and deepened its vortex into a gate void of color. Silence encased the area followed by a shrill blast of sound erupting throughout the courtyard all at once, returning in a rush and leaving an annoying, piercing ringing in the ears. The ringing couldn't drown out the sudden onslaught of warrior cries and flapping wings that attacked us. Where the silence was only eerie a moment ago, the sound of death was even more terrifying.

I felt a blast hit me and blue hues clouded my vision. I stumbled against the rock wall and reached for my daggers. My chest pushed tightly against sweat-sodden leathers with every rapid inhale.

Something was draining my magic like fire reaching deep inside and siphoning power. I looked at the portal and could feel the pulses of blue radiating from it. That was a sign old magic, dangerous magic. The naïve giddiness I previously felt about being drained had been replaced with a motivating mix of fear and expectation.

Spreading my fingers out in a splayed, palm down motion, I felt around for an idea of how many new players we had and how much magic it would take to save us all. The answer was more than I had at my disposal.

The good news was that the Gentry quickly trained any doubt out of me, and I was ready for the fight ahead of us. I had more than my magic; a woman should always have more than one weapon against the unfairness of the world.

I had to get to Safamir and get us out of here. The only way to him though was through them.

I assessed the new fodder pouring in from the portal. They had shorter, smaller, winged bodies. They appeared similar to the humanara in their shape, though the gray toned arms were hanging lower in a decidedly not humanara way. Their skin was smooth and their noses perky, but the eyes were tiny slits glowing with a sickly yellow light. They weren't quite goblin, not quite human.

The taller ones pushed through their smaller comrades. There was no sense of loyalty between them as they stormed a path straight to Safamir. Several smaller soldiers stepped through the portal in a blur of muscle and wings, each hand grasping a club or axe. Noxious gas spilled out behind each monster and my eyes watered with the pain of it.

I took a deep breath and spread my feet a bit, palming throwing knives into my right hand with the left elevated to cast a blast as soon as the time was right. It wouldn't be a cast equal to the power I put into taking out the first wave because I didn't have that much power left, but the bomb of magic would decimate many on the field at once.

There had been two slight lulls in the blasts from the gateway, indicating a period where the portal would be powering up before spitting out more soldiers. The next one was due any second, which meant now was my window of time. By some miracle I caught Saf's attention between blasts. He looked determined and very tired. I took a chance and lifted my hands to sign to him: "Be ready to go when I reach you."

He slung his hands out to renew his defensive shield and signed back: "You'll get yourself killed, get Kian and meet the others at the temple."

Men are so dumb sometimes. Like I could just walk away from this.

We didn't have time for this kind of ego battle right now. I sighed to myself and decided to at least try and behave rationally. Lifting my fingers, I responded: "Take cover in... five, four, three, two, one!" I took in hot, dirty air into my lungs in large gulps. My weapon hand tightened its grip as I let my best blast loose. It was a lesser blast due to my weakened magic, but I struck true.

The opening to Veill began to wobble and every injured body, minus about a dozen, dropped to the ground dead or close to it. We wasted no time taking the offensive.

I whipped a long dagger from my thigh and set my sights on the shaman that Safamir still fought. He never missed a beat during my blast, but the intruding magic wielder seemed to be slowing.

Slicing low into the abdomen of two Veiliri grunts on either side, I ran through them into the fray, my blades dripping and shining in rattling unison. Muck covered my black boots and my hands were sweating. A mixture of sweat and blood dripped from my wrists, wetting my face and caking my suit.

Turning left I dropped and barely avoided a jolt of lightning from the fighter blocking any shots I had to the open portal. Shots pierced the moment spent deciding my next move. We were simply out of time. I focused on the blue energy pulsing around the courtyard. The sounds crowded against my senses, so I focused on a single target, drowning out the clash from the few grunts still fighting a small group of hardy locals.

The target took notice of my approach and dropped a white-hot lightning shot towards my feet.

This is going to hurt like a bitch," I thought as I dropped into a crouch, grounding myself before connecting both open palms with bright, hot, incoming death.

I only had seconds to reach into the well inside and pull out the heat of the moons. My own magic seared to life in a nearly unexpected swell, given the intensity of fighting since the ambush. Pushing everything I had in me, into the strike of the shaman, I directed the heat to him in a rapid reverse current.

The kill was instant. The thud of his dropping massive body reverberated around the courtyard and the portal made a loud sucking sound before collapsing on itself. Activity seemed to pause briefly before the surviving Veil were sucked back into the closing portal. Safamir approached at a run and I looked up at his beaten body from where I sat catching my breath.

"I'm weak, but I'm not dead. Give me a minute and we can go," I nodded.

I tilted my head toward the group of locals watching us. Two women stepped forward and introduced themselves as Ilia and Mollie, mothers of the village schoolhouse and asked me when they could be taken to their children. I shook off dirt and looked towards the courtyard that had been emptied of the portal that shimmered feet away just moments ago. I swore I saw a body fall, but now there was just a sparkle in the air where a body should be; almost like a whisper of his magic left behind. I shivered, but I had a job to do. I must pull my thoughts from the direction they were headed back to a soul-destroying night of surprise attacks; the night I lost every connection to who I was. The fates did not shine well on that night as they did this day. Here I saw no bodies left and assumed that we hadn't lost any locals and the Veill's magic had taken their own fallen back with the defeated shaman and his port.

Lady Cyneil would have some cleaning to do, but I had no doubt that this town would come together to make the villa better than it was when she took our little team in.

Our team! I begged a moment from Ilia and Mollie and spun to look for the rest of my team. I tried to think of the last time I'd saw them and was rewarded with images of their bodies whole and pursuing soldiers on foot to the outer edges of the chateau.

"Castilen has your Sky Knight and they will meet us at the temple outside of Sirione." He looked around again before finishing. "The rogue lives, but that is all I know of him for now."

My face pinched in thought and I tried to relax my features while I thought about his message. Safamir mistook this for some animosity toward the rogue, a member of my own party.

"He is a rogue, did you expect him to remain seen? He will do as rogues and rangers do, fighting from the shadows until they are ready to be discovered."

I reassured him that I had no doubts that Marli would do exactly what he was created to do and none of us would know him again until the missive had been cleared of threats. No, my thoughts were slamming against the wall of logic I had tried to remain anchored to. I knew that the gate was our destination. I still confirmed it with a look of confusion, tinted with cold, sweaty dread.

A flash of frustration temporarily hardened his beautiful verdant eyes into a cold, faded amalgam as his trepidation mirrored my own. It was not our own fear that darkened the door of tomorrow, but the desperately dark memories of losing droves of people and being helpless to stop the carnage attack mercilessly. The night the sky fell was a problem for everyone, and no one would forget the raid's destruction soon. Not even battle-hardened magi and warriors.

I allow for a moment of weakness to pass through me and wonder if it's worth all of this.

"Yes, my grace, it is," Safamir's voice cracked with fatigue and emotion when he responded to the rhetorical request.

He spun before I could ask any follow up questions, so I turned to trek back to the school mistresses and gathered them in each hand. I advised each of them that the ride may be bumpy, and I caught a cackling, hushed reply. "That's the only way to ride."

I was too tired to laugh fully, and the wind smothered the small scoff I mustered as I tried to figure out which one said it. Both faces were set in stone when I studied them closer. They were both tall and stately with elegant manners and deadly with a weapon in hand. The ruby ring on Mollie's left-hand dug into the open wounds of my beaten palm when I squeezed her hand, sending waves of discomfort through the open injuries to my skin. I gripped tighter despite it and stepped through the dark again into a warm living space full of cozy flickering firelight and plush rugs.

This day was getting weirder and weirder.

. I was pleased to hear a warm voice call my name when we arrived.

"Skarlet!" Kian's voice was demanding. "What took you so long?"

He wasted no time in greeting me, as though he knew exactly when and where we would emerge. That would be impossible since all of space and time sets an unbreakable rule of infinite causes and conclusions, the greatest one being that an entity made of the skies cannot be tracked against its backdrop. He couldn't track me. Not with this kind of magic.

Yet here he stood peering at me as though the only thing he had ever had faith in was my return to him.

Deep, deep breaths girl.

Wrong time.

Wrong place.

Wrong person?

I knew few things in this moment, but given the chance I knew I would go to my knees for that man and not just to pray for him. Maybe fall to my knees was more accurate at the moment, which made the errant thought even more ridiculous.

A familiar heat lit my face under the mix of mud and blood.

Wrong environment for my wretched mind to process this rather than the words and sounds around us. I needed to rest, and, in this moment, I knew that I was safe with this male that I didn't really know in a town with citizens both unfamiliar and reassuring.

All the reasons to be ashamed of this moment, of myself or my choices, threatened my common sense. Shame never did anything for anyone but keep them from seeing a misjudgment for what it was asking you to learn instead of focusing on the emotion of it. Shame made you forget all of the good things you innately were, like knowing when to berate and when to educate is where the secrets of happiness lie, or when to avoid the things that don't settle well with you and the things that keep you calm will be more bountiful.

Despite my fierce subscription to a model of internal balance, my core monologue refuted the basic proof of this. Regret, shame, and criticism were the enemies at the gate guarded by rest and clarity. Unfortunately, I was super low on both rest and clarity.

I inhaled to focus my mind, the hitch in my breath shifted black material against my aching chest. Slices in the leather tunic bunched together in pools, sticking to the blood starting to slow and dry from the gashes that weren't healing under it. Great strips of exposed skin alerted Kian to the extent of damage done in the moments since leaving him to return to the fight for the Countess.

Ice couldn't have cooled his look any faster than understanding did. I looked away, leaving him to think it over. I'm not sure what it was, but I couldn't think of anything so I might as well let him work through it on his own.

Beginning to shake gently, I pulled a blanket from an outstretched hand of a little boy with blue-back curls and opaque eyes. I'm forced to admit to myself that my opinion of the tiny villagers may have been undeserved, formed under the pressures of being on the defensive, rather than the one ambushing a target. The efficiency with which the people jumped to defend their land, family, and rights was admirable. In this moment, the factions occupying this area seemed extraordinary. Were they taught by the Countess's court to fight and respond the way that they have or were they warriors all before that life we knew was mercilessly cut by the attacking Veiliri? They could be from anywhere on the continent, with nomadic groups of refugees being immersed in non-occupied settlements like this one frequently now.

These villages are harbors in a storm of hardship for these families. They are next on the Veiliri scum's list, too.

Every inch of Tannira lost something the night the skies opened, and soldiers were flown, marched, shipped, and otherwise delivered to her every region for an attack in mass by Veill scum. They should never have even been able to enter, yet here we were.

I saw no portals that night though, still unsure what that means for the threat we may be facing next.

All regions fell with the exception of the forests in the farthest reaches of north Tannira. Prince Dekren had the most elite forces, the greatest wealth, and the forests of ancient ways creating his kingdom, providing everything the prince needed to wipe out the Veiliri when they descended upon the north in their unified attacks, leaving his home pristine. His policy on accepting refugees amongst his fair constituents had been less than agreeable since then, with some revisions causing a rift in Gentry business.

It was likely that no one would be granted extended stays in the forests now, exceptional, or not.

I focused on the children and noticed their attention was drawn to a singular spot, listening intently to stories despite the peril that surrounded us. Children of war were desensitized to its destruction in a way that silenced their cries, kept their sleep light, and created humor where ordinary decorum said there shouldn't be any. Laughter erupted at a joke with questionable content, but no adult spoke against it, instead rallying their spirits to join in. These kids were my kind of people.

"Kian, we need to talk," I whisper harshly, noting all the little faces beginning to turn from their places spread out about the room.

I heard a quiet voice speak up over the others and recognized the little cave bandit that landed with me first. She cradled a large tome in her hands and my eyes blurred as the scene became clearer. A smokeless fire was lit in the hearth, keeping them warm and toasty against the brisk evening wind. The steam rising from the ultra-thin cups of swirling creamed chocolate danced with the light of the flames, drawing the room into a subtle movement between bright illumination and shadowy darkness. As the lights dimmed, the leader of the knee high bandits moved her hands so that the shapes were displayed on the walls, her words projected around the children at her feet, bringing them close and providing the kind of heat the soul needed.

I tried to turn back to Kian, to ask him questions about his injured wings, his Shaman, my crew; the list was growing the longer I considered his face, but something kept me from raising my voice, demanding answers.

I blinked my eyes at the dancing lights and slowly took in the room again.

The scene was eerie, off somehow. My arms and legs felt as if the children still clung to them. The sensation did not compare even mildly to the fog digging fingers into my head. The words from the salty little storyteller were gently floating whisps of the tale coming my way, pieces coming in of the name of a great Shaman, her kingdom threatened by a traitorous friend and her family broken, a handsome lover. I recognized something about the story and continued to stare blankly over my bloody left shoulder and into the stone walled parlor where she was perched on a high-top marble table. I wondered what her name was, but it wasn't the time to ask.

"Skarlet," Kian's voice broke through the daydream. "Skarlet, turn around. Are you alright to move?"

The gentle shake he gave was barely hard enough to move my body, but the pain that radiated from his touch nearly ruined me. I swayed backward, my energy draining more by the second. I heard him, but my body didn't want to listen. Instead, I fixed my gaze more firmly on the scene in front of me.

"Who is the fierce little girl reading the story? She packs a mean punch and I." My words were cut off by the hands circling my waste. Warm breath brushed against my neck, contrasting with the cool feel of his hands. My eyes closed despite my need to hold them open, and I inhaled his scent. I tried to make sense of the way I felt now, the way I felt the first time he put his gorgeous ass in my way. How could I have been so instantly smitten? I didn't know this male. I barely knew his name, but nothing in this moment sounded better than giving in and allowing him to coddle me. I leaned slightly back, dropping my head gently against the soft leather pulling against his taut chest, unwilling to respond. He growled my name again, close enough that no one else could hear the heat behind it, but I didn't miss it.

How long had he been calling my name? I tried to think and could only recall the way his kiss felt just hours before. He was so close and what a shit time to be thinking of those lips moving in to take a bite of my exposed neck. Regaining some control over the fog infiltrating my senses, I grasped the overwhelming urge to move. Kian was right. This wasn't over and there wasn't time to spare for me to shut down right now.

I dropped my head to release the moan of frustration. Whether the frustration stemmed from my faded well-being or because of his proximity was a mystery I couldn't spare time for solving right now. Pushing forward and breaking my contact with Kian, I was struck again by the oddity of the moment. The children, the brazen fire, the calmness with which this small group of villagers were waiting for an all-clear to resume their activities was puzzling. It was as if nothing more than a freak storm had interrupted their evening.

Though it wasn't a storm, it did arrive swiftly, and had now seemingly departed with that same suddenness.

The merriment picked up and I found a place to sit, no longer wishing to depend on the green-eyed snake relentlessly trying to situate me into comfort after swaying twice into him. His hands caught me right after I leveled a glare at him to be sure he knew how fine I was. I was just fine. Capable even. Graceful all the way until I wasn't and landed in a heap on the cushion of a faded cream settee.

I lolled my head back and sucked in a laugh. Kian's lips twitched before his visage softened.

"Alright grace, what's the plan?" he asked.

Me? A plan from me, right now? I tried to lift my head, but the reward fell short of the effort. Scrambling for a cover, I chose one he saw through immediately.

"Ok, but first let me hear your plan, sir," I asked with a grin.

A sigh of tolerance softly escaped his dark lips and he began to pace slowly. The view was perfection. At the moment, I was not capable of moving my head up and down, but the left to right movement worked just fine, and I followed his form. Long legs swathed in layers of black and tucked tightly into matte black laced boots. A tunic and jacket in layers of black and deeply darkened browns left no doubt to any eye that he was lethal as he was sexy. On his pace back around, he stopped in front of me and crouched. I sighed and lifted my head to look at him.

"My plan is to move out of here swiftly. We need to go. You go back for Saf and I will organize the efforts here. We need to be on the road before dark if we hope to make it the caves before danger wakes." His eyes softened a bit when he continued. "I have mounts coming. You're exhausted and don't need to try to carry us that distance."

"What about your wings?" I asked, looking at the conspicuously bare space above his shoulders.

"Hidden so that they heal faster, and unable to fly for a while." He responded. "You took the most damage of all of us. My concern is with you being able to make it out of here."

Despite the concern in his response, I scowled and used the aches coming back in waves to distort my face at him. Kian's brows pulled together in deeper concern, and he decided to move closer.

I waited until he was inches from my face before moving.

"I'll grab the boy," I winked to him and stood, stepping back towards the settee, the movement testing the boundaries of my wrecked balance. With a blink, I left him to faceplant into the furniture, through a space that no longer contained me. I could feel his laugh follow me into the courtyard of the villa.

Safamir and the elders had made remarkable progress. The scene looked like a play of characters on a stage all pushing, pulling, grunting, and humming together to completely restore the efforts to damage the grounds and façade of the hospitable Countess. Saf approached in much higher spirits, either hiding that he feared for his life or proving his dramatics were not to be trusted. The quiet, pleasing sounds of the courtyard soothed my insides a great deal and I rolled my neck, taking a deep breath before willing tired feet into motion to greet him. Was it not years ago that I raced him to a chair for no reason in a home more perfect than a museum?

No matter how many times you fight a fight, you forget the healing power of learning from ungraceful moments and trying to mature. I would try not to play foot race games with strangers, in the home of more strangers, surrounded by mostly strangers, anymore. Fate had dealt us a hand that gripped tightly to a nonstandard form. There was no room for strangers, and we met now as allies, if not friends.

His smile and eyes told different stories when I searched him for injury. Warmth and terror, fear, a brazenly adventurous spirit, fear, and desire were written on his face. These were all emotions I had become intimately familiar with since the fall of the Mountain. I reached out my hand to him, aware of a tickle of nerves beginning to form from idleness.

He spoke and I felt a wave of heat prickling against my neck. I nodded, the fog from battle seeming to form in front of my eyes. I shook to clear the sensation and felt the rough strap of a weapons sack drop into my palm. Thin black gloves did little to protect the woven strap from pulling the open skin. I jumped at the startling weight of it.

His features softened with mischief when he suggested that I carry it for him in my magic closet.

"Come on babe, I'll toss it in on the way," I chuckled and grasped one of his full hands, we walked into the darkness, and I released the weapons bag before facing whatever lie beyond today.

XXIX

We left in a frenzy of packs and gratitude, and the entire event couldn't have unfolded faster. Within moments I settled upon the white leather saddle of a white steed of equal beauty as its mount and matte-white bit. It's hooves were covered in the work of a Northern smithie, hardened and enchanted to withstand any terrain without making a sound. This was an expensive mount even for a villa like Lady Cyneil's. It gave me hope of better days. The dash into the mountain passes will need to be deathly quiet if we were to make it through.

Packs were secured and stuffed with extra comforts, including leather canteens of creamed chocolate and wine, as though it had been just any other solstice celebration, plain and routine. I couldn't help but smile as we trotted out into the trees opposite our clandestine entrance from a few days prior. It seemed like a lifetime ago that I feared Castilen and first met Kian. Now we quietly made our way back into the cavernous mountainside to rendezvous with her and Vance with the anticipation of a friendly reunion.

Our best chance would be to coordinate on the best plan for discovering what activity at the Southern Gate was bad enough to encourage the unexpected attack of settlements far outside of its boundaries. We had headed North right out of the gate of the village and rode like the wind to the edges of occupied mountains that will lead us through to the temple.

The eastern region, full of verdant valleys and clear lakes, bordered by underground ruins with tunnels built in the first war of monks, lay as dormant reminders of how we got here. Reflecting on the second war had long seen their temples in ruin, but the routing of families into homes and camps of warring factions demanded action, with one family rising to leadership through a platform dedicated to peace and longevity of beliefs for everyone involved. The Azullons.

It's their story that brings us to today's events, I shield my eyes of the cold wind blasting them as I push my mount through frozen trails and up further into the mountain. Quietly.

Once the revolution began, it couldn't be contained, and the construction of the gates began. Magic bearers of all sects gathered under a ceasefire to provide the energy needed to create a small bridge to the plane nearest ours, an ancient place named Telseneir. Lore claimed that all the planes were once harmoniously aligned, allowing for easy travel through a great bridge dotted with time-ports and guarded by Knights. The fall of a kingdom that immense would have been well documented by scribes and scholars, yet nothing more than a children's poem had ever mentioned it. Despite this, there had been many lively debates and theories over the truth of the story and its origins and the truth of its existence was ardently believed to be true, giving rise to the idea that another such existence could be rebuilt against the wishes of the gods. Some believed bending the sanctity of magic to extremes that could be apocalyptic and stood in opposition of the movement. Despite this, the magi gathered and the spells were cast and the gate not only took form, it spread, causing little bubbles of gates to appear. In some areas the bubbles joined form, expanded and created such large gates that decades were spent exploring and fortifying them. Nothing of use was discovered across the years, and regions stopped battling over who would control the lands around each of the substantial gateways. Rangers began to take the unwanted guard contracts, and soon, growing bored, found reason to begin new expeditions into deeper areas. Some of them were lost to the things that live unknown in the dark, and some emerged the night the gates and skies opened to allow the attack of Tannira. Like a door between two bedrooms, the paths through time and space must be locked from both sides to avoid surprises. The magic, unstable from the casters engaging in combat while casting, left the door open to Tannira. The sides are wide open now and the only deference to discovering the truth of the dark side of the gate is in the form of Veill scum.

The Gentry has long been responsible for sending small teams to infiltrate weakened areas around the gates as identified by other teams of Gentry intelligence. Their arsenal of knowledge bases on the Veill infiltrating our regions grows weekly thanks to the teams settled in the default discovery division when the Gentry were founded.

Going over the details of the last hours in the silence of our ride out, I frowned in the dark. The hooves of our steeds were nailed with hardened tourmaline, the enchantments of silence and swiftness swirling in the protective crystal's grooves, and the smoky opaque cover it provided was priceless. Mountain streams lined up underground and sailed through the nooks and crannies of the steep mountainsides to our left and right, with a mossy path below that seemed to make its own breeze in spite of the tall crags and peaks above blocking the sun and wind from fully reaching the damp pathways. It settled oddly on my nerves that the Gentry's near omniscient operating standard of tracking had not landed at least a handful of scouts here to pry, if not one entirely hostile extraction team.

My eyebrows creased into another frown, the fatigue finally allowing me a stream of coherent thoughts. I focused on the establishment that should be looking for us and wondered if the threat at the southern gate was growing more fatal, drawing the elite teams of the Gentry into the fray. Agreeing to go underground until the mess of the sabotaged flier had been cleared up was a fantastic idea. I truly thought it would never work and now I worried at its sheer effectiveness. Too many times had I been injured, separated from Vance, or unable to communicate a new extraction plan, and the Gentry had always found us.

Except this time.

Which left me asking myself whether or not I wanted them to find us.

Had I been using the resources of the Gentry for several seasons now? Of course! Did I want anything more from them than that? Absolutely not. I subscribed to the creed of the OG because it was relevant to the job I must do. It kept me safe, employed, and unnoticed.

Others lived by creed because it was a way of life. The Order of the Old Gentry had members older than the settlement of Tannira if the histories were meant to be believed. Thankfully I wasn't forced into an education by the Gentry, being raised in a different world of power, I was led down a different path in adolescence and would eternally be thankful for that opportunity in education with a family who loved me. Children that were accepted into Gentry training in adolescence all exhibited extraordinary gifts. They were chosen and recruited by other children with extraordinary gifts and so much so that the acceptance into a Gentry program was only for the best, the crème de la crème, of babies who made the mistake of being born powerful. The choice was never really their own.

The Gentry halted all programs of affluence when Veill attacked. Lifting into the air for a fight no one thought would ever come but showing up late because of the necessary evacuation of hundreds of families living amongst the chartered air schools of melee and magic run by the Gentry.

Now, however, it was these families that had been driven far into the mountains and villages that were home to their extended relatives, hiding from a future that became unknown with a crack of thunder across the skies. These families were the foundation of our rebel network and the key to eradicating the threat of the Veill on the continent. It was my guess that we fought alongside refugees of the same ilk at Lady Cyneil's that were trained by the Old Gentry code.

Locating the Gentry-trained elite amongst the rubble of their leftover lives was my current plan. I had hunted hard, traveled fast, and fucked loudly for months with the Gentry's agenda a hard front for the real goal of building an army of people who didn't want to be found. An army full of exiles and veterans who were also biding their time, waiting for the right moment to strike back. My ardent hope was that the rebel flanks would be Gentry trained by proxy, each one taught one and our resurrection could not fail. Reports from leaders of scattered fronts indicated there were groups doing exactly that. They passed on their intelligence and training to others, aiming to eradicate any weakened links.

Both melee masters and mages bunkered with their families in towers, each teaching sword tricks and alchemy basics to even the most magic challenged underlings, giving anyone at any ability level a chance to fight back. They were also creating loyalty. An army that was loyal was an army that was victorious.

Finding a place for the like-minded to use their other differences as learning tools for one another established a regime of might organically, and that was where the magic happened. The links that belonged were simply the links that wanted a place at your table when it served hard, contemplated revenge.

The sun had dipped evenly in a deep purple sunset over the grassy valleys below us hours ago and the temperature was dipping now into an uncomfortable whipping cold. The chill settled uncomfortably around my fingers and I noticed the healing had almost completed its work. Not even a scar would blemish the peachy cream of my complexion when I finished. My hair had already returned to its original blend of white-blonde, cleansing the faded pink of blood splashed from the tips again. We had made excellent time, but I still mourned the loss of my portaling magic, its ability to get me somewhere instantly or out of somewhere dangerous even faster, and had I not been so damaged from the surprise onslaught I would have had us in a tavern with a hot meal hours ago. Alas, here we were.

I wondered again at how we got here and thought of our missing companions. Castilen and Vance must be traveling by horseback, too, so we wouldn't lose any time, but a mountain cavern was never my favorite place to sleep.

I pressed my lips together and let out a low and steady whistle, quickly grabbing the boys' attention. Kian didn't look my way, but his dark head dropped in a silent nod, and he pointed to a space above and to the left. The light of a single crescent moon shone on a flat space much wider than the trail, indicating a common camping spot must be nearby. A cavern in the wild that often housed travelers would display its safety validation by way of runes, markers, or messages left by prior visitors.

My favorite common camp was one I found nearly by accident while on assignment in the North. I had traveled at the behest of the prince of the wild, Dekren, to handle a matter of familial security with discretion. After delivering on the contract, I was mesmerized stepping out into freshly falling snow and immediately decided to spend the night watching the white of the snow catch the sparkle of a dark twilight. Snow was to the top edge of my boots when I turned a curve and spotted the glowing, waxy entrance. A common cave with doors that moved against the rock to seal in the heat of the fairy flame fire. Jars of additional flame lined the wall behind floating glass doors and iron shelves. I slept that night on a white fur bed that felt like a dream and bathed in a hot spring tucked away behind another waxed door.

Looking at the common cavern now in front of us, I scrunched my nose at the disparity between the luxury of that snowy evening compared to what awaited tonight's respite. The muted blues and greens of the mountain surrounding the camp drained gently away into dull beiges as the mouth of the cave sat darkly at the bottom of a steep decline.

Dismounting from the smooth seat of the cream and gold saddle was painful. My rush to get inside was suddenly dampened by the wobble in my legs. Grasping the horn to steady myself, I tried to settle the queasiness overtaking me and barely registered the warm breath on my neck. Kian's large steadying hands grasped my hips and settled my spinning dark world. As the feeling came back to my lower body, I felt washed out, nothing but fatigue registering against the thick slowing of my thoughts again.

"The air is heavy here, grace," Kian whispered. I hadn't seen him leave his mount and now he was holding me against him like a rag doll so that I didn't hit the rocky front porch of a dank common cavern. His large fingers gripped my chin to angle my head against his shoulder and before I could close my eyes to take a steadying breath, he locked his sea green eyes with mine. "I got you," he murmured.

His breath was warm against my cool neck when he lowered his eyes and stood stoically as a protector while I gathered myself. His whisper clamored loudly through my thoughts and I recognized it as both soft and demanding. For a moment I accepted the feeling of safety found in the hardness of his chest, experiencing a rare recharging energy in the movement.

The smell of magic tingled my nostrils when I took a deep inhalation, slowly releasing my breath and finding Kian's fingers to remove them from my waist. The cold was beginning to cling to my fingertips, and they startled him when I settled my hands against his. His little yelp made me smile and I released his hands to take a step away. Knowing that I had never met anyone who made me feel safe and dangerous at the same time was an accident waiting to happen. There were consequences to be suffered when a girl lost herself in a man like Kian. I couldn't afford the kind of punishment that would break my heart and diminish my cause by replacing thoughts of retribution with those unholy thoughts of sucking off a man large enough to break all of me in half.

Kian's gruff voice cut in and I sighed again at how draining the loss of my magic could be when it went so far as to dull my senses. "If there's a water spritzer or a bathing pool in there, you should have first access. I will take care of the mounts and grab your packs while you get cleaned up," he uttered.

The moment reminded me of the first cave we stayed in and how attentive he'd been to me. We were less than strangers then, having only met moments before when I went limp in his arms, my blood more poison than not.

I looked over my shoulder to see full lips pulled tight and his seafoam eyes glowing under dark, arched brows. I stopped at the lead mount and pilfered through the pack until I found a navy-blue satchel of bathing needs. I didn't look back as I walked through another waxing door with runes, its porch simpler than the first I'd experienced, and into an enormous cavern with rooms divided off a long rocky hallway by boulders carved into willow trees. Beveled amethyst, citrine, and pink ice crystals sparkled in all hues of their relevant colors, creating a painted glass garden of blooming roses, irises, dahlias, and wildflowers.

I was so startled by the disparity in the porch and the opulent layout greeting me that I nearly missed the six steps descending from the waxing door down onto a waiting oversized rug in verdant shades. The memory of tumbling onto Kian in a cumulative display of every ungraceful moment I've ever suffered at once flitted through my thoughts. There was no first impression like it out there. I couldn't keep making a stumbling fool of myself like that, but the surprises just kept coming.

Training had never failed me in tough times before and I didn't expect it to now, but I had been unable to keep my thoughts straight and ordered for hours. Resting would help, but resting without the blood of Veiliri under my nails would only help more. There were no signs or clerks like you would find in an inn, but the direction of the wall only continued one way. The carpet narrowed and continued past the doors and wrapped to the right and left before coming to a stop in front of a much larger door.

The scent of so many people lingered and it was hard to tell right away if the space was being occupied by anyone else tonight. I checked each of the six rudimentary doors that lined the rough hallway and each pushed open easily, and to my relief, all were empty.

My hair brushed my ears as it fell back out and away from my face when I exhaled. It' had been a long ass day and I wanted an equally long bath. The thought of the heat unwinding my tense and sore muscles after today was more than I could handle. A small groan escaped at the luxury of the thought.

The carpet led me to openings on the left and right of the hallway, each with a staircase leading up. A marking on the wall identified both as the cave's common hall. My mouth watered at the thought of a warm meal.

There was only one door left to open and it sat before me like a sentinel over the others. Sharp edges pushed into the low point of the cave roof where the door came flush with its edges, and no light escaped below the seam at the bottom. The size of the handle dwarfed my fingers as they wrapped around its brass shining against the dark swirling engravings of trees and dancing grasses under a moonless night. How strange to have such a monumentally pretty common cave tucked away on a long non-descript road out of the city no one visited anymore. Most of the work was hand hewn, meaning hours and hours were spent in the details here. Someone appreciated its remoteness enough to hide a small treasure here of their own design. I couldn't help but thank them for it when I opened the doors and hot steam hit my face.

Stone steps had been sunk into the middle of the room and opened wide, welcoming me into a steaming, swirling blue pool. It was meant to be a bath, but it was large enough for several people to soak at once. The pool's water was so clear it reflected the white painted cave walls lining the rear, cut into images of steel cloud across the water.

I jerked my head up when I caught movement in the reflection of the painted wall. I couldn't help another weak smile. There were spouts carved out of the stones where water rolled down the mountains. Normally pooled into underground lakes and used as a resource for locals, the water was the most delicious and cleanest you could get. The spouts gurgled slightly and there was a steady hum that I noticed now. I closed my eyes and breathed the heat in before finding a bench located off the smooth path circling the pool. The bathing bag wasn't heavy, but when I opened it to find it full of unscented oils and crushed petal soaps, I knew who packed it right away.

XXX

Lady Cyneil. I worried often about her during our ride here. A resourceful woman, I don't doubt she was uninjured, but I didn't think she would have been in a place good enough to manage this for me. It was more touching than I wanted to admit. It was more than I wanted to feel.

Lady C reminded me too closely of another strong, beautiful Lady; one that gave me everything and then left me. I would give anything to have her back with me telling me what to do and giving advice that I won't take. I missed the comfort of having the option to feel safe in someone else's decisions. Thinking of safety made me think of our small crew and the green-eyed stranger who kept intruding on my thoughts.

Pushing all thoughts of Kian away, I selected soap petals for my hair and an unscented lather for my body. The benches were tucked in against the wall with hooks hanging there and outside of the spritzer doors. I didn't want to walk barefoot across the rocks until I could check for injuries my boots may be hiding. I angled to the back right corner to a spritzer stall that turned slightly around a corner, making the whole area dark, steamy, and lit with fires around the floor that would warm the space entirely once a shower started. A small bench curved inside the right edge against the face of the mountain's interior. Its seat is white like the painted walls, the only bright décor in the space. I sat on the edge and leaned against the wall to pull off my gear. There was a warmth to the rocks where the hot streams ran behind the facades and were directed through channels to provide for travelers and settlers alike.

I undressed and determined the extent of my injuries from hours before that hadn't been discernible until this point. However, what still hurt had begun to heal, though much slower than normal. I reached for the spout and moved the few rocks around to get the water to flow in fast and hot. I needed it to be steaming hot. I needed it to burn and wash off all that today had taken from me. I needed it to wash off the fear still coating my skin, so I moved a few stones into the cold spout, blocking it, and the steam rewarded me instantly.

The soap petals shimmered and blushed as they hit the water, dissolving into my palm. I ran the silky shampoo through my hair and inhaled deeply. The smell reminded me of the garden lunch we shared at the Villa and I wondered if they were made from the roses growing there. It felt like a lifetime ago and smelled like walking into a memory.

The waters were waking me and tension was rolling with the steam from my shoulders. I opened the unscented lather and it smelled of nothingness. I was in a cave in the middle of nowhere, on the run from ghosts, and traveling with the puzzle of mercenaries, but I would not spend my night smelling like a dull hopeless void while I recovered. I put the bottle back on the shelf with a little more disdain than I intended, its pouch deflating a bit upon impact with the rocks.

Time was distorted and it made it difficult for me to keep up. Struggling to keep the timelines in order made it feel like this week had lasted for months, and that it had changed everything, though I had no idea what actually had changed. Being so far removed from any outside intel was beginning to make me jumpy. Well, it was adding to the jumpiness.

To think about it rationally would be to admit that I was in over my head. I was on the run from an organization I was intimate with and who may be trying to kill me, while being hunted by a party that I didn't understand who definitely wanted to kill me. I needed to meet back up with Vance as quickly as possible.

My power was as volatile now as the night it was amplified, changing my course forever to one I wasn't ready for. My only safety depended on two males that I didn't know but must trust to survive and possibly build my cause without catching the notice of the Gentry in all the wrong ways; ways that would have me executed for treason.

My stomach growled taking me away from thoughts of the Gentry and reminding me of how long the day had been. I turned around inside the stall and realized that I left my clothes in the bag with the other shower supplies, but I heard no one come in, and the dry benches were just around the corner.

I covered my tits with one arm just in case, and made a run around the soaking pool with all my greatness on display. I snatched my bag and clothes and spun back toward my stall, barely making it back into the water when a deep voice dipped softly through the chambers. Bumps erupted along my neck when I heard Kian call my name.

The dim lighting set the ambiance for a relaxing evening and the secluded overhangs extended the coverage of the waxing doors along the rock face, but his form filled the frame of the stall. The stream of steaming water felt cool against the heat blooming in my center. Was it magic or lust? A spell he cast? I couldn't deny the pull Kian has had on me from the moment we met. What would that have meant if there had not been a rogue attack on the Villa? Would I have gone so far as to screw him without knowing him?

I scoffed and it vibrated around the cavernous bath. Of course, I would. It was the dance I learned out of necessity for keeping my unexpected gift of magic under control, and even after training with the Gentry for months, I still relied on it.

None of that mattered when Kian's gaze searched mine across the distorting film of the doors, lighting flames of red dancing desire against the cool blue heat of my power. The magic swelled, filling the tiniest bits of me with heat, and it was still not enough to compare with this headiness.

"Tell me your joke. I want to laugh, too," Kian grinned at me over the water.

"The joke is you, sir," I replied.

His eyes flashed, but his smile grew. "Come eat when you're done. Saf is putting out a meal upstairs."

He didn't give any further details, but he also didn't turn to leave immediately, so I turned to face him and his smile changed into something dangerous at the curves I displayed. I stood there with water and soap the only things between the two of us until he abruptly dropped his eyes and walked away with his hands in pockets and eyes down. I imagined him walking right into the bath and the little laugh that escaped had him shaking his head without bothering to look back and see if I was watching him walk away, laughing at him.

The throb he left behind nearly took me out. I could not let myself get wrapped up in this boy or any part of him. The timing couldn't possibly be worse.

Yet...

I stepped away from the water with a sigh and resigned myself to dressing in clean leathers before supper. The shower did the work of the gods and the meal Safamir prepared was a delightful distraction from green eyes and dark attacks. The hearth blasted warmth into the room and chased away the cold winds creeping in through the cracks.

Kian's low snores drifted across the room and I leaned against the wall, opting to take my respite in the central main room with him and Safamir. While Kian rested, his shaman stared awkwardly at me across the room.

We were instant allies in battle, but barely acquaintances in times of peace. People who learned to live in the chaotic times of war often had a difficult time associating with the outside world in times of peace. Camaraderie, adrenaline, and purpose were not things that could be replicated in the same way at home. All the things that made life worth the effort existed within the destruction of war. They exist outside of it, too, but it was often a long damn time since anyone had time to practice their social manners.

A city-state held under the rule of a malevolent hand would never prosper. Holding battle grudges in your heart will turn you sour. Forgive others so that you may tear down obstacles rather than one another. This was all good advice I would give an apprentice, yet I loathed to take it to heart myself.

I sighed and met Safamir's eye.

"I've never met a shaman before. I've seen your kind in battle though, the control of your powers is phenomenal. Is your magic elemental?" I asked nonchalantly. It was already awkward in this room.

He tilted his head in acquiescence. "Indeed. I am an elemental shaman. I can channel and control the magic of the elements. You saw my fire totem. I can also summon a totem that shoots rocks as projectiles, and ones that shock those that come within a few feet of it."

"Is that at all?" I asked.

"Not at all. There is ice with water magic and more moon power than I could list. What about you, Skarlet? How did you take out half an aerial squad in a single blast?" he inquired.

I grinned at him, determined to keep my secrets my own without needlessly making an enemy where there wasn't one before. There was no need to appear pretentious. People don't like it when one kept secrets they couldn't manipulate; it had a way of making people feel powerless.

He waited patiently, rolling a blue rock from the front of the fireplace across his fingers.

"My powers are old ones, though I am not as old as they. Some of them were gifted to me the night Veil attacked, some I was born with. I burn hot all the time because my magic is a flame that devours anything in its path. Sometimes I have to really put in work to control that part, but not when I can expel the excessive energy in a fight. It's why I stayed and trained with The Old Order of the Gentry after Abruzi fell," I explained.

"You weren't a child candidate?" he asked incredulously.

"Absolutely not. My family would never," I scoffed.

"Where is your family now?" he asked. I instantly felt the old sting of grief overtake me. I recognized the flash of pain that darkened his eyes. Safamir has lost someone, too. Maybe a few someones. Still, boundaries existed even among new friends and I wasn't ready to talk about this.

I tilted my head and Saf straightened up at my admission. "Not here. And don't expect anyone to come looking for me. I'm alone now." I allowed that truth to settle over me in the heavy silence of the room. Timbers crackling in the fireplace were the only sound in the room.

I often think about the time that's passed since I left the Gentry's aerial base. It wasn't a lot, but it seemed that life had irrevocably changed. Yet, I didn't know anything about where my companions traveled from. It wasn't a question we asked one another often, since Abruzi fell we all belonged to one mission, one goal. Where you started at before this no longer mattered. All that mattered was where we were all going.

This wasn't like any other assignment I have ever been on before, though. I've never been separated from Vance this long while on mission and I wouldn't be able to find the rogue if he didn't want to be found. I was stuck with strangers and operating with the blind trust afforded to friends in times of peace. I decided to act against my own better judgment and ask him a question that had been on my mind. "What about you, Saf? You have someone to go home to? Is it difficult for you to get back to them since the attacks?"

I grabbed the corner of my blanket and wrapped it around my shoulders. I considered pulling an extra pillow out of the void but decided that one is plenty. I was still very tired. My eyes watered and I fought off a yawn. That would be rude to do while Safamir's telling me his story. Except he hadn't acted like he heard me. The room had grown silent and there was a chill settling over the previously warm cavern. My arms pimpled with warning.

I wrapped a hand around a small chelcei dagger and sat up, turning toward Kian and nearly took my skull off with a low hanging rock shelf. My eyes lock with Safamir's and then Kian's. A warning was held there. The light burned bright to his side, the hard edges of his mouth set against the question in the shaman's own.

I put my dagger silently back into its scabbard with a scratch against the rock. The bubble of danger popped and the room went warm again.

"I apologize, boys. It was rude of me to ask. So many have lost so much. Stolen by the Veill. It's easy to forget we don't know each other very well, sharing a common trauma can make for fast intimacy," I croaked.

"It's not that, Skar, you were right to ask. I asked first. It's just not the place for our story. We have a long ride ahead of us tomorrow. We should say goodnight and focus on making it to Castilen and Vance. She should have information that will determine our next steps. The temple is a sanctified location, so we should be safe from any attacks there. We will figure this out. Goodnight," Saf said.

One glance at Kian's blank face assured me that this conversation is over. It never really got started, but there would be hours of slow riding through and over the peaks into druid lands. Most races stuck together, but the druids had built a city of stunning allure, enchanted its lands, and invited all to come and find worship in nature alongside them. Strong magic prevented those people from fighting one another on their land, ensuring a blanket of peace remained in a cold war forgotten by peace in all of her other corners.

"Goodnight," I responded. I knew I should feel bad for leading the conversation in that direction, but I just couldn't find the space to hold onto any real remorse. I fell asleep with something tickling my memory, but I lost it to the grasp of slumber and thought of it no more.

But the morning always came.

XXXI

The morning arrived quickly, sweeping away the unpleasant memories of the night from our minds. It breathes fresh air into the room, causing the stale awkwardness to flutter away with the soft breeze that flowed through the open balconies.

I dressed in an extra layer under buttery soft riding leathers. The morning's respite was interrupted briefly by the message relayed by Vance on the wing of Jeweled Beak Berserker. I snatched the message from the huge, annoyed bird before it could land. Either Vance was just fine and had time for jokes or he could be sending a warning. I didn't have the patience for not knowing.

The message was simple, stating that their route had been compromised, and they would go under with the rogue. The temple was still the end-goal. We should expect no contact until rendezvous.

It was standard Gentry protocol when a mission went under, but we haven't been on Gentry protocol since the flyer went down. Not really.

Why now?

What changed to make Vance alter plans that he knew would be harder for me to find safety. Had his safety been compromised? If the Veill have infiltrated the Gentry as had long been feared, who would they be after first? The officers of the Gent would be the obvious answer. What would the old ones want with destroying everything they've built for an alliance with Veill that would leave them bleeding out from the knives in their backs in years to come? What was the long play?

Or maybe Vance was just being himself. Hovering over me like a puppy when all I wanted was a dog in the fight, a loyal warrior.

The note promptly crumpled itself into a tiny marble and exploded before I could think more of it. Nothing more than silence would come from the other three now, though if I'm being honest, I was surprised that Marli was still in group with the other two. Vance, Castilen, and Marli would take to the shadows and wouldn't be seen until they were ready to be found.

Apparently at the temple of Samora.

I considered our options and decided I'd rather take the mellow miles road passage around and into the druid capital and regroup there. The temple was a short northern ride across the southern boundaries of Prince Dekren's court from the city center. I proposed the plan to my companions and no cry against it arose. So, in an awkwardly returned strained silence, we packed up and rode for the clouded bridges granting entrance to the last friendly pass before the Druid capital.

The common cave was the last bastion of respite before entering through the yawning rock face painted in color of grays and blues and stacked level with the white peaks of the mountain. No chelcei crystals formed here, but light bounced about opaquely from crystal formations that caught the rays from their hiding spaces between mammoth boulders and worn path stones. The roof was open though conclave. The remnants of a stained-glass tunnel that ran the length of the eastern entry to samora. The Veil's attack destroyed anything that resembled the art of those who would not kneel to them. At the end of this climb, we would have to change directions and travel back down to connect with the remainder of the road that would take us into the valleys. The connecting bridges were destroyed though the terrain was still safe to travel.

Safamir took to his saddle and we fell in line behind him. Cool winds blew from behind and whipped about, floating dead leaves in a macabre dance about our party. Smooth white arches marked the entry onto the Drendals, a series of mountain paths, bridges, rock faced taverns, and valleys filled with Dunelin Wraiths.

The wraiths weren't worrisome, as long as you don't get close to the edge of a sky-pit... that bony white ruins they frequent.

They throw the bodies down the sky pits, but they weren't killers in life.

The story was that they haunted the temples where they were once revered for their knowledge and beauty. Heroes traveled all the worlds to search for them and beg to compete for their love. The belladonnas living there would discourage their pursuers to the one, knowing that their death would be tied. All but one failed and he was the heart who won priestess of the unknown lands. She allowed herself to be chosen, laid bare and prepared to share all of her worlds' secrets and wealth with her partner: the first transference of such a power since the beginning of the world. With her arms lifted above her head, small pink buds pushed through virgin white linen. He leaned in for their first kiss, the kiss of true love, and as he cradled her tear-stricken face, a blade slid silently into his lover's throat. The priestesses reacted as quickly as they could, calling home their warriors and taking up arms against the invaders. The fight was over before it began. Each priestess that chose to live in the tower chose that life with their partner. Each connected in irreversible ways. When the priestesses were murdered, their lover's hearts shriveled and died. There was a large underground labyrinth of untold wealth and knowledge buried on the other side of the angry, envious wraith-hold now. In several hundred years, words still have not been discovered to put the ladies to rest, and traveling through their homes, even with benevolent intent, just doesn't sit right with me.

Someday, when the power of the moon was strong and bright in the sky again, I would return. I vowed to learn the story of every love here and promised to give it new life amongst the eternity of the stars someday.

For the morning ahead of me, I had to stay focused on the beauty of the terrain. That is where most of the trouble lie. The boys would watch for bandits shoved into tiny crevices or dragons patrolling paths covered by rock ceiling, but I would be the one checking the obvious places for trouble.

The wraiths weren't harmful unless you enter a nest, and traditionally their nests didn't move from the tumbled turrets of their temple homes. It was the Limlits and Potes that would cause your horse to falter, or a rider to step right off an edge to get some space, ultimately finding more than space at the bottom of a long rocky drop.

The Limlits, also known as potes, were sticky little bastards that took the form of anything they touched, conforming to match it exactly, with a sticky secretion that could hold a surprised traveler hostage with the tacky arm of a broomstick, using the bristles to tease its captor. S

Any other number of pixie-type could have made home of these mountains since the route. Their homes had been bulldozed and razed like a lot of smaller townships, pushing them further into environments where they were seen as harmful nuisances, being run off to cause mischief in the trees and valleys. The druids kept most of the bitey ones on the side of the valley closest to the water.

A weed grew along the rocky white outcroppings that smelled like cake baking against the waters, but could kill you in a bite. The naturalist sprites used the weed to draw in beachgoers by offering them bites, then devoured their bodies over days with no one able to smell the rotting corpse over the terrible sweetness of the Tonks weed.

My daydreaming took me to lands far beyond the ones my eyes could see, where Blue Mountain and her halls held true. Fields of blue indigo flowers that reflected in perfect pools tucked into the valley where I hid, where a voice still called for me.

It wanted me to return, though I couldn't. Not yet. I shook the melancholy of days past for a study in the beauty passing me by now. White arches continued to climb up and across the trails we took despite the steep incline. Loose leaves hung tightly to trellises that ran up to meet the ceiling, dripping small vines of the memory of grand plants where they filled in cracks and open space when the paths were tended regularly.

The trails remained narrow enough to keep two horses from riding abroad for miles into the mountains. Safamir rode in the front, his elementals darting about like shadow creatures and reporting back to him on what the turns may have in surprise for us. Behind me rides Kian. Silent, gorgeous Kian whom I knew nothing about. I was spending my time studying the two, determining which to make my appeal to. I wanted to know what they knew. During our time together, it had been more than mentioned that there was a plan, and those in charge of the plan were doing no more than mentioning its existence to me.

This clawing sensation had taken hold since we mounted this morning and I had tried to give it time to be something I feared, not a thing that was actively happening, but I couldn't deny it anymore. Something was draining my magic. No one should even know how. What I told Saf about my power was true, but not the whole truth. The goddesses of the double moons was family to me, and a lunar power burns in me always. Until now. I was being drained and I couldn't place the source to stop it.

If the clouds would clear from my thoughts, I would have pieced it together by now. I've always been quick to come out of a magical stupor, but this time was different. This had taken hold in places I couldn't get to. Places I needed to be in control of for my plans and my magic to work. They were co-dependent and something felt like it had attacked both.

Nothing, other than me, had ever drained my magic so far that my thoughts are affected, and even then, they return, loudly and normally correct.

I reached through a muddled recall of events and tried to think of the last time I felt full with my power. I haven't had a clear thought since the Shaman.

I looked back and aught Kian's eyes on my retreating form. Looking forward, I could see Safamir slant his eyes past me to hold Kian with its meaning. Maybe the conversation I needed to have was one they were bouncing out of their saddles to have with me.

The white stone of the mountain began to change to a smokehouse gray and tall blue spruce trees lined the trail where it sloped into a connecting fence and gate opening to the merchant trail. The path widened across a golden swaying valley. The city of Druids stood as the only neutral stronghold on this side of the continent. The Northern province was the only other to have retained its beauty and culture as thoroughly as the City of Sirione. Kian and Safamir rode to take a place on either side of me before the dust turned to gravel, and for a moment we were speechless, each lost to a time when this was just another ride amongst companions into town for some fun at a tavern. It's a memory, a moment, that felt like it could belong to anyone on any timeline.

This ride was over now though and it was real. The feeling of loss slammed into me and I stumbled in guiding the white beauty that's gotten me here. She shone with the sweat of the ride but corrected my error and pranced ahead of the boys as though she had just been pulled from the yard.

We waited at the gate to catch a breath before opening it up across the fields. With little coverage we will have to ride hard to avoid any aerial advances. I leaned in to check my packs and a blast of freezing ice grasped winds rushed me.

The rocks rumbled and in the distance a lone black figure landed on the top of the temple of the wraiths. A second priestess joined the first in another gush of air, but neither approached us.

Through the distance I could feel a slight chill sink into my body, catching hold of my bones and shrinking, freezing them so that any touch would shatter me. I reached for my heat and found it lacking. I looked up in time to catch the chelcei pommel Kian tossed me. One look at Saf told me that he would be no help. His aura was blue, the freeze radiating from him; he was closer to broken death than I was.

I squeezed the chelcei and called on the innate powers I possessed, but it felt like the limit of my magic was near. The crystal warmed from the inside, touching the heart of power. My arm trembled and barely aimed toward the winged figure dozens of feet away. I shot and dropped the stone to cover my ears when the wraiths began to scream at the loss of their temple and the memories stored there. It bought us enough time to get into open fields where they won't follow.

I leaned in to charge the valley, but Kian already had us rounded up and was whipping the horses into a frenzy across the gate. Safamir's horse followed in blind terror. My girl didn't have to be dragged; she knew it was time to get the hell out of there. I think I may try to keep this one.

"What was that!?" I yelled, but the wind ripped the words away.

I leaned into the white beast and couldn't remember its name. I was head-to-head with my companions in seconds. It only took a few more seconds to see what was on the temple ruins since it was following us high above with wings like a Veiliri, but with a body like a man, like Vance with his large wings and enormous body.

"Vance?" I called loudly, confusion and hope marring the strength meant to project it upwards.

"Veill, but kin to your Skye Knight," Kian announced. He was suddenly in my ear from across the swaying valley grasses separating us.

Too much was happening at once. Kian was in my head and Vance's twin was trying to kill me. I didn't even know he had people outside of his world. Fuck! I was a terrible friend and it's never bit me like right now.

"Where's it from?" I asked.

"His homeland is the same as Vance's," Kian declared.

I could almost detect a grin in the message. What a bastard. He knew I didn't know and was delighting in my terror.

"I'm not enjoying your fear, Skarlet, but you make riding look like a sport. It drew my attention to you. I didn't mean to intrude," Kian continued, even though I didn't trust his word. He seemed like the kind of guy who would love nothing more than to intrude some other time.

I cut my eyes toward him and pushed my mount to a faster pace. I felt for the crystal he was using to get into my head. Stupid communicators used between paired partners to avoid detection. I had one for Vance that was lost in the crash over the mountain.

"Shit. SHIT!!!!!" I screamed internally.

Kian whipped his mount to come up beside me immediately. His eyes met mine with expectations. "No way you heard that!" I yelled.

His answering look drew my face up in time to see two wraiths and an enormous, winged beast beating amongst the clouds tracking us.

"I was wrong, Kian. Very, very wrong," I answered him, still staring at the sky.

Kian looked up silently. Two wraiths? They've tended their temple since death, never to leave the confines of the rocky, hallowed ground. But there are two barreling toward us on the heel of the winged beast. I shook to focus my thoughts and slowed my mount, allowing a plan to come to me.

The wraiths were coming after the beast, and we were twenty yards from the gates of Sirione. We needed a distraction to bring them close enough to have the archers drop them when we cleared the valley. We needed to stay alive long enough to get them there.

I slowed my borrowed girl down more and gave her whispered instructions. She hesitated for a moment, and I wondered if my hunch about our connection was wrong.

It was not, and as soon as I was off my mount and grabbed the back of Kian's for a ride in, she was off, shining brightly and drawing the attention of our pursuers in a circle for a brief moment. We took off for the gates in that small window. We no sooner had the chance to pull our mounts in the small space before the torso of a man the size of a wyvern stopped mid-air, staring straight into the face of Kian and I. Arrows and magic were aimed at him, dancing lights across his bare skin.

He looked toward the city and nodded, then shot straight into the sky, leaving scratches two inches deep in the stone where he gave a warning swipe on his way out back to the hells he came from.

XXXII

Sweat was still assaulting my eyes and dampening my undertank when the Prince of the Sirione himself greeted us by walking straight out of a poof of blue smoke. It was a beautiful blue like a cerulean lake before the water was broken under the dew drops and the sunrise. His clothes were all dyed to match. His eyes though were golden and bright in the darkness of the last few moments. He looked at us as though he didn't need the amber orbs to see us truly. His assessment lasted but a moment past awkward and I was ready to go back out with the wraiths by the time he spoke.

"You two bastards did THE thing I said to not do. THE thing. And now, here we are," he sighed. "Welcome, I guess."

Honestly, I was not sure if I was one of the bastards or if he was just mad at the boys. I was ready and willing to blame all of this on them if his druidness would let me in for a nice bath, though.

I waited with less patience than I should, but not rudely insistent. Poor manners would never be a good look. He snapped magic into the globes guarding either side of an ornamental door. The perfectly matched sconces lit before we came under them as we were guided down a long narrow, covered walkway. The boots echoing above us confirmed that we were being led into the city in a covered tunnel with the city visible through slotted openings.

I had traveled hastily through Sirione in the dark of night before and seen images of their Master Druid, even met some of his court before on Gentry business, but nothing compared me to the sounds of the city floating down from the streets above us.

Offers of goods could be heard being listed to passersby among the ding of chapel bells ringing in lofts all across the city. The city hums more quietly than others, its residents mindfully tending their needs with spirits tempered in consideration for the practice of druidism throughout the hallowed streets.

Padded feet scuffled across in tune to murmurings to the sun, the gods, even the bounty of the harvest by those dedicated to praying for the hope of a kind future. Carts ran on a system of magic that whirred them quietly on systems of unseen rails. Not even the clomp of hooves could be heard this far from the gates.

I hoped they had my horse, not that we could hear her if she were prancing straight above us with her enchanted horsheing. I'd seen her wait until the winged hellions were properly secured before returning to the guard house gate. From there I hadn't seen her. I would have to assume she is stabled alongside our other two mounts, as they were removed for handling once the man-beast had taken flight. We were told that the way was too narrow for us to ride in on horseback like a normal, courteous reception would have granted us. I doubt that's true based on the cold reception we've gotten so far. I glance ahead at the stormy stance of the druid. We've definitely pissed our new ally off, still not sure why. I was sure, however, that the handsome rats I've been traveling with will be giving me an explanation. Even I have to beat it out of them.

The constant fear of betrayal I carry with me is draining. I don't know what they are actually behind and what they are innocent of. They haven't been exactly forthcoming, and I have lazily adopted too many of Gentry's contradictions, it seems. Allowing people that I serve missions with personal space on a home we all share could be different than the space I've been allowing Kian and Safamir, assuming their stories were as sad and tiring as mine, and that they didn't want to share. Perhaps I was wrong to go all in on instinct alone with these guys.

I tended to live by the philosophy that you will never increase your own happiness by bothering with someone else's. I don't make friends easily and that works in my favor. It's easier to become a ghost in the field when no one is looking for you on a Friday night. This philosophy may have led me dangerously astray this time. My intellectual disadvantage is an uncomfortable one. Despite the time we've spent in the company of one another over the last days, I know so little about any of them in my party.

And as well as I worked with Vance, I couldn't say I knew him much better than I knew the others. It's an understated naivete born from the desire for things to be safe again; normal and youthful. None of those things were true any longer. We know people the best way we can, and my effort was largely lacking.

Maybe I just didn't care, which was an even bigger disadvantage than ignorance.

The advantage was in the hands of everyone in this tunnel that held tight to truths and facts that had been kept from me. Kian and Safamir knew more about me than they should. They knew a lot about a lot of things that shouldn't be common knowledge and I've let myself be distracted from that. I needed to know what they knew, and why they cared enough to have traveled all this way with me to retain that knowledge.

Thoughts of Kian's voice in my head drew my thinking to him in a different way. I started to push him out of my mind and focus on putting together the puzzle in front of me. It felt different this time, and I let myself explore the memory. His voice felt like it sounded, warm and a little dangerous whenever he spoke to me.

The problem? I didn't have a common transmitter crystal, and If Vance said our communicators were broken, Kian shouldn't have access to me so easily, despite his magical typing.

That's what's been trying to push through the fog. This knowledge about crystals, communications, and protocols, especially when on mission.

It suddenly hit me.

Our flyer went down and we still don't know who was responsible for that, but it took out everything on the way out. The explosion was enough to render the night sky sunrise red for several long moments. I haven't had anything other than verbal communication with Vance since then. He couldn't have tracked me to deliver a message. With the cloaking saddles and protections from Safamir, no one should have been able to precisely track us.

The timing was inconceivably convenient.

It was perfect. Too perfect.

We came to a stop in front of another ornamental door, this one with natural light shining through its bars. I cleared my throat and cleared my thoughts of the message's logistics. With a smile at the druid, I asked politely. "My apologies, sir, but I don't think I've caught your name."

The sunlight and splendor reflected onto the druid's face from the courtyard welcoming us to Sirione from the other side of the tunnel. "Caben, Master Druid of the First Light. Too busy to be coming down here to rescue this trash from a Veil scum they've dragged to my front door, but here we are. Wasting my time."

Kian's laugh mingled with Safamir's long-suffering sigh. Before I could throw the correct amount of side eye at this, Kian pulled me to his side and guided me through open paths of blooming dahlias and peonies toward the closest building.

I scrambled to keep my balance while being dragged toward a white brick arched entryway with dark wooden doors suspend from them. I tried to compare the shapes and movements of the city in the sunlight to the bulky skyline I'd spied from the darkened road as I'd traveled by it in the night.

The smells were the same, with most of the city being focused on creating and perfecting magic, most mages chose to buy their supplies from caravans rather than depend on local gardens for them.

Caben opened the doors and dismissed the guards and a few scholars studying at one of the massive desks in the center of the room. Bookshelves lined with scrolls and text arched like a hug around the entire room. Once the doors slammed behind us, Caben spun, his blue robes creating an illusion of stormy days. His eyes were equally stormy when he took in Kian to my right and Saf slightly behind him.

"Really, I'm the shield? I'm your secret weapon against the tiny fury of the druid prince?" Both move to either side, dwarfing me between them.

"Children. Both of you," I sighed.

A smile slowly appeared across Caben's face, revealing a grand, handsome look. "You make my job harder than it has to be, old friend." He looked at Kian and I knew I was right about their connection and that they had to be close as Kian's grin lit up the whole room and his cheeks dimpled slightly.

"Old friend, thank you for accepting us without notice. We were unable to communicate our location and did not expect to be chased into your protection by your little pets," Kian chuckled. The accusation hung in the air, everyone afraid to breathe it in.

The druid shrank in front of Kian's stoic stance before straightening. The room let a collective breath. "My churlish friend, you try to scare me for answers, but it won't work. I don't have any for you, therefore I cannot be cowered even by the gaze of the ocean herself." He straightened taller before continuing. "In fact, I have made many warnings to you, specifically you, about the kind of company you attract and what I will allow in my city. Now, I must allow wraiths in my city because you have destroyed their home."

Kian tried not to smile when he answered. "They make a nice chorus, you're welcome. What about the winged one? Was he not a handsome gift?"

It was Safamir that broke the slight tension. "Kian, we didn't come for this. Caben knows we didn't bring a winged Veiliri Shaman to his front door on purpose. And I think he can help."

"Nuisances, all." Caben sighed again and I wasn't sure if he meant Shamans or Veiliri.

I didn't know the story here, but I really hoped I could get out of this city when they were done with this pissing contest. I also didn't know the Veil had Shamans with that much power. I had met two in less than that many days. I couldn't say I'm a big fan.

"Of course, you didn't set an attack on my city, with just one Veiliri, but one cannot be too careful in such a place of splendor. Can you agree?" Caben loosened his shoulders and grasped Kian around the wrist to pull him close. When they released one another, the druid asked how he could help.

I spoke up first. "Do you have a map room? And do you have my horse?"

Three heads turned toward me with blank expressions, but I barreled on.

"Honestly, Caben, you seem to have a wonderfully stylized version of friendship with these two that I really want to stay and experience, but I must leave you all here. My timeline has shifted with newly received information." It sounded weak, but I stuck with it.

"New information, grace?" Kian asked quietly. His expression was now soft and curious, but his eyes were not. He raised an eyebrow and finished. "You would be breaking protocol to leave on your own now."

I responded, "Sir, I am not on your protocol. I'm barely on The Gentry's. You may try and stop me, but you would only be pushing my agenda further."

"Skarlet," Kian's face was all concern now. He grasped my elbow and pulled me closer to him.

"Don't speak to me like we are friends. You have been lying to me." I accused him in an attempt to free myself. I didn't know what he was lying about, but the flush in his face told me I was right to listen to instinct. I reached for my magic just in case and got nothing but a throbbing headache in return. I took a step back, still held close by Kian, and grasped at my pommel. My magic wasn't responding and the Chelcei should help,

He let me go and lifted his hands slowly away from my body. "I have been lying to you Skarlet, but you won't get the truth from me until I have Castilen back."

I felt the shock down to my toes. "Have her back? From whom?" I asked the question to the room, not expecting an honest answer.

The air in the chapel stilled suddenly, a current electrified my skin, boiling my blood and locking me in place for several seconds before freeing me abruptly. I wasn't sure what happened until the slide of steel against its scabbard drew my attention away from Kian. Caben held Safamir at the tip of his sword. Saf had him surrounded by a blue current of electric power. Blue current like the color he was glowing when hit by the beast in the valley. The same blue emitted by the portal in the courtyard. The same blue that floated across my dreams when I dozed off now. The same blue of the portal and the foggy light that shone from Kian's sword when he drove it home. I looked to the men that had led me to this moment and everything fell together. I hadn't been driven to these two by happenstance, someone led us there and everything since that moment had been based on a lie.

"You!" I pointed at Safamir.

"What villain have you brought to this court, my friend?" Caben was enraged and staring directly at me, his arm wrapped around Safamir to hold him in place. He looked between the three of us.

"Caben, brother, the girl is out her depth. She doesn't know the story. I need you to listen to what I'm saying to you and this will all clear itself up," Safamir addressed the panicked druid but he ignored his pleas. The temple shook with the force of the peaceful magic straining to keep the men separated. The city of peace was fighting for her title against a magic more powerful than even she was accustomed.

Caben slammed the flat of his sword against a wavering blue streak cast from Safamir and the charge traveled up his arm, burgeoning veins and muscles. He tried to retain his grasp on the Shaman but the pulse of the current drove him to drop to his knees.

Kian's attention was drawn toward the madness for only a second, but I saw the moment he realized I'd figured it out.

"I guess bringing a sword to a magic fight makes sense if you know that your opponent can drain magic! You're not as stupid as you look in all that hot metal after all, sir!" I screeched.

"Skarlet!" Kian reached for me, but I'd spotted the stables and he would never catch me before I could call my mare to me. I jumped the ledge of a tall living fence and came up in a roll. I didn't bother slowing the momentum before rolling up leaping onto the saddle. I won't doubt this connection again. Less than a day together, and I know she's the one.

The gravel flew behind us as she tore out of the center of the city away from the gate we came through, back out the opposite side. I leaned into the ride, white hair flying up, mixing with my own as the wind carried us over the cobblestone paths in the city. The rear gate loomed over us, our approach maybe a little too fast for them to open it.

I swung my head around to check for pursuers.

Kian. He rode like the hounds of Veill were on his heels. His stare was aimed straight at me.

I couldn't use my magic, not after the shaman had been siphoning me of it since we met. Kian had to know since Saf was his.

Why did I trust Kian over everything? It felt right until it didn't. Now he was chasing me out of a city of flowering beauty older than the Gentry gardens, and I could not stop. I felt a small push against my consciousness and knew Kian was reaching for my thoughts to speak to me. I focused all of my mental strength on the feeling and pushed against it. It felt like the sting of a rubber band snapping when it broke.

I tried to reach Vance, though I had no idea if he had a transmitter. I did not, but that didn't keep me from throwing a prayer to the goddesses for him to hear me. I needed him to be there at the temple. I needed him to have my back. Something I have taken for granted for too long.

I didn't hear anything, but I knew Vance heard me call for him. I could feel it in the way my hair stood on end, and the clouds churning in the sky darkened, as if they obeyed the thundering Sky Knight's presence. He was supposed to be there, just ahead, out of reach from here in the city gates. I turned my face away from Kian's approaching form and focused on getting out of the lumbering doors without hurting anyone. I inched closer to the white beauty and tightened the reins.

No one was stopping us, but if we were stopped, I doubt Kian's intentions are good ones.

Carts and wagons sat in line to be loaded onto the track system that would bring them into the city, blocking the overgrown path leading back into dark forest, toward the only road to the rendezvous. I pulled to guide us around the troupe, but she tensed, and I felt a pulse of power vibrate through her capable form. The shocked faces below us were the last thing I saw before ducking into the cover of the forest road. We didn't go around; my girl took us straight through to the solution on the other side.

I think I'll name her Stella Cait. It sounded nice, and I once loved a Caitie B dearly.

I whispered her new name in her raised ears and she shimmied. I took a deep breath and patted her gently, encouraging her to continue on this wild ride with me. She pranced forward and I leaned deep into her mane again. It was time to fly to Vance the only way I knew how. The sounds of hooves not far behind kept the pace faster than I've ever ridden before, but I knew Stella Cait wouldn't let me down in the same way I once thought that Kian, Saf, and Castilen would be the most important people in my life someday.

What an idiot.

I ignored the negative self-talk and focused on my next attainable goal; figure out how to take out the asshole chasing me and go back for his shaman. That kind of power shouldn't be uncensored.

Stella Cait outran the wind, she outran my fears, and she left Kian chasing our dust miles ago. I had only ridden the paths to the temples on the other side of the garden city once, but I didn't need to worry. Stella had stayed true to a singular path and purpose since she went off the trail and into a crowded row of oaks that opened to a tight mountain pass.

The blue and white rocks that guided us into the valley, then the city, were a display in contrast against the black and moldy grey rocks we now followed up the path. She plodded along silently while I reached for my magic over and over. If I could trixxt out of here, I would be there by now.

Stella whined at the thought. I supposed if I could just blink myself out of this mess, I wouldn't have found her. It was a painful thought for the both of us as we flew across jagged, uneven terrain, faster than the wings of Asti's dragon could fly.

XXXIII

The sun was sinking lower in the sky, casting shadows across the path, the trees, and my thoughts. I couldn't place the moment that Safamir started to drain me. The blast at the onset of the attack had been witnessed by everyone while I tried to hide my identity. I never thought about someone tracing my identity back to me with my magic. I don't think Safamir did either, but it wasn't until after the power display that I started to lose control. But when? What was the moment?

It was blue, that's all I knew. Whatever he had tampering with me was still with me.

Frustration swelled up as tears, hot and ready to streak weakness down my cheeks, rolled out of my eyes. I let them fall and my thoughts weren't any clearer, but my feelings on things certainly were.

Caben was right, those two bastards were naught but trouble: Kian with his green eyes and Saf with his magic. I should have....

What? What should I have done with the circumstances? Removed from my team by my own selfish desires, drained of magic by a magi I've willingly spent several nights with, and distracted by the gorgeous man down on the trail chasing the ghost he thinks is me.

What does Kian want with me, if not sex? What kept him by my side the last days, pushing me toward this place, this moment?

The hoot of a large owl broke into my thoughts. I listened again to be sure and my heart leapt with hope. It was a message; the kind Vance and I agreed upon in the event our comms were ever down. I answered back and heard a rustle in the darkening tree line ahead.

Stella Cait stopped in the road, her head down and a snarl threatening whoever was on the other side of those trees. I rubbed her gently and encouraged her into a slow walk, but she refused to move, instead backing down the dangerous path we just ascended. If she lost her footing, we would both be crushed. I cupped my hands and licked my lips to sound another chirp to sound as a message and tried to calm Stella while we waited.

She stopped moving us backwards toward imminent death but became strangely still and quiet, not moving even a hoof forward.

The trees were very quiet now, and even more still than before. I risked whispering Vance's name, still holding onto the hope that he answered. Nothing else came from the path and eventually movement returned to the trees and the wind pushed a breeze through the path that felt like a held breath.

"No way to the other side but through the dark, kiddo," I said to Stella. I meant this as an encouragement to her, but also for myself. She huffed, stomped, and took off so fast that I bounced for several seconds before pulling myself back down, palms wrapped in the stark white of her reins. The color from around them seemed to swirl and darken where my palm rested, as though they moved from the dirt caked below my nails. Maybe they would be forever clean, that would be an enchantment worth whatever price.

As I settled back in and hunkered below the passing branches, I tucked myself close to Stella. I might always be questioning my own instincts, but hers seem hardened with the confidence of being the best. We rode so quickly past the dense spacing of the forest that I was unable to see anything past the dark tree trunks, their back and needles grasping for me as I flew by. Maybe I needed to tamper down these emotions. With no magic to distract me or depend on when my intuition wasn't so sure, I felt raw.

I wanted to look into the trees for Vance, or the owl, but night began to blocked my vision into the forest as we flew by, and I got the feeling that this wasn't the part of the forest you just hang out in. This part of the forest is nothing like the sparse grouping of trees stretching alongside the road I would normally travel when coming around Sirione, but this was Stella's way, chosen after I whispered a prayer to her to get me to the temple, alive. Stella didn't need any kind of reminder to get us away from danger; she flew across the stone and dirt like mist in the night.

The sun continued to dip into a sunset, drawing colorful lines across the sky that seemed macabre in the black forest. I focused on that, the colors swirling and dancing with the clouds. Nothing came of my message, no owl or Knight or other fowl appeared as we exited the woodland.

My thighs burned when I straightened in the saddle to clear my view. Hair whipped tears from my eyes, but still I stared at the horizon as it closed quickly. Just below the colors of the night rising, I finally could make out the temple lines. Tall, rounded turrets jut into the purple and pink sky like skeletons reaching for a beauty they'll never have again. White stone stairs led up one side of a tall building between the turrets. Its stained windows told the horror stories I grew up on, demons and veil hounds and war and life, in colors that felt too real.

Thankfully, a lone, winged figure stood tall against one of the broken pillars littering the courtyard. His hair rustled against his ears and a dark cape flew behind him and the first stars twinkled to life above making Vance look like a savior.

Wasn't he though, hadn't he always been there just on the other side of my bad choices, waiting on me with concern. Hadn't he always been a friend to me?

The thought made me feel markedly better in a moment where I felt like a failure. I misjudged Safamir, and more importantly, I'd misjudged Kian. Not Vance though, his friendship is solid, dependable.

I leaned forward, close to Stella's twitching ears and urged her to rush to him and as she moved I peered ahead with unbridled excitement. The emotions were unexpected and tears fell hard before I could reign them in. It's easy to say that you know a mission may end in your death, but to feel that truth several times over in a handful of days is enlightening. There were so many things left unanswered, but they could wait until tomorrow until I've had backup getting home, true backup to my home amongst the Gardens. I raised a hand to wipe the tears away and wave to my partner, but it was caught by another rough hand. I'm jerked from Stella Cait and put in the saddle in front of Kian with an explosive scream.

I couldn't think, I couldn't call my magic, so I did all I knew to do which was fight. I struck anywhere I could hit, aiming for his eyes and leaving deep scratches behind his ears and bites on the hands that were trying to silence me. Finally, Kian threw me from his mount and took off in the direction of Vance.

My only real partner was in real danger. I watched, magic drained, ordinary weapons with no helpful magic forthcoming and completely helpless to do anything but run to him. Stella was too far to mount, and I was drained. I lifted a hand and aimed for Kian, shooting just enough magic to light the area. No blast of death, but a big blast of fear and confusion hits me.

The Vance waving back to me is not my partner at all. It's the winged beast from the valley, and walking slowly at his side is a cloaked humanara. He is about the same height as the Knight, the same enormous shoulders that stretched the silken seams of his cloak.

I could hear his command dance across the wind meant for me to hear. "The girl will end it all, get both of them and two worlds will be ours."

The winged shaman nodded once before the cloaked figure disappeared into the night air. I sensed the hit before I felt him draw in the power. I ducked against the trunk of a giant tree and barely got out of the way in time. I try my magic again, but it is an empty promise. All I have is myself.

That's never been enough though, just me, without the sex and magic and blades forged by fires more ancient that history could recall. I had nothing on my own despite my claim of ladylike preparedness, I had nothing to fight this. I could hardly breathe. This is what it feels like to be stuck in a fight you didn't ask for with no way out; someone making choices about your life for you while you sit and hide.

I may not know enough of the secrets of this world yet, but I've never hidden from anything. The snow from the mountain peaks above float down in large clumps, settling across my face as I stand there thinking through my options. I swipe to dislodge them from clinging to my lashes, blocking my view.

A groan reached me to break through my thoughts again. I know it's Kian, and I know he isn't on my side, but at least he didn't try to kill me twice today. If he goes down, that thing will have a straight shot to me. I need him to live so that we both have a chance.

I palmed a few rocks and my throwing daggers and stepped boldly into the clearing. I took a breath, cocked my arm, and tossed my daggers straight into his left eye. One hit dead center while the other went wide and sliced his ear. It was the only surprise attack I would get in and I jumped to use it. Running, I hauled rocks at his body.

Kian saw the distraction for what it was and reacted by using magic I'd never seen him use before. It was intense magic that glowed an identical shade of blue as Safamir's. His look was instantly full of guilt, regret, and hope. It was the last look I saw before he charged at the Shaman. I followed suit and sprinted to the right, setting up to take him from the side.

Before I could make it three steps, I was knocked off balance and rolled into a tree, pinned against it by a heavy black paw. A long tongue licked my face, giving me a second to gather myself.

"Castilen?" I asked softly.

The panther growled close to my face then slowly released her hold. I watched her lop into the fray with enthusiasm. If she was here, then so was Vance!

I see him across the courtyard, coming up behind the shaman on silent feet, a black scythe grasped between both hands. I've seen this move before, helped him to make it successful, but the sound his weapon makes when it slices the head off of the giant Veiliri still makes me dizzy. I avert my eyes to save myself the memory later. I'm a tough bitch, but everyone had a limit.

Before I could pull myself up from the tree and join the others in the temple ruins, a whirring sound filled the sky. I clenched my teeth and ducked back behind the tree. It wasn't not wings though, it was the Gentry lighting up the night sky with an entire fleet. Were they here for us? Finally?

I looked around for Stella Cait, forming a backup plan, but she was hiding. I was grateful, yet disappointed. I had never needed to escape from the Gentry. I even went so far as to allow them some semblance of control over me. None of that meant I trusted the Order, though. Maybe before the sabotaged mission, bombed flier, silence in the face of agent losses; maybe I could still believe that they sent an entire fleet to precisely the right place at precisely the wrong time and still could manage to rescue us.

Maybe I just have a lot of new trust issues to work through.

I shrugged and made another decision I knew I would grow to regret. I walked out from behind the tree with my hands loose at my sides. They didn't know that I didn't have magic, the only one here that knew that was Kian. That would have to be my wildcard in my otherwise ineffable plan; the thing I would have to figure out once back in the strategy room with Arike.

All lights shone toward me before splitting again between me and Kian. Why would the Gentry want Kian?

A voice suddenly called out for us both to stand down, and I looked at the man with the ocean green eyes. He was looking back at me, inching his way closer. He gave me no reading and I couldn't place his next move. I couldn't help us to get away if he didn't let me in.

I inched closer to him as Vance did the same from the other side. I wanted to ask him so many questions in this moment, but only one kept coming up, insistent on being let out. I didn't open my mouth, but he heard me, and the answer was the last thing I heard from Kian.

"Why?"

Because I need you more than they do.

I was still staring at him, trying to find my place to run with Gentry descending in a circle around us. He was inches away now.

I could do it. I could just grab him and blink us far enough away to give him the chance to get us out. I lifted my palm to reach for him and he grasped it tightly, pulling me into him, face to face. It was the sorrow in his eyes that I felt first. It hurt so badly I barely registered the small blue dagger he ushered into my back.

The pain was complete when it registered and I hit my knees, reopening little wounds from days ago that still hadn't healed. I could hear the screams and the orders to give chase. I could hear them give the order to kill him. I could also hear his whisper in my mind reminding me that he needed me.

I opened my eyes at the rustle of wings around me expecting to see Vance, but he and Castilen were fighting with the Gentry. I had no idea what's happening, but Kian was rising above me on dark leathered wings, supple and shimmering like Stella Cait's fine coat. I tried to rip the blade from my body to slice his throat with, but the movement only left me paralyzed in the middle of a battle.

The fighting only lasted for seconds longer after Kian's betrayal, with most of the force taking off in pursuit of him. I tried to lift my head to follow the action above but could only make it to the tree line. There, a dark mass moved along the shadows and further into the mountains. I stared at Castilen as she fled to the safety of darkness. For a brief second she stopped, her golden eyes focusing in on me and blinked. Once, twice, then twice again. I followed her loping form as long as I could before the black began to creep into my sight, threatening to have me crumpling to the freezing ground in a pool of my own blood.

It only took mere seconds for Vance to gather me up in his arms, cradling my tired, broken, and betrayed body against his. Skipping the fliers the Gentry brought to carry us home, he lifted straight into the air and flew me home.

EPILOGUE

My memories of the days before the temple event have come to me in pieces. Some are a rush of lusty heat, and some are overwhelming moments of crushing shame. I have balanced between the two steadily since returning to the ship. Few people have come to visit. Whenever I often asked about Marli, I get zero response every time. When a Rogue went underground, no one could find him apparently.

Still, I have the blue blade that stole my magic, but outside of Arike confirming that it had blocked me from accessing my gifts, I'm no closer to discovering how it works or why someone was in possession of one. Healing has been slow and my only companion is Vance. I've begged him for more information, a trail to follow, for anything, but he continues to deny me.

"Skarlet, I will tell you when I think you are strong enough, and that day is not today," he sighs.

It was always the same thing: Him avoiding me for days, showing up like a knight, and then leaving me unsatisfied. Soon, though. Soon I will be back on my feet and I'm bringing hell with me when I come for answers from each one of them.

ACKNOWLEDGMENTS

First, I need to thank the Mister, for all the hard work, for the unconditional love, and for believing in this dream with me. Vic, without you, this project would forever have remained just a dream.

Dearest Vittoria, my Boots, my Blue Girl, you're my everything and any good thing I have ever done in my life has been to impress you. I couldn't be prouder of you. I love you endlessly.

To the girls that have climbed the mountains of time with me, Sambob Squarepants, Aunt Jatittiema, and the Headless Bikini Queen, for reminding me that love exists in tragedy and that humor can fix anything.

Endless gratitude to all my family for loving me in all my wildness. Through the years nothing has shown up in my life with more assurance than my brothers, sisters, and extended family.

To Georgia: Bubby and Hala, Nikki, Mama, Aunt Carlene and all the other rowdy Dowdy's, you're truly my heart. Thank you for building the woman that had the courage to follow her dreams. To the in-laws, Vince and family, Mike and Jenny, Joe and family, thanks for teaching me your Italian ways!

To Florida: Nana, Pop-Pop, Grand-Millie, PJ, DD, and kids, Lynda (Mom), Tim, Marcus, Brooke, Jeannie, and the most precious nieces and nephews, have held space for me to come home over the years. You could never know how much that has impacted me. Thank you.

I'd also like to thank Wednesdays and Fridays because on Wednesdays we go to Pilates with Tracey (Pam, Bree, and the Inspire family) and on

Fridays we have coffee with Sherrie. Without these two allowing me to keep coming back, I would have already fallen apart.

To Tara for allowing me to see the world one client at a time. Thank you!

This acknowledgment would not be complete without thanking my friends! Amanda, thank you for believing in these crazy other worlds I think up and for never letting my imagination take me too far. For Brittany, I don't know how I could love you more and I'm proud of you. You will build empires before we're done! To Liz, I began with a handful of people that believed in me and you were the cornerstone of that. I'd cross oceans to celebrate this win with you! I'll see you soon for my hug! And to Emily, the other love of my life, the girl that shows up, the girl that wears her sass like a pretty picture of chaos, thank you for being all that you are.

To Jaimie and Victoria at Between Friends Publishing. When I walked through your door years ago, I felt immediately at home. I nurtured the tiniest secret hope even then that someday we would place my books on one of your shelves. Over the years your quiet support has been priceless. Thank you for those years and for believing in your community.

And to Jennifer, thank you for reading that first stack of papers and continuing to push me into making the leap that terrified me. I appreciate you!

ABOUT THE AUTHOR

You can find Miranda in South Georgia complaining about the heat and reading instead of adulting. She shares her house with an Italian husband, a rotten teenage daughter, and one bad kitty.

DEAR READER

When I was a kid, I knew I wanted to tell stories. It was the age of Stephen King and J. K. Rowling and big blockbuster releases, but the life of a writer seemed so unattainable. Before the rise of alternative publishing, a creative life appeared fickle, unsure of what it could offer as a real future. There were people in my life that cared for me deeply, and in that love, they discouraged the path of the creative for something guaranteed. I tried to follow that wisdom into a more lucrative career, and struggled endlessly, never quite finding my place. When Skarlet came to me, I knew I had to tell her story. Having you join me on this journey means everything to me. When I started working on Skarlet's story, I felt like I was meeting a new friend. She came to me in a way that couldn't be ignored, and I knew she would feature in my debut novel. As you get to know Skarlet and her gang, please know that I thought of you while writing her, because without you, none of my stories would matter. With all of my heart, allow me to say thank you, thank you! This has been a dream for me, and I thank you for giving me your time.

Miranda Spaventa

Made in the USA
Columbia, SC
13 December 2023